Paws for Consideration

Amy Butcher

got
g'nads

Paws for Consideration
ISBN: 978-0-9852075-4-0
Got G'nads Press
2261 Market Street #80
San Francisco, CA 94114

This book is a work of fiction. Names, characters, places, and incidents either are products of the author's imagination or are used fictitiously. Any resemblance to actual persons, living or dead, events, or locales is entirely coincidental.

Set in Palatino and Cracked using Adobe InDesign
Cover design by Amy Butcher
Cover illustration by Amy Butcher
Chapter and flipbook illustrations by Amy Butcher
Author photo © 2012 Marisa Aragona

For Frieda and Joe,
old-school neighbors of the highest order.

Paws for Consideration

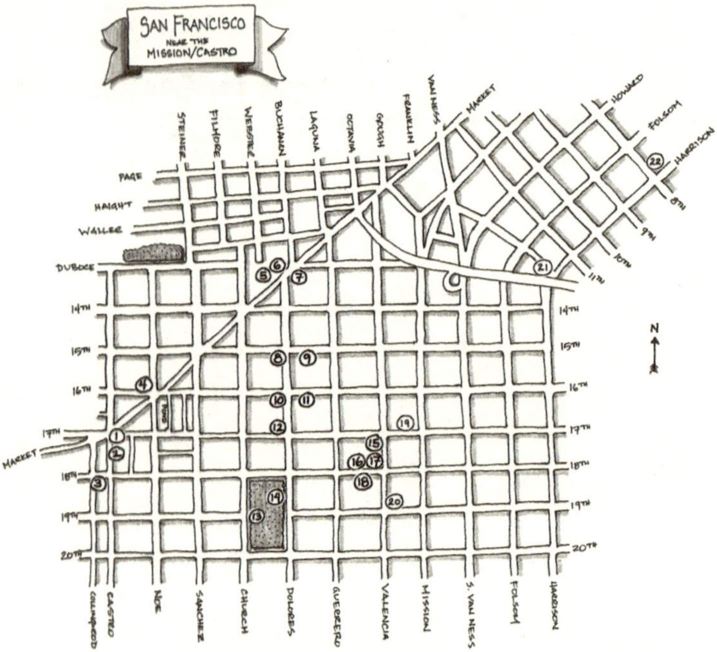

SAN FRANCISCO
NEAR THE
MISSION/CASTRO

N

LEGEND

1. TWIN PEAKS
2. CASTRO THEATRE
3. THE EDGE
4. LOOKOUT
5. SAFEWAY
6. STARBUCKS
7. PET FOOD EXPRESS
8. VACANT LOT
9. DAISY'S APT.
10. MISSION DOLORES
11. TINTIN
12. MAYFIELD'S
13. HIDALGO STATUE
14. DOLORES PARK
15. MISSION POLICE STATION
16. FARINA
17. LUNA PARK
18. THE WOMEN'S BUILDING
19. PIED À TERRE
20. ALI BABA'S CAVE
21. EAGLE TAVERN
22. MR. S

San Francisco, November 2008

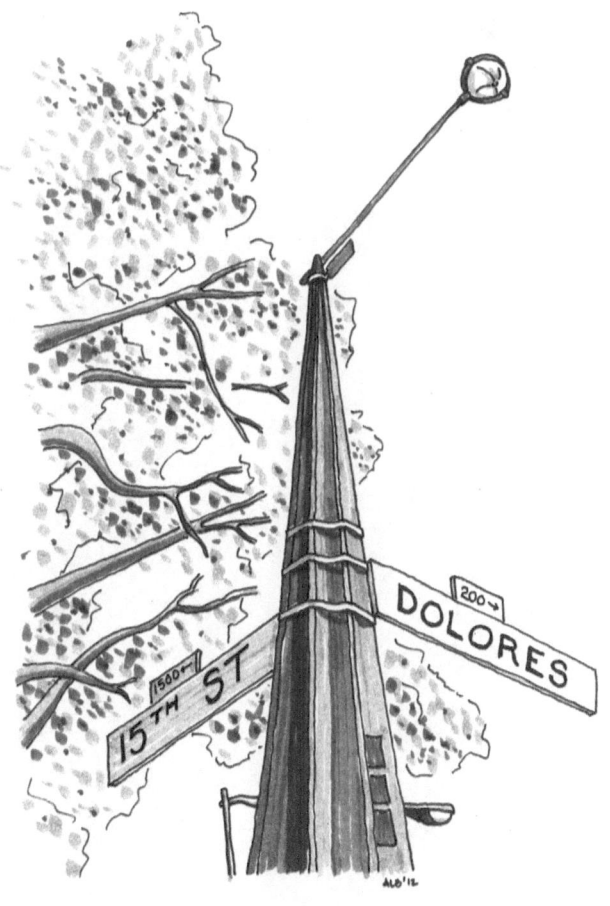

FOR THE BRIEFEST OF moments, a question hung in the air between two damp noses. Daisy-the-person joysticked her electric wheelchair a little closer to Daisy-the-dog. Daisy-the-dog danced one cautious step backwards in response, slid a long tongue across the tip of her nose and tasted the dampened air, trying to decide if this hulking combination of vehicle and person was to be trusted. Daisy-the-person snorted too, and wiped a sleeve across her own muzzle. "Come on over here, you cutie, and give me some love!" she said, beckoning low with an outstretched hand.

The voice of Daisy-the-person carried way beyond the dog in front of her. She was the morning wake-up call for her neighbors, as regular as the bells ringing out from the steeple of Mission Dolores, only higher pitched. She patted her generous lap again, encouraging Daisy-the-dog to come closer.

To the canine, it wasn't clear where chair began and person ended. The way this creature moved, the wheels and the whir, were disconcerting. But she smelled good—of oily chicken scents and warm lint—and she wasn't moving now. Daisy-the-dog decided to take a chance.

"All the dogs love me. I know all their names," Daisy reassured the woman who stood tethered to Daisy-the-dog. While the woman might remain a stranger, the two Daisies— one scratching behind the furry ears of the other—were now bonded for life.

After a few minutes, the tethered woman found her voice, "OK, now. We've got to get going." She smiled sheepishly as she urged her dog out of range.

"See y'all later!" Daisy yelled out, her southern twang

rising above the traffic noise, not the least bit offended by the woman's eager departure. Grasping the joystick of her Permobil Chairman HD electric wheelchair, she spun neatly on a dime and drove off down the sidewalk in search of her next dog friend.

This had been her morning routine ever since she had moved into the city housing high-rise on 15th Street near Dolores some twenty years ago. Back then, Daisy could still walk but it wasn't long before the diabetes and fibromyalgia had made that nearly impossible.

The chair had been her savior. She could zip uphill to Muddy Waters on Church Street for a cup of their double-brewed coffee (strong enough to raise the dead) and be back down along Dolores in no time. Dolores was the dog highway. Dotted with palms, a strip of green grass ran down the middle of the street. It rose and fell over the Mission hills like a verdant stream. Most dogs, having both delicate sensibilities and definite habits, preferred this grass over the sidewalk cement for their morning business. Daisy-the-person, for her part, preferred most dogs over their people.

It wasn't that she didn't like people. She did. Rather it was that she liked dogs better. Their love was simple and true. A good scratch, abundant praise and pats, and most any dog would meet her halfway. That was more than she could say for most people. Seeing her large body and chair rolling towards them, most people tended to make an abrupt change of direction or suddenly stare intently at their phone. Most had the good manners not to make the aversion too obvious but some, especially the little kids, were more obvious.

Granted, she told herself, her appearance was a sight. Her short gray hair stuck out in tufts, still growing out from the self-inflicted buzz-cut she'd given herself one day last week in a fit of DIY barbery. And lack of exercise and repeated indulgence in her favorite garlic fries had only increased her girth. Sitting in the chair, everything about her just flowed from head to toe: jowls flowed evenly into the double chin that flowed with equal ease into the lumbering torso, the mass gathering momentum like a skier on a jump, sliding headlong through her lap, launching over the lip of her knees, only to land and finally come to rest in the thick ankles and feet on the foot rests of the wheelchair.

Dogs didn't seem to care, though. They assessed the situation utilizing a completely different set of aesthetic standards. Sure they noticed the gray whiskers sprouting from her chin but took that as a good sign. And the pleats and folds of her housedress were a promise of secret treats from the crumbs that had fallen during Daisy's last meal. And the thick ankles above the foot rests? Well those just clearly marked the entrance, the front steps, into the world of endless pats and scratches. Even her piercing voice was a comfort. A dog never had to wonder if he'd missed Daisy that morning. If she was around, her bark would penetrate even the noisiest of days.

LISA STEPPED out of her apartment on 15th, her ancient shepherd Rocco so close behind that his forehead touched the back of her knees. It was a good strategy, she thought. His eyes were so clouded now with cataracts that it was hard for him to judge the stairs. Gluing himself to her legs at least provided some guidance, a kind of canine banister.

In his prime, Rocco had pulled eagerly on the leash to get down to the complex olfactory landscape of Dolores. Now, at age 14, he seemed more content to explore randomly. Often he would squat to pee just a few steps from the front door, the warm trail of urine snaking down the cement and steaming

in the cool morning. Lisa remembered a time when he was a pup and they'd visited friends in New York. She'd taken Rocco out for a walk and he was positively beside himself, unable to find any grass to piss on. No self-respecting dog peed on the cement. It just wasn't done. But in his dotage, all such vanity had fallen away. At a snail's pace, they headed down towards Dolores. Pausing, Lisa smiled thinking of the sweetness of old dogs. There are some lessons for me there, she thought.

DOWN ON Dolores, Daisy rolled across 15th, heading south.

"Hey Lisa. Hi Rocco!" she yelled. Lisa waved back. Rocco lifted his stiff neck slightly, curious but unable to locate the faint familiar sound of Daisy's voice. Eventually, he gave up and returned to his random sniffing, lost in his own sensory world.

Normally, Daisy would stop and visit but today she just kept on rolling. She'd spied a particularly nervous Boston Terrier that she'd met only once before but was intent on befriending. This dog was young and unsure what to make of this wheeled human. He'd just turned onto Dolores farther down the block, and she sped off after him. "Skittles!" she called out as she hit full speed.

Allen, the owner of the dog, a youngish man in a tailored suit, gave a pained smile as she approached. He'd been hoping to slip by unnoticed as he was in a bit of a hurry this morning. No such luck, though. Skittles cowered behind him, waiting for a clue from his owner as to how to proceed.

"Skittles, you remember me! Get over here and get up in my lap! Such a good dog." Daisy leaned forward in the chair, snapping her fingers low to the ground, hoping to entice

Skittles to take a brave step forward.

Skittles twitched his black nose, scrunching his wrinkled flat face in confusion.

"Go ahead," Allen said, stepping sideways to encourage Skittles, hoping to get the encounter over with as quickly as possible.

"Come hear, sweetie!" Daisy said at a volume that would scare even the bravest of dogs.

Skittles shook subtly but persistently. Although Daisy did smell interesting to him, he wondered where to begin, how to approach.

"Come get some love!" Daisy pleaded.

Skittles took one tentative step forward, just enough to make contact—wet nose to cool hand—then scurried back behind his owner.

"He's just a little shy," Allen said, hoping that would be enough explanation to end the experiment, at least for today.

"Don't be afraid of me," Daisy squealed. "You're just a little scaredy cat!" Just a little at first, and then more fully, Daisy started to chuckle at her own joke. The man and the dog just stared. "Scaredy cat! Your little dog is a scaredy *cat*!" Nothing had been funnier to Daisy that morning and her body rolled with laughter.

"OK, baby, maybe another day," she said, conceding that the dog wasn't going to budge.

"Scaredy cat!" she said to herself again, turning and rolling off, still giggling.

It took Allen a moment to shake himself back to life from his stunned state. That woman was a piece of work! He looked down at Skittles who looked back, his wide eyes silently imploring "What just happened there, man?"

"I'm not sure," he said aloud in response as they hurried

in the opposite direction from the retreating Daisy.

THE MORNING commute was winding down and with it the dog traffic. Lacking any more canine company, Daisy headed towards Joe's garage halfway down the block on Dolores.

Joe had retired about a year back and now spent his free time on small projects in his garage. He'd worked for the San Francisco Municipal Railway as a bus driver for most of his career, the last few years driving MUNI's infamous 22 Fillmore line, so the last thing he wanted to do now was anything requiring a schedule. Now he reveled in just puttering about in the garage repairing small items, re-organizing the already-neat tool bench, or simply washing his immaculate black Ford F150 truck. Although it was early, he'd already rolled the truck halfway out onto the wide sidewalk in preparation for her bath, which was why he could see the reflection of Daisy in the black fender as she rolled up behind him.

"Good morning, Joe. Sure lookin' shiny today," Daisy said with a grin.

Joe enjoyed Daisy. She was easy company and that was something he missed from his MUNI days. Just shooting the shit with someone, no real agenda or purpose to it all, just one human to another passing the time.

His wife was still adjusting to his presence at home during the day. Sometimes he came down to the garage not so much to get to a project as to get away from the sense that his wife didn't really want him around. He couldn't really blame her—she'd had years to establish her own routine—but it still made him feel lonely. Daisy, at least, was a bit of easy company and nothing about her would make his wife jealous.

"Did I tell you about the toaster oven I got? $12.50 over at Walgreen's on Castro," Daisy said.

"Not yet," Joe smiled as he wandered back into the garage for the bucket and sponge. He had already hooked up the hose to the spigot just inside the garage door. Stopping just beside Daisy, he plunked the nozzle of the hose into the bucket and began to create a whirlpool of soapy water.

"I was over there yesterday," said Daisy, "and they were having this sale. I figured I could just put it on the counter in my kitchen next to the sink. We're not supposed to have a lot of appliances or nothing but I figure a toaster oven is OK." Daisy tweaked the controls as she talked, making minor adjustments to the seat position, a sort of electronic twitch.

"Figure it is too," Joe said as he eyed the water swirling, long after he'd shut down the flow.

"I can use it to make me some Pop-Tarts. Or maybe even something healthier, like those little spinach pies they have over at Safeway."

"Me? I'd make one of those mini pizzas. You know, the frozen kind. I like those." Joe dipped the sponge in the bucket and began to make wide circles across the hood, imagining those mini pizzas grown large.

"Me too. My doctor says I really shouldn't eat that many carbohydrates. With my heart and my blood sugar, I'm supposed to be eating more vegetables and grains and stuff. But it's hard. Who wants to fire up the big oven and do all that cooking for just one person?"

That image and its implications sat heavily between them for a moment: aloneness, loneliness, choice. Joe broke the moment, splashing another soapy sponge-full, this time attacking the front left fender. "It's amazing how dirty this truck gets, even though it's just sitting in the garage." Joe squinted at the hood, eyeing a spot he'd missed.

"Joe, I do believe you have more vanity about that car than you do about yourself. Why just take a look at those pants." Daisy pointed to a large oil spot on the right cuff of Joe's khakis.

"Well, shoot," Joe said as he bent over to see. "Must've rubbed up against something in the garage."

"Or maybe you're just an oily old bastard!" Daisy laughed and Joe did too.

She reengaged the motor of her chair and turned. "I'll see you later," she called as she wheeled off for home, her morning visits—dog and human—complete.

ROBBIE STEPPED out onto the sidewalk and paused; in part, to feel the temperature; in part, to settle back into her body. You would think that after years of this daily routine she'd be used to the sound of the iron gate slamming behind her, but it still startled her each and every time. If it didn't slam it didn't catch, and her apartment building had suffered enough break-ins to make that catch important. She sympathized with her neighbors in the street-facing apartments but there was so much noise and hubbub out here that the sound of the slamming gate was probably just one among many annoyances.

Robbie looked up at the high-rise looming across the street and watched as Daisy rolled along the exterior hallway on the third floor. In a squat city of three-story apartments and condos, a ten-story apartment tower seemed seriously out of place, dwarfing every building around. Like in a cheap motel, the doors to all the apartments opened onto exterior walkways. This may have been good for security but no architect familiar with San Francisco's thick fog would have designed open hallways facing north. It was so L.A. But then again, Beck's Motor Lodge up the Castro had made it work. Of course, privacy wasn't the goal in that design. As one of the Castro's notorious cruising spots, the goal at Beck's was to see and be seen.

Robbie turned right and headed up 15th Street. This was an old habit from when she had her spaniel Molly. Every morning the two of them would head out: Molly to pee and Robbie for coffee. It seemed a win-win. They'd meander down the center strip of Dolores, Molly hunting the ripe smells of the well-pawed urban dog trail and Robbie stepping carefully to avoid dog poop and keeping an eye out for foxtails.

Foxtails had been an unfamiliar menace when they'd moved here from the east coast five years back. Benign-looking grasses, their sallow barbs were actually mini-spears intent on a one-way trip into a dog's skin. They'd latch onto the coat and then slowly pull their way down through the fur until hitting their target. If Robbie didn't find them and pull them off, in a few days they'd burrow beneath Molly's skin, causing pain and risking infection.

Even though Molly's life had ended three years ago, their morning ritual had not. Robbie still headed north for coffee each morning, rain or shine. She thought it wasn't such a bad habit. At least it got her outside every day. Of course, as the dedicated morning runners passed her by she had her moments of doubt, but coffee and the paper still seemed a more appealing way to start her day. The imagined running could happen later.

A COOL wind rose up from the street below carrying the sound of a slamming gate to her attention. Daisy knew without looking that it was from the brown brick apartment building across the street. Probably Robbie-without-Molly

heading out per usual. Daisy's apartment in the high-rise was the last one down this end of the exterior hallway. A few plants stood sentry around Daisy's door, hand-me-downs from neighbors long since moved on.

The largest plant, the potted lavender, had been Jerry's. He'd always stopped to chat with Daisy before his daily poker game down at the Vet Center. They'd been joking buddies, had even shared some pizza and TV on occasion, but once Jerry started dating Shirley it had all gotten a bit complicated. Shirley was the jealous type and didn't cotton to Daisy. Absurd really, as there wasn't one volt of erotic charge between them. They were just company, one lonely person to another, that's all. But now they weren't even that. Last month, Jerry's body had been found slumped in his bathroom. His friends had become worried when he'd missed three poker games in a row and had come to check on him.

Daisy took the key from around her neck and opened the gunmetal gray door. She paused for just a moment to take stock of the silence of the place before flicking on the light and heading in.

Personal hygiene evidence to the contrary, she liked to keep her apartment neat. The kitchen alcove was over to the left, toaster oven now wedged on the counter beside the sink. The beige walls weren't so hard to take except where they led towards the bathroom. Daisy always thought it might be nice to have the walls a bit more vibrant over there—perhaps yellow or teal—but city ordinance didn't allow tenants to paint their own apartments. And with the rent she was paying, she couldn't afford to cause any problems.

The bedroom was all the way to the right. There was just enough space between the dresser and her bed to be able to pull her wheelchair alongside the bed and transfer herself from one to the other, just enough space, to pull in but not enough to turn around.

Daisy rolled into the kitchen and filled the kettle. She placed it on the front burner and set it to boiling. Another cup of coffee right now sounded good: a little pick me up before she got much further with her day. Lately in the mornings she'd been thinking about her cousin Adeline back in Kentucky, how they used to argue for hours over coffee about whatever silly article was on the front of the paper. She missed that banter.

She rolled into the gap-toothed spot at the table where a fourth chair would normally be. No need for it since she came with her own. She spread the *San Francisco Chronicle* out before her and surveyed the front page, hunting for something provocative. Just three days after the election— little else managed to squeeze in around the photo and article about Obama. She was a proud to be a Republican, even if she didn't always make it to the polls, and considered herself a good Christian woman. He seemed like a decent man but some kinds of change just took a little longer to wrap her mind around.

Below the fold, the latest installment of a series on cost-cutting in the home caught her eye. With the economy going to hell in a handbasket, it seemed that the latest chic thing was to figure out how to compost, grow a garden, and make your own clothes. She hated the articles that instructed hipsters on how to do what she'd known how to do forever, get by on less. Every time one of these items ran it meant there'd be more folks down at Community Thrift on Valencia, more folks with money to burn skimming off the best of the new items. It irked her.

Down at the very bottom of the page was an article on Iran—or was it Iraq, she had a hard time keeping the two

straight—more car bombs leaving more carnage. Daisy wasn't quite sure what could be done.

Next to that, a smaller article profiling a new mini-tapas place opening down on 16th. What were mini-tapas, she wondered. She tried to picture the location they described. Must be around the corner from the Lutheran Church, same side she figured, but not as far down as the Taqueria. It seemed like an odd location for a new restaurant.

She flipped the page, searching for some news that would be more to her liking. Maybe the entertainment section, she thought. Daisy loved her celebrity dish.

J.B. BENT over, flipping her wet hair into the waiting towel, gave it a quick tussle, wrapped it up tight, and flipped the whole turban right-side up. She had just stepped out of the shower after her morning run along the Panhandle. Even though it had been a still and foggy morning—and her run had felt enveloped in cotton candy—she was alert and filled with endorphins.

She took a moment to admire herself in the full-length mirror. Neat, taught, toned. The jeans she planned to wear today would ride right at her hip bones, leaving just the tiniest suggestive gap as the waistband bridged the curve between hip and flat belly. It was a subtle tool—this exposed flesh—but one she could work today, if need be.

J.B. leaned closer to the mirror and scrutinized her face. Sharp creases chiseled between her eyebrows. She put one finger on each side and pulled gently towards her temples. Better, she thought, but I'm not quite ready to do another Botox treatment. The last injection had produced an odd pustule, which had taken weeks to go away. Even now, she could still see the spot of faint red. For now, she told herself, just drink more water. That'll have to do.

Most mornings, J.B. would catch the special Bauer Bus that Google hired to shuttle the young, eager techies down to the Peninsula headquarters. Clever of Google—the WiFi-enabled bus felt like a perk but actually extracted an extra hour of work during the commute.

Three years ago, an eon in the tech world, when she'd first been hired on as a Marketing Strategist, she'd been seduced by the freebies—the bus, the chef-prepared meals, the celebrity speakers, the laptop, even the on-site dry cleaning. They made her feel special and exalted. But over time, she'd noticed a shift. J.B. had become jaded by the food, wishing some days for the dirty pleasure of a Big Mac or just a sandwich from home. The laptop had been great perk until it had been stolen from a friend's car one night while they dined at Foreign Cinema on Valencia Street. Dealing with the police about the theft and then IT about the potential security breach had been such a hassle. Each week, the perks had come to feel more and more like chains and she, more like a cog in the machine. She longed to feel special again, like she was at the center of what really mattered, but was at a loss as to make that happen.

The catalyst had come six months ago in the form of graffiti stenciled onto the sidewalk beside the Google Bus stop. She'd just stepped off the Bauer Bus at Dolores Park Café. She'd been looking down at her iPhone and would have missed it but for her smooth-soled stiletto skidding over the fresh painted surface. In bold lettering above a big, black "X", the neat stenciled statement: "Mission Exploitation: Trendy Google Profs Raise Housing Prices!" Suddenly, it had all become clear. She was tired of being made to feel guilty for her professionalism and success. This was her neighborhood too, she had thought, and it's high time for her to mark

her territory. It was time to return to a dream that had started way back in business school. Back then, she and her classmate Allen had fantasized about starting a restaurant. They'd even written a complete business plan as part of their Entrepreneurship class. But right out of school she'd gotten distracted by high tech and moved west while he'd stayed in Boston and been involved in several successful restaurant launches already. The day after her graffiti epiphany, she'd spotted a newly vacated appliance store on 16th and she had known in her gut that it would be a great restaurant location. She had called Allen back in Boston and convinced him to come out to San Francisco to take a look. The timing had been right—he'd been looking for a new challenge—and she'd convinced him that with her local connections and his restaurant know-how they could finally make their class project a reality. Best of all, she wouldn't even need to let go of the Google gig. He had agreed so readily that she had to remind herself that it wasn't her feminine charms that sealed the deal. After all, Allen was gay, and even if the two of them had once had some sort of chemistry, it had always been of the neutered kind.

J.B. pulled herself out of her reverie, finished drying her hair, and quickly got dressed. She picked up her new Jimmy Choo bag and headed out the door. As she turned toward the Google stop a mere fifty yards from her door—a requirement she'd given the realtor who found her this place—she pulled out her iPhone and clicked on Allen's text message thread. She was eager to see how things are shaping up with the restaurant this morning.

ALLEN CLOSED HIS MACBOOK Air with a little click and traced his fingers across the sleek surface. Then he reached across his desk for his Americano and took a small sip. For a moment he held his breath, savoring the silence and the feel of the lukewarm liquid on his tongue. He swallowed hard and let out a loud sigh.

Skittles was asleep on the Aston Martin DB6 couch across the room, his Boston Terrier blackness set off against the red leather. The dog stirred when Allen sighed, stood up, turned completely around once then curled back into a sleepy ball, assured Allen wasn't going anywhere just yet.

Allen and Skittles had been up early and out for a walk, unable to avoid the strange woman who pressed for Skittles' attention then called him "scaredy cat." Since their returned home, Skittles had been sleeping on the couch as Allen worked at his desk. He'd had an early Skype call to investors in Boston whose decision-making moved at the pace of molasses, a hurried call to his wine buyer trying to lock in the best lot-price on that spunky Merlot Allen had discovered last week, and a text barrage from his business partner J.B. who was way too high-maintenance. He stretched back in his slate gray Aeron chair trying to ease the kink he'd had in his lower back for the past week. It's probably just stress, he thought. Clicking the home button on his iPhone, he flicked the slider to unlock, and tapped on the Facebook app. "Let's see what everyone is up to . . . ," he said to his sleeping dog.

Malcolm was "feeling tired and hunting for a better double latte." John was "annoyed with the dry cleaner who can't get the creases right." Andy was "thinking of the hottie I met last night," while Rebecca wondered "is a facial and

Mani-Pedi too much for one day."

He wondered why this drivel calmed him down. Some neurologist might be able to explain how, when he reviewed the minutia of his friends' lives, certain pathways deep in his brain stopped firing while others lit up. All Allen knew was that this addictive break took him to an alternative universe and left him refreshed when he came back to this world.

His new restaurant was just a week away from opening. They'd chosen every detail carefully, including the name: Tintin. It was an homage to the Belgian comic-book series created by Hergé in 1929. Tintin was the protagonist of the series, a clever reporter who travels the world with his trusty dog Snowy. They'd chosen the name for three main reasons. First, the adventurousness and whimsy of the series matched San Francisco's own culture. Second, the series had a following amongst a certain set of the sophisticated gay elite, probably from their boarding school days, which pleased Allen to no end. Third, and most important, the pronunciation of the name made it easy to define those in the know. If some pronounced it *'tin-tin* like two cans of beer, they were out. But if they offered up the smooth nasal *tah(n)-'tahn* then Allen knew them to be part of the in-crowd that mattered.

Allen had started and flipped restaurants before— one in New York (Eclectica) and two in Boston (Barcode and Namaste). He knew the flow, the chaos that was to be expected especially during these final few weeks before opening. This was his first San Francisco project, though, and he was finding the politics of the whole thing unbearable.

Since he'd moved here five months ago, it had been nothing but hassles. First, there was the permitting process. Those vultures at City Hall had gouged him for an arm and a leg. In other cities, permits were a flat fee but here they were a percentage of the size of the project. The more upscale the project, the more it cost. It made him fume. Why should some plebian Taqueria pay so much less for the right to build out the interior of what was essentially the same space? If this city ever wanted to get out of its indolent 1950s ways, they'd have to realize where the real value was, who the real players were. Hadn't they heard about trickle down economics?

Then there was the construction crew. The foreman was OK but refused to take responsibility for his crew, who were rarely the same men from day to day. Half the time, when Allen did a walk-through with the foreman and pointed out quality issues, the workers couldn't even understand what he was saying. He'd heard about the day-laborer economy here on the West Coast, but this was ridiculous. Couldn't these people speak a little bit of English?

Worst of all, there were the neighbors. They had nothing better to do than complain about the construction. Weren't they "compadres" with the crew after all? But they bitched about the noise, the parking, even the color of the exterior—it was like they thought they should have a say about this project, what it should look like, and whom it should serve. He'd be damned if he was going let his vision get watered down. He'd done his marketing plan and he knew his target audience. If they weren't it, that was their problem.

Allen stood and moved over to the window. He stared out across Dolores Park towards the slumbering container ships that were anchored south of the Bay Bridge, waiting for their chance to be loaded. Tintin was in pretty much the same state—all built out and just a week away from their opening, waiting for their human cargo to come aboard. On the couch, Skittles had rolled over onto his back, his long pink tongue lolling out of the corner of his mouth. "Lucky bastard!" Allen grumbled.

He crept over towards the sleeping dog and, bending low, blew coffee-scented breath directly into Skittles flat black nose. The dog sputtered awake, snuffling and scrambling to his feet.

Asshole! Skittles thought, *I hate when he does that.*

Allen laughed at the dog's obvious discomfort. "C'mon buddy, let's get out of here and go for a walk. I need to move."

Skittles gave one last snort of annoyance as he bowed forward and arched his back into a stretch. Things could be worse, he thought, surrendering to his human's strange ways.

ALLEN DECIDED to swing by Dolores Park Café for yet another Americano. There was a chill in the air and he couldn't tell if the gray clouds were high fog or actual rain clouds. The weather here continued to confound him. Since he'd left his umbrella at home, he hoped the enveloping grayness was only fog.

As he walked, he had formed a plan—head to Tintin, work in the back office there for a bit, then take Skittles back home and hit the gym. At least at Tintin, even if things were still not quite finished, he'd be surrounded by all the tangible proof that they really were making something happen. That might calm his jangled nerves.

Just as he placed his key in the restaurant's front door, a throaty voice called out from across the street.

"Yoo hoo, handsome! If that's your place, stay right there for just a sec!" Three remarkably tall drag queens dressed in nun's habits strode into traffic, confident that drivers would screech to a halt from shock value alone.

"Do you work here?"

Allen just stared.

"We've been trying to reach the owners for weeks but to no avail. Perhaps your fabulous gay self could make the introductions for us?" This from the tallest of the three, her face painted white and set off by broadly applied magenta eyeshadow with matching lipstick.

"I'm the owner," Allen said, his lip practically curling as he spoke, "and I can't begin to imagine what you might want from me."

"Oh girl, you've offended him," said another. "Where are our manners? My name is Sister Ophelia Love, and this is Sister Dee Light and this—" she said pointing to the tall one who'd started the conversation off on the wrong size-fifteen stiletto, "is Sister Sasquatch. Please forgive us. We are with the Sisters of Perpetual Indulgence, and we're collecting prizes for our Halloween Bingo Extravaganza! We're hoping you might be willing to make a donation."

Allen had heard of The Sisters of Perpetual Indulgence, how could he not—they'd been an irreverent fixture in the Castro for almost thirty years and they were pretty hard to miss. From what he understood, they were a service organization—the Shriners-meet-Beach Blanket Babylon; where initiates took their vows, their Sister name, and then dressed in the most insane drag queen/nun outfits imaginable to raise money for worthy causes.

Skittles stared up at these unusual women with keen interest. He sniffed around the hems of their habits, detecting a strange mix of masculine and feminine scents. It took him a moment to notice the small miniature Chihuahua peaking out from the flowing wimple of the shortest of the sisters. They exchanged quick sniffs at a distance, curious about their respective humans.

Allen was less inquisitive than his dog. "I'm not

interested," he said firmly.

"But it's for our community!" Sister Ophelia Love said. "It benefits P.A.W.S., Mission Cultural Center, The Women's Building, and a whole host of others."

"Aren't you straying a little far from your homo 'hood?" Allen asked. He tolerated drag queens in the Castro but was offended they were venturing so far afield.

"We're coalition-building, we can't just stay in our gay ghetto and pretend we're not part of a bigger community. Times are tough all over and we queers need to support our Latino neighbors, especially with all the gentrification happening in this neighborhood . . . and even in our own."

"Well, the way I figure it," sniffed Allen, "opening Tintin is donation enough. So it looks like you 'sisters' . . ." —he coughed and surveyed them roughly, head to toe— ". . . are shit out of luck." With that he turned, unlocked the door, and disappeared inside.

"Well, I never!" Sister Dee Light said, stroking the head of her perpetually trembling Chihuahua. "And him being family and all."

"That guy is a prick," said Sister Sasquatch, straightening her tunic. "I think we ought to tell Sister Radical Rage about him. She and her people might want to take a slightly closer look at Tintin."

Sister Ophelia Love hesitated only slightly. "I hate to say it, but I think you're right." She knew that Sister Radical Rage and her splinter group—Sisters Who Reap What You Sow— did not always follow the rules, but she had to admit they got results. Sometimes it was good to have a few outlaws in the convent. She just didn't want to know the details.

THE GRAY CLOUDS HAD finally decided: rain. Darkness fell as the skies opened up, the water puddled on the pavement, soaking up all light from streetlamps and headlights, making them equally ineffective. A car honked, blinded, barely missing Allen as he sprinted across Valencia and into Luna Park. The restaurant's heavy red velvet curtain swirled around him, sucking hungrily at his damp clothes. The winter rains had begun in earnest and he without his umbrella.

"Damn!" he said as he wiped the dripping water off the end of his nose and shook out the rivulets running off his fingertips. Glancing across the small, dimly lit restaurant, he spied J.B. and made a bee line for her table.

"You look like a drowned rat!"

"What is up with this weather?" Allen tried to wipe the already soaked-in raindrops from his shoulders. "It's like they take a fire hose to you!"

"Welcome to our winter," she said. "Do you think you'll melt or something, princess?"

"Whatever," Allen scowled, and turned to flag down the waitress. "If I'm going to get soaked like this, a drink is a must." He ordered a Roadrunner, hoping the Don Julio Blanco with chili in the drink would warm his bones.

J.B. couldn't wait any longer: "So let's hear, how are things coming? Did the workers get the lighting fixtures over the bar installed yet?" She'd designed the interior fit-out and was eager to know if the final look was all she'd hoped for.

"To be honest, they're behind. I've been riding the foreman's ass—which believe me is no pleasure—he tells me they can only work so hard. There's always some lame excuse

for a holiday I've never heard of slowing things down. First it was Día de la Raza, then Día de los Muertos. What's next, Día de los Assholes?" Allen took a long slow sip of his drink and yes indeed, the chili began to warm his core.

"Just so we're ready for opening next week. We cannot— I repeat, cannot—miss our deadline! We've got too much on the line."

"I know, just chill. We'll make it." The final week before an opening was always the most stressful. He'd come to expect that, but this time it was over the top. There was something about San Francisco that just got on his nerves. There was a way that the whole city felt a little seedier, a little dirtier, than jibed with its rep for being on the cutting edge. Certainly the homeless were part of it—they were just everywhere and so in-your-face. But it was more than that. There was a way he felt tugged at in this town—like a pack of imaginary dogs was nipping at his heels. It unsettled him, made it hard to know friend from foe, made it hard to find his bearings.

"We have a placement on SFGate and in the Guardian. I'm working viral on Chowhound and Yelp. And I think— keep your fingers crossed—that we'll get a mention in Leah Garchik's column. The buzz is building!" J.B. said, the PR short-hand flowing confidently from her lips.

Allen scanned the menu as the subject of food and the lubrication of the Roadrunner cocktail were beginning to make him hungry. "That's great. Pedro's got the seasonal menu finalized and I think you're going to like some of the things he's come up with."

The waitress, tall and lanky and dark, subtly pierced on her lower lip, glided quietly over to their table. "Are you ready to order?" she asked.

"I'll have the Salade Niçoise," J.B. said distractedly.

"I think I'll have the beet salad and the cassoulet. It's

a good night for cassoulet, don't you think?" Allen looked up at the waitress and arched on eyebrow, trying to induce a glimmer of life from those dark, inscrutable eyes. When she didn't reply, he pressed. "The richness, the warmth, the perfect match for the wetness all around. Are you wet tonight?"

The waitress wasn't taking the bait. "Cassoulet then. Another drink?"

Allen shook his head silently, and the waitress turned and left as quietly as she had appeared.

Allen looked across at J.B. and winked. "Never hurts to try."

"You're such a prick. You wouldn't even know what to do with her if she responded."

Allen shrugged. "I always like to keep my options open."

"Anyway, you were telling me about Pedro finalizing the menu," J.B. prodded, frustrated by Allen's arrogance. When they'd been in school together, at first she'd been confused by his sexuality, thinking him a metrosexual.

He'd responded to her cues but then it never seemed to go anywhere. Kind of like releasing an unknotted balloon only to see it sputter and fall to the ground when you let go. Finally she'd figured out that he was a closet case, and that explained the draw for both of them. She liked gay men, they were easy and safe and certainly better dressers than most of the men she dated. She was willing to meet his need to feign straightness every now and again because, professionally, there were still times and places when discretion remained the better part of valor.

"Oh yeah, the menu. He's got the usual—mini ahi tacos, Neiman Ranch sliders with Morbier cheese, thimble cassoulet. But he's mainly working the French angle. He's figured out

how to get these perfect mini baguettes with sliced Brie. And get this, this is brilliant! He's found a periwinkle source so he's going to make mini escargot. People are going to need tweezers to get those fuckers out of their shells!"

"Impressive!" J.B. said, biting her lower lip. "Has the stuffed Snowy arrived?" she asked, referring to the white dog that was the Tintin's sidekick.

"Arrived yesterday. We're going to put it right at the end of the bar so it's visible when people walk in. With that, the reporter's notebook menus, and the ligne claire prints, we oughta strike the right balance—you know, without hitting folks over the head with the concept. You want them to think they're on the inside of the joke, after all."

"Definitely. Let's meet down there tomorrow morning and you can finally show me firsthand. You know, I'm beginning to think this is going to be fun!" J.B. smiled, kicking Allen lightly in the shin under the table. "Let's toast to Tintin, our big adventure!"

The clink of glasses echoed the glint of their perfect, conspiratorial smiles.

DAISY WOKE UP HAPPY, grateful for a break in the rain, and eager to face the day. She left her apartment, rolled up to the corner of 15th and Dolores, and hit the brakes. She looked left, towards Dolores Park, checking to see which, if any, canines were about. Tall, skinny Rich and his black shepherd mix were down on the grassy median now but they were headed toward the park.

A young Asian-American woman with an over-caffeinated Chihuahua ricocheting on the end of a delicate leash had just crossed towards the vacant lot directly across the street. Daisy thought that if she were such a little thing in such a big world she would be that frenetic too. She didn't recognize the woman or the dog, but that never stopped Daisy from introducing herself and pulling them into her canine community. But before she could catch up with them she looked right and broke into a big grin. Marty and his two-dog entourage were coming her way.

"Morning, Daisy!" Marty called.

"Morning, Marty. How are my babies today?" Daisy yelled this with such enthusiasm that Marty's Great Dane Tim stumbled in his lumbering gate. Tim was short for "Tiny Tim," Marty's attempt at irony.

"Come here, Tim, you big cutie you!" Daisy patted her left thigh with one hand while twirling the joystick to face the fast–approaching giant. The Dane was gentle and generally tried to keep his eagerness in check, but even so, his sheer mass pulled heavy on the leash. His droopy red-lined lids were pulled back wide, as were the corners of his mouth.

"Tim, I could almost swear you're smiling!" The big dog offered his massive skull into her lap like a gift. She laid a

hand on his cranium and expertly began to find his magic spots. He didn't move, leaning heavier into Daisy's lap. The scratches she was applying behind his right ear were particularly satisfying to him this morning and he was in no hurry to go anywhere.

"He's so spoiled," Marty said. "You know, he won't move a muscle as long as you keep that up."

"Now slide over, Tim," Daisy said gently, "we've gotta make room for Stubs." With this she patted her thigh with her free left hand. Almost instantly, the smallest, scruffiest, blondest mixed terrier she'd ever met launched himself up into what little space remained next to Tiny's head.

"That's a good boy! You missed me, didn't you?" Daisy cooed. "I haven't seen you in days, you little Dickens."

Stubs worked hard to try and lick Daisy's chin but couldn't quite reach. He could tell she'd had chicken in the not-too-distant past and he wanted whatever leftovers remained. But he could also tell that Tim was getting annoyed at the clambering. Stubs long ago learned the hard way to respect the boundaries that the big lug set, knowing that his protection was worth all the rules and etiquette. Odd as they were together, they were loyal pals. Yes, Tim protected Stubs from larger more aggressive dogs, but Stubs provided Tim with comic relief, and a bit of an ice-breaker for those who found his size intimidating.

"You love me, don't you boys?" Daisy continued showering attention on the two dogs.

"Morning Daisy," Robbie said as she stopped beside them, coffee in hand. Although the exact time might vary, Daisy could always count on catching Robbie either on the way to or the way back from picking up her regular morning coffee and bagel.

"Will you look at these two?" Daisy said proudly. "They

are such a pair, aren't they?" She continued scratching Tim and hugging Stubs. "Have you met Marty? Marty this is Robbie. She used to have the sweetest spaniel named Molly. She was such a good girl," Daisy said, giving Robbie a sad smile to acknowledge Molly's passing.

Robbie nodded in nostalgic agreement, and took a sip of her coffee.

"This is Tim, and Stubs," Daisy offered with the utmost politeness, true to her Southern upbringing.

"Are they both yours?" Robbie asked, turning towards Marty.

"Yup, had 'em both since they were pups. They make quite an odd couple, don't they?"

Robbie raised her eyebrows in agreement, and then some. She tended to be of few words first thing in the morning. While she appreciated Daisy's neighborliness, sometimes she didn't feel quite up to long-winded conversations. Daisy would get on a topic Robbie found awkward or other times simply go on for too long but if someone else was there, or if dogs approached, that offered her the possibility of escape.

"You'd be surprised what a disarming pair they can be," added Marty.

"Disarming?" Robbie queried, curiosity filtering through her not-yet-fully-caffeinated stupor.

"Yeah, I work with kids, mostly in the East Bay—suburbs, like Hayward, violence prevention. I take Stubs and Tim here along to model possibilities. You know, the whole gentle giant thing. The kids really connect with the dogs and, god knows, they need something to connect to."

"How so?" Robbie was curious. Teenagers scared her some, so any insight was welcome.

"Like just the other day, one of my kids came in with a big fresh X tattooed on his neck. Now that's certainly not

gonna help his job prospects but I tried to play cool. 'What's that signify?' I asked. 'X marks the spot?' Know what he said? 'Nope, X as in crossed out, incorrect, X as in nothing matters.' It's sad when they can't even see their own fundamental value as a human being."

Daisy paused for a moment, thinking. "Well for me, God provides that kind of assurance of value. I mean, if he made me in his image and all then I must have some purpose."

"Do you ever go to church, Robbie?" Daisy continued. "I find it comforting and Mission Dolores is just around the corner."

"Hmm," Robbie said noncommittally. She'd learned that often, if she just waited, Daisy would move right by some touchy subject without even noticing. It was almost as if Robbie was a sounding wall off which Daisy simply took pleasure in hearing the echo of her own voice. This time, Daisy pressed on.

"Have you been?"

"I don't usually go to church," Robbie offered. "Really not my thing." Hoping to leave it at that. But Daisy was on a roll.

"Marty here was raised Catholic, so he's used to the formality of the services down at the Mission. But me, I come from a different tradition. I was raised Pentecostal. In comparison, these Catholic services are dull with a capital D! No one singing, no one speaking in tongues, no one writhing on the floor . . ." Daisy chuckled at that last image. "Can you imagine?"

Robbie tried not to.

"What were you raised?" Daisy queried.

"Heathen." Robbie's stock response. It was in fact technically true. The youngest in her family, by the time she'd arrived her parents had lost interest in what little spiritual training they'd given her older siblings. So nothing, not even a smattering of Unitarian indoctrination, had come her way. As an adult, one girlfriend had insisted on dragging her to Catholic services year after year. Though the Christmas Eve candlelight services were beautiful, the experience of organized religion never had captured her imagination.

"But don't you miss having something to believe in?"

"Not really." What Robbie really wanted to say was, "How could I believe in something that doesn't believe in me?" It was too early in the morning, and not enough coffee had been drunk to get so worked up. She really didn't want to get into a long discussion with Daisy about homophobia and the church. Plus the whole genderqueer thing was just too much to try and negotiate in such a conservative environment. The thought of dealing with the stares of some middle-aged Christian woman as she used the ladies room after a service was about the last thing she wanted to do.

Robbie took a long swig of her coffee. No one spoke.

Finally, Daisy relented. "I guess I just like the routine."

Tim had started to get restless, pulling his big lug nut of a head out of Daisy's lap. Stubs, of course, remained there, happy as a pea in a pod.

"OK, kids, I guess it's time to go!" Marty said, casting a direct stare at the recalcitrant Stubs, who tried to avoid eye contact.

Robbie, seizing this opening, took her leave as well.

"See ya!" she waved behind her as Marty and Daisy worked to untangle the knot of leashes and dogs and wheelchair.

ANOTHER NIGHT'S RAIN HAD passed but yet the air was still strangely warm and moist. A light steam rose off the damp sidewalk where the sun was beginning to strike the cement. Daisy shook her head in wonder as she looked up the length of 15th to find nothing but blue sky framing Buena Vista Park. No matter how long she lived here, she didn't think she'd ever get used to San Francisco's weather. One moment it was pouring, the next sunny. Unlike the predictable weather of her native Kentucky, San Francisco's was whimsical and stealthy. No big thunderstorms to announce the rain. Just a soft insistent dampness that gradually nudged its way into deluge, then just as quietly morphed into mist and blue sky and puffy clouds.

Daisy's plan this morning was to head up to Safeway Plaza, pick up some coffee at Starbucks, and then make the usual patrol back down Dolores Street to catch up with her canine pals. She counted any day as an excellent day when she saw the majority of her pack. Not that the dogs were better than people, that wasn't it, rather, they were just more straightforward. Clear in their affection, clear in their annoyance, clear in their distraction.

Of course, the people who were attached to the other end of the leash were pretty interesting too but she'd found them a bit skittish in this town. In the South you could just go up to a person and say "Good morning. How y'all doing today?" and get a polite, languid conversation out of the proffer. But here folks were a bit wary, in a hurry, insular. Talk to their dogs, though, and all those defenses melted away. Daisy had all the time in the world and was happy to play this game.

She nudged her chair carefully across to the sunny

side of Dolores Street. The steady stream of luxury SUVs, impatient hybrids, and over-powered BMWs were in their usual hurry this morning. Most had just dropped their kids off at the upscale preschool down the street. Once free of their precious cargo they sped along Dolores, cell phones pressed to ears, oblivious to all but their own agendas. On more than one morning, she'd been forced to a screeching halt halfway through the crosswalk. Their kids were treasures worthy of all indulgence but running over someone else, that didn't seem to matter.

Daisy turned and headed up towards Safeway. The sun silhouetted the high horsemen on the Volunteer's Memorial statue at the end of Dolores Street where it met Market Street, the main diagonal route cutting from the Castro down all the way to the Ferry Building. She liked that statue, in part because of the beautiful winged horse but also because it was so incongruous right in that spot. Were those warriors set on attacking the Ford Dealership? Or defending the Petco store on the other side? Or maybe they were leading a charge of the homeless lined up at the bottle collection station across the street? It seemed a sad final location for their frozen bravery.

Bumping across the cable car tracks Daisy debated whether or not to do some shopping this early in the morning. Part of the fun of going to Safeway was the people you might run into. But she had a feeling that it was a bit too early for a very interesting crowd. "I think I'll come back later," she said to no one in particular, making a bee line for the Starbucks next door.

After squeezing her chair through the doors and up to the counter, she paused to survey the pastries on display this morning. She really shouldn't. Her doctor said that her blood sugar was definitely on the high side and that her heart wasn't as strong as he'd like. He'd scolded her and told her to lay off the sugary treats. So far she'd been pretty good about it but this morning that sticky bun was just too good looking to be denied.

She looked up at the barista, who was busy looking down at her nails.

"Good morning!" Daisy said with her usual vigor.

The woman looked up and gave her a half-hearted smile. "What can I get you?" she said with a decided lack of enthusiasm that perfectly balanced Daisy's excess.

"It's such a beautiful day I think I'll indulge and have a large coffee and one of those sticky buns, sweetie."

"One grande daily blend!" the barista translated. "Room for cream?"

"Yes, please!"

The barista retrieved the bun with long metal tongs. She struggled to wrestle it into a paper bag that was far too small and fragile. Daisy took a certain pleasure in watching the barista's feigned indifference battle against her growing aggravation with this nearly impossible task.

The barista slid the slightly ripped bag across the counter, then the coffee. Daisy paid, then rolled over to the cream and sugar counter. She held the glass sugar dispenser over the coffee for a count of five then added half and half until the coffee rose just to the cup's edge. Stirring carefully, she blew across the top of the cup hoping to cool it just a bit before snapping on the lid. She liked to be able to drink her coffee, not carry it around like a scorching hot water bottle. She wedged the distorted bag with the sticky bun into the corner of her chair next to her ample thighs and retraced her route back out of Starbucks.

Today, she figured, was going to be a good dog day. When it rained, folks shortened their dog walks to the bare minimum. So when the sun had broken out this morning, she

could almost guarantee they'd all be out in force.

Daisy backtracked down to Dolores Street, staying on the west side. She hoped she'd see Rich and his new dog.

For years they'd chatted while he walked his two black shepherds, Sodom and Gomorrah. She'd watched as both had gotten older and a lamer. Some days Rich would be walking them, some days his boyfriend, but the dogs were out there every single day. Then about a year ago, she'd seen Rich with only one dog in tow.

"WE HAD to put G. down yesterday," Rich had said, the tears flowing easily while Sodom sniffed at the grass. Rich ran his fingers absent-mindedly though his ponytail, seeking solace in his own dark fur.

Daisy had felt for Rich but she was more worried about Sodom. His brother was gone but he didn't seem distressed. Usually dogs did mourn. They could feel loss every bit as acutely as their human companions. But Sodom had seemed calm, even content. It wasn't until the next week that Daisy had understood why.

She'd passed Rich again walking slowly, this time dogless. Rich was tall and lanky but he looked even more so this day.

"Did I miss my baby today?" Daisy had asked.

Rich just shook his head and hurried on. "I'm late," he'd said, coughing slightly.

Over the next few weeks she'd seen Rich or his boyfriend or occasionally both but no more Sodom. They both looked so sad and long-faced.

Then one morning last week, election morning if she remembered correctly, she'd seen Rich at a distance being pulled along Dolores by, what else, a young black shepherd, and Rich was grinning from ear to ear. Even from a far, Daisy could tell he was in love once again.

THAT MORNING last week, they'd turned off before she could catch up but this morning, just a few block away from Starbucks, Rich was heading her way, barely in control of his new charge.

"Finally, we meet!" Daisy said. "Are you going to introduce me to your new baby?" The dog was still so puppy-scatter-brained that she hadn't noticed Daisy approaching. When the chair whirred to a stop in front of her, the shepherd jumped with alarm, did a 180 in the air and let out a high-pitched squeak.

"It's OK girl," Rich said, smoothing the raised hackles on the shepherd's black neck.

"Daisy, this is G.M.. G.M., meet Daisy. It's short for Gay Marriage. We figure if we spend every day saying 'Here, Gay Marriage' and 'Come, Gay Marriage' and 'Stay, Gay Marriage,' it might send some karmic message out to the universe to overturn this hateful Prop 8."

"Well, regardless of the name, she sure is cute." Daisy wasn't sure exactly how she felt about gay marriage but Proposition 8 had passed, creating a constitutional amendment that said it was illegal again in California. The Bible certainly said marriage was supposed to be between a man and a woman—that's what the priest down at Mission Dolores had said just before the election. It wasn't like she couldn't see that Rich and his boyfriend were a steady couple, she just didn't think it was quite the same as her marriage to her first husband, or her second, for that matter. "You could have called her C.U. instead!" Daisy laughed.

"See You?" Rich asked, "Like 'come see you'? Sounds like someone with limited grasp of proper grammar."

"No, C.U. as in Civil Union. She'd be more likely to stay, that way." Daisy slapped her thigh as she laughed at her own joke, rustling the Starbuck's bag she'd totally forgotten.

"Nice," Rich said, only slightly amused. He now realized Daisy, pleasant as she may be, was probably one of the two-thirds of Christian voters who were responsible for passing Prop 8. He really didn't want to go there, not this early in the morning.

"Got me a sticky bun this morning." Daisy said, changing the subject. "Bet that would get G.M. to come, sit, and stay all at once." Daisy took a large bite, crumbs raining down to her ample bosom.

G.M. did take notice, but, just as quickly, was distracted by a squirrel that was poking around the base of the date palm across the street and about twenty yards farther up on the Dolores median. She took off like a shot, dragging Rich stumbling behind her. His lanky build no match for her youthful dogpower.

"G.M., no pulling! Shit. See you later Daisy."

Daisy laughed and took another bite of the sticky bun. It was particularly good today. She washed it down with some coffee, which had just reached the perfect temperature. By holding the bottom part of the cup in her right hand, she could use her little finger to press the joystick left and spin herself in a complete, but slow, 360. The battery must be getting low, she thought, even though she'd charged it overnight. She hoped it wasn't getting to what the repair guy called "over conditioned." She never could quite understand when it was better to let the battery run down all the way and when it was better to charge it fully. All she knew was that replacing the battery cost close to $500 and she didn't have that kind of money.

Daisy surveyed her domain from the corner. Rich had

crossed over Dolores to the sidewalk on the far side and he and G.M. were in a tug-of-war on their way home. No other dogs were coming up or down the length of 15th. On Dolores, the action was equally slow. No dogs were in the median as far as she could see, but down near the synagogue on the corner of 16th she thought she could see the woman with the Chihuahua. It was hard to tell, but she might as well head that way and see.

She crossed over 15th, narrowly avoiding being run over by a skinny guy whipping down the hill on one of those crazy bike messenger bikes. He skidded slightly, doing a neat little wiggle around her, before accelerating through the intersection with no regard for the stop sign.

Crazy kids! As she paused to collect herself, she noticed something odd—for whatever reason the fates of urban coincidence had aligned and, in that moment, no car passed, no plane flew overhead, no fire or police sirens cried, no Harley roared by, no wild parrots squawked on their way to the park, not even a breeze stirred the noisy palm fronds. For just the briefest of moments, everything was absolutely still.

It was because of that unusual silence that Daisy was able to hear a very quiet but unmistakable canine whimper, almost more of a vibration than a sound. She turned her chair slowly and tried to locate the source. She couldn't see anything on the median, and it seemed to far to be the source of this noise, and there was nothing along the sidewalk. She had stopped right next to a vacant lot, the one that used to house the Baptist Church, before it burned down in the early '90s. It abutted the burned-out Victorian parsonage that still stood. Peering into the shadow between the bottom of the parsonage's steps and the chain-link fence that surrounded the empty lot, she willed her ears to see what her eyes could not. The sound again, slightly louder now, seemed to echo off the tan bricks

of the porch. Daisy rolled closer to the weeds and listened again. Yes, there it was. As she looked close she could see one tall clump of grass quivering inexplicably. A paw was just barely visible amongst the roots.

"Pst-pst-pst," Daisy called softly. "C'mere. It's OK."

She patted the side of her leg, trying to entice whatever was in the weeds to emerge. A small black nose pushed timidly through the foliage.

"Skittles—what are you doing in there? C'mere, boy." Daisy held out her empty hand in encouragement but the dog was frozen in place, shivering terribly, and unable to move.

Daisy broke off a big piece of sticky bun and held it down towards the terrified creature. "Come here, silly. Come get a treat."

The hot smell of cinnamon was enough to tip the balance and Skittle shot out of the grass directly into Daisy's lap. His body trembled so violently that it radiated through hers, splashing coffee over her hand. Daisy poured the remainder of the coffee out onto the ground, tucked the empty cup and the pastry bag in tight beside here thigh, so she could give Skittles her full attention.

"What's up, little buddy? What are you doing here all by yourself?" Skittles big black eyes in his flat Boston Terrier face looked up at her in stark terror. His shaking did not abate.

This was strange. How did Skittles get out here by himself? Even though she'd only met him a few times before, attached to that tall guy who was a bit of a cold fish, Skittles had possessed that combination of qualities that always captured her heart—cuteness and playing hard-to-get.

Daisy hugged the pup a little closer, trying to get his trembling to stop. He remained steadfastly terrified.

She spun the black leather-studded collar around, until

she could read the small brass dog-bone-shaped tag. It had these three lines, "If I'm loose, I'm lost!" then "Skittles" followed by the phone number "415-979-9550." No address.

"Well, that's not much help without a cell phone. Where's your dad?" Daisy surveyed the street, hoping to see the tall guy running from one direction or the other. What kind of person let their dog get loose? Sure, sometimes leashes broke, doors got left ajar, but these little animals, god's creatures, needed our protection. There was no one searching for a dog as far as the eye could see. Strange.

"Well, we'll just have to take you home and give your dad a call. He's going to be missing you for sure!" Daisy gave one last look around, holding Skittles close as she turned her chair this way and that, just to be sure. Something glinted back in the weeds, catching Daisy's eye.

"Look, I do believe that's your leash! We better grab that too before we go."

Daisy rolled closer to the grass but the chair was too big to get far enough in. Even from a distance, she could see the end of the tooled leather leash that matched Skittles' collar.

Just then, Lisa and Rocco meandered slowly around the corner. Nothing would hurry Rocco along in his old age, and Lisa patiently walked at his funereal pace, just a few steps ahead. Seeing Daisy, she raised one hand and waved hello. No need to yell out yet, as it would be several minutes before they'd covered the twenty-five yards to where Daisy was parked.

"Hey Lisa, can you come here?"

Daisy rarely referred to Lisa directly by name. Her sweet attentions were almost always for Rocco. Lisa tapped Rocco on the butt, encouraging him to leave off sniffing at the bird droppings on the sidewalk and instead to focus on Daisy.

"I need your help!" Daisy yelled, squeaked really, with

that shrill twang of hers.

Like a slow-motion replay, Lisa and Rocco steadily covered the distance.

"Hey Daisy, who's that you got there?" Lisa reached over to scratch the head of the quivering thing in Daisy's lap.

"This is Skittles. He's lost. I found him over here in the bushes. I think he belongs to that tall guy, you know—the new guy."

"I don't think I've seen him before. Where is he?"

"I have no idea," Daisy said with clear indignation, "I think I see Skittles' leash over in those weeds. But I can't quite reach it. Do you think you could help me?"

"Sure." Lisa pushed in slowly by the fence and kneeled down to reach the leash's end. Rocco had only just taken note of the small furry creature in Daisy's lap and was sniffing at him clumsily. This didn't make Skittles any more comfortable, having some wrinkly old stranger-dog's nose up his butt.

Lisa had to turn sideways to squeeze in far enough to reach the quick-release clip of the leash, the only part she could get a hold of. She could just barely grasp it between two fingers, but when she pulled it wouldn't give. Reaching in a little farther, she pulled harder. Nothing. She pulled again, leaning back slightly, then suddenly something let go. Lisa fell back, landing with a thump beside Daisy's chair, one end of the leash still in her fist while the rest trailed back toward the grass, silently pointing back to a now visible—and decidedly dead—pale hand.

Daisy and Lisa screamed in unison. Skittles shook even harder than he already had been. And even Rocco, the screams falling on half-deaf ears, turned his clouded eyes to see what might be the matter.

SITTING AT the built-in Formica table of the breakfast nook in their Dolores Street apartment, Joe struggled to hold his paper upright. He gave it one good shake before giving up and laid it flat on the table. With one hand he lifted the mug to his lips, blew on the coffee's surface before taking a noisy slurp, while the other hand traced a path across the newsprint, feeling the news before reading. The smell of cooking bacon made his stomach rumble.

Joe's wife Janet stood before the stove, meditatively turning the bacon strips with a fork, trying not to get burned by the splatter of hot grease. Her thin nightgown hung out from beneath an oversized plaid wool shirt, which she'd added to fight the morning's cold.

After the crackling fat of bacon grease, the next loudest sound in the kitchen was Joe's hand running over the paper. The steady brushing sound annoyed her to no end but she said nothing. She rarely did.

Joe flipped another page, coming to the editorial section. His attention was only half on the paper, half somewhere else completely. This morning routine was so familiar that he was on autopilot. Not the relaxed "put your hands behind your head and lean back and enjoy the view" kind of autopilot. More like the dentist's "open wide, this won't hurt a bit" autopilot.

Janet and he had perfected this routine over many years. It worked, but it was an uneasy peace. In the early days, they'd laughed and danced across the floor of this same sunny kitchen, but they'd grown apart over time. His retirement had made that all too clear. Before, when he'd left each day in his brown uniform to drive his route on the 22 bus, it seemed like Janet liked him at least a little bit. Now that he was around most days, they barely talked. He wondered if she missed him in uniform or if she just missed his absence every day. So

now there was a new part to their routine—after breakfast, he'd retreat to the garage and putter about while she stayed up here doing God-knows-what.

As Joe flipped to the sports section, Janet set a plate of bacon and eggs next to his coffee and turned away. Joe opened his mouth but no words emerged. Instead, he looked back down to see what crisis the Raiders and their crazy owner, Al Davis, had suffered overnight.

The wail of sirens this morning was nothing unusual— the urban equivalent of morning birds twittering—so at first he barely noticed as the sound approached. It was only when it came on full bore and then stopped almost directly in front of the house that the sound registered as something out of the ordinary.

As the sirens unwound, he went to check out the front window. He hadn't heard any cars skidding or gunshots so he guessed it was probably just overly enthusiastic cops come to evict the homeless, who often camped beside the electric box over by the vacant lot. The cops didn't usually go at it with full sirens though. He pulled the curtains back and was stunned by the crazy scene across Dolores. Cops were coming from all directions. The curious were rapidly gathering. And there in the midst of it all was Daisy, clutching a small black dog who he could see—even from this distance—was trembling violently.

Joe was out the door in a flash.

AS HE crossed Dolores, Joe saw that the police cars were parked all over the place as if they'd been tossed down in a wild roll of the dice. One squad car was diagonal across Dolores facing against the traffic, another up on the sidewalk, while a third sat blocking Dolores at 15th with its lights still flashing. He guessed that the coroner's van had arrived last because it was parked more discretely ahead of the scattered black and whites.

He could see that a crowd had gathered at the edge of the yellow tape that the cops had stretched from the fencing out to the Acacia trees on the edge of the sidewalk. Having seen his share of accidents, Joe knew that the casual onlookers, sensing no immediate action, would usually get restless and wander off while only the patient would continue to gawk. He also knew that, normally, that was where Daisy would have been—gawking—had she not been right smack in the middle of that circle of onlookers.

DAISY STILL held Skittles in her lap but had tucked him in under her fleece jacket, hoping that a bit more warmth could stop his shivering, knowing that it wouldn't. She watched the huddle of officials over near where she'd found Skittles. The man wearing the black nylon jacket with the words *Coroner* in yellow on the back and a cop were squeezed in tight between fence and stoop.

"OK, I think I'm ready to move the body," she heard the coroner say. "Rick, if you step over here, I'll grab his arms. As we move him, try not to step in the area under his body. There may be evidence there."

They'd already wheeled over a low gurney and unzipped the black plastic bag that rested on top.

"Ready? On my count: one, two, three!" They lifted the wedged body out of the space, carried it over, and laid it atop the gurney. The soles of the victim's shoes squeaked as they settled into the rubberized material of the bag.

The coroner looked young, like a geeky science student, complete with glasses held together with tape on one corner.

He pushed them back up his nose as he examined the body more thoroughly than he'd been able to when it was stuck in the bushes. The detective stood quietly beside him, note pad in hand. He was older, his gray suit rumbled and shiny at the edges from wear. He waited for the coroner to speak.

"Well of course there will be more in the full report, but for right now I can tell you the obvious: white male, 30 to 45. Judging by the body temp and rigor, I'd say he's been here overnight. Take a look at this, though." The coroner lifted the right arm of the victim and pulled back the loose sleeve of his jacket. A deep X, complete with horizontal cuts at the top of each diagonal, had been carved into the soft flesh of the inner forearm, directly over a tattoo of a red heart on a blue and black flag. The edges, though caked with dried blood, were neat and clean.

"Someone used something pretty sharp to make that happen," the detective squinted to get a closer look. "And, it looks like they might have had some training in typography. What are those things at the top called? Serifs?"

"Indeed!" acknowledged the coroner. They both stood still, admiring the precision of the wound.

"I won't have the official cause of death for a few days," added the coroner. "But a young guy like this with no clear marks, it often ends up as an overdose, but the way the body was wedged in there ... doesn't seem like he could have crawled in there on his own." He wrestled with the heavy-duty zipper of the bag, trying to get it all the way closed.

"OK, well let me know ASAP," the detective replied, flipping his notepad shut.

DAISY HAD been listening but watching all this out of the corner of her eye. She didn't really want to see the body directly, in case it was all bloody. Not her thing: blood. It made her squeamish as hell. Vomit really didn't do much for her either, but she could deal with that. Blood, though, sucked the very life out of her—as if their blood loss was her own. She had seen the face when they'd placed the body on the gurney. It had the same angular features she remembered from the man she'd seen leashed to Skittles.

"Ma'am, I'd like a word with you," the detective said as he approached, licking the tip of his pen before bringing it to rest on the notepad.

"Of course," Daisy said, twirling her chair in his direction. She didn't really trust police that much—who did after all?—but this was another time where her Southern manners kicked in automatically. She found herself sitting a bit more upright and smiling up at him as they began.

"So you found the body. Can you tell me what time that was?" He looked down at his pad rather than at Daisy.

"I think it was probably about 7:30. I'd gone up to—" Daisy started.

"I'm sorry, can you tell me your name again?" he interrupted.

"Daisy Catsimatides, a good Kentucky name," she said proudly.

"Is that with a C or a K?" the detective asked as his pen hesitated above the page.

"C, of course," Daisy said, slightly insulted.

"And you live . . . ?"

"Just over there, 1863 15th, the high-rise. I'm the 'busybody' of the building. You just ask anyone."

"So, Ms. Cat-suh-muh-tee-deez," the detective struggled with the unfamiliar name, "That was about 7:30?"

"Yes, thereabouts, and you can call me Daisy. Everyone does. I'd gone up the street to go to the Safeway but I

changed my mind. My feet were bothering me all last night. See how swollen they are?" Daisy pointed toward towards the sausage-like ankle, snug in its blue corduroy slipper.

"Yes, ma'am." The detective gave a cursory glance and then looked back at his notebook.

"I was going to get me some celery. It's a natural diuretic, you know. But I changed my mind. I ended up going to Starbucks and getting coffee and a sticky bun instead." Daisy paused and looked down, slightly ashamed as she confessed her sin.

"Anyway, I came back down this way, just like I do every day, to see me some of my people. That's what I call the dogs—'my people.'" She could smell Skittles from inside her coat and held him a little closer. It was a funny smell, the distinctive odor of dried spittle from too much anxious licking.

"I was just getting started down this way when I heard a sound. It was coming from over there, where I found the man." Daisy pointed towards the trampled grass between the building and the empty lot's fence.

"So I rolled over to take a closer look and that's when I found Skittles." Daisy pulled back her blue fleece, revealing the terrified terrier. "He was just sitting there whimpering. I tried to get him to come out but he was too scared. Good thing I had the sticky bun—that's the only thing that did it."

Curious, the detective started to reach towards Skittles but the dog shrunk back, deeper into the warm place between Daisy's breast and arm. The detective shook his head and continued, "You said 'Skittles'—you know this dog?"

"I know all the dogs!" Daisy said emphatically. "Now this little one, we've only met twice before and we were just getting acquainted. I didn't even know his human's name yet."

"OK, we'll get back to the dog in just a minute. So is that when you saw the body?"

"No, I didn't see that at first. Not at all. I saw the leash and figured I should bring that along too. I figured Skittles had escaped somehow and I was going to get him—and his leash—back to his owner."

"So when did you see the body?"

"Not till Lisa pulled it out. Lisa, she has the dog Rocco, I think you talked to her already. Lisa comes by and I ask her to reach in and get the leash. I can't get in there, you see, because of the chair and all."

The officer surveyed the wheelchair, turned and looked at where the body had been, and nodded in agreement.

"Anyway, Lisa—she's just a little slip of a thing—she reaches in and she was able to just grab the end of the leash. It had that nice, fancy buckle on the end, so she could just get a hold of it. But it was stuck. She pulled harder and that's when it broke free . . . and the arm appeared. We both just screamed!"

"Yes, ma'am, so I've heard."

Just then, Joe approached and placed one hand gently on Daisy's shoulder. "Are you OK?"

Daisy turned, surprised. His touch caught her off guard.

"Oh, Joe. Hey, can you believe it? I think it's that new guy, the tall one. Skittles' dad."

Joe shook his head. He didn't know dogs the way Daisy knew dogs.

Daisy pulled back the edge of her jacket again to reveal Skittles to him. The dog's round moist eyes stared imploringly. Joe reached one hand forward, very slowly, and allowed Skittles to sniff at the back of his hand. It smelled like bacon to Skittles. Joe could feel Skittles shaking, but it slowed a bit as he reached around and tugged gently at the soft skin at the

base of the dog's ear.

"Ahem." The detective cleared his throat, the moment between Daisy and Joe had disrupted his train of thought, sending the unfinished business of the dog's disposition rolling down the tracks forgotten.

"Well, I guess that's all I have for you for now. I'll probably have a few more questions in a day or so." He handed her his business card. "Detective Rendell, ma'am. I'll be in touch." He gave a quick salute with his notepad and turned back towards the coroner, who was trying to wrangle the stretcher into the back of his van. "Hold up, Pete, I'll give you a hand!"

"Isn't he going to take the dog?" Joe whispered to Daisy.

"Shh. He's focused on the humans and I want to keep it that way. Skittles here is coming home with me for now. I don't want him having to go to Animal Care and Control. They're nothing but trouble, those hard-hearted bastards."

"Well at least come across the street to the garage. You can tell me what happened and I'll get you some coffee."

Joe lifted the yellow tape and Daisy wheeled under. The crowd had thinned now that the coroner had departed with the body. A few of police were doing the final sweep for evidence but they'd be finished soon and by afternoon, there'd be no trace that anything had happened. No indication that a body had been laying here. That Skittles, poor little thing, had cowered for God-knows-how-many-hours at his master's side.

Joe and Daisy crossed back over Dolores, and over to his garage. Joe unlocked the T-handle latch and pulled the door up and away. Inside the garage, he put some water into the Mr. Coffee machine he kept on the workbench and set it to brewing.

Daisy told him the full story of her morning. She was

beginning to get a rhythm to the tale, this being about the third retelling. It felt good to run over it again with Joe. It calmed her.

"But how are you feeling now?" he asked, concern evident in his eyes.

"I'm OK, I think. Certainly not how one wants to start one's day. But I'm better off than that guy. At least I'm still here kicking and screaming." Daisy laughed, but it was a hollow sound.

"So you'd met him before?"

"Just a few times. I think he's relatively new to the area. Another one of those yuppie types, but pleasant enough. I remember I called Skittles a scaredy cat. Well look at him now." She peered inside her jacket where the dog had finally stopped shaking. His eyes were dropping slightly. Exhaustion was beginning to take hold.

"He's been through a lot, poor little fella, and so have you!" Joe said. He poured two cups of coffee into the "We Are Family" rainbow cups he'd found at a yard sale. The colors had pleased him at the time, bright and cheery. He figured he'd misread the words, thinking it said "All in the Family"—like the TV show—instead. He had been doing that more and more since retirement. He'd look at a sign or a headline in the paper and it would make perfect sense, it just it would be wrong. Just the other day, he'd been surprised by a bumper sticker that said "Preparation H Energy Source!" Who knew a hemorrhoid treatment might be the new Viagra. Only later did he realize that the bumper stickers was referring to *Prop*osition H, the ballot measure about energy independence for the city, and not a new treatment for erectile dysfunction.

"Well Skittles and I've got each other, at least for now," Daisy sighed. "I figure the guy's family will come looking for

Skittles as soon as they hear about this, but meanwhile he can hang with me."

Joe sipped on his coffee and stared out the open garage door towards the vacant lot. "Seems like an odd place for a person to end up. That building's been empty for years, but it's a busy corner. You'd think someone would've seen something."

Daisy nodded in agreement.

"If it had been a gunshot," Joe continued, "I would have heard it for sure, but you say the cops didn't mention that?"

"No, and I didn't see any blood, except for that mark on his arm."

"Strange," Joe said, falling silent.

"You know, Joe, I think I better get myself something to eat. I'm beginning to feel a little spent." Daisy was looking noticeably paler than usual.

Again, Joe put his hand on Daisy's blue fleecy shoulder, giving a gentle but insistent squeeze. Daisy felt herself relax just a little more. Inside her coat, Skittles snored gently.

"Well if you need anything, don't hesitate to ask. You know where you can find me," Joe said.

"Thank you, Joe. You're a good friend. God loves you." Daisy pulled out of the garage, turned and wheeled towards home.

Joe stepped out into the middle of the sidewalk, its cement squares all askew from the fast-growing roots of the Magnolia trees in front of his place, and watched until Daisy rounded the corner. He took one more sip of his coffee then headed back into the coolness of the garage.

BY THE TIME ROBBIE had dragged her sorry ass out of bed, showered, gotten dressed, and pulled her hair up into a half-decent faux hawk, it was almost eleven o'clock. Even so, she stuck with her regular routine, taking herself on a dogless walk up to Muddy Waters for the regular coffee and bagel. It was only on the way back home that she noticed the yellow crime scene tape on the corner of the vacant lot.

"Wonder what happened there?" she muttered to no one in particular. Crossing Dolores, she waded through the flock of pigeons that regularly congregated on the sidewalk outside the corner apartment building. They avidly pecked at something, but she could never see just what it was. She assumed that someone in one of the apartments whose bay windows hung over the sidewalk must have tossed something down for the birds each morning. Whatever it was, it was either too small to be visible or so delicious that the pigeons kept searching long after all traces were gone. All she knew was that as she passed they gave her a light, airy, and slightly dirty feel when they fluttered up all around her.

She unlocked the apartment door and pushed in past the pile of shoes, the cotton grocery bags lying on the floor, and the bike in the hallway. Her cat, Mr. T, was fast asleep on the couch and didn't even bother to look up.

Like a sacred offering, she put her coffee on the table and unwrapped the bagel she so loved. The crinkle of the paper was just as oddly pleasing as she knew the bagel itself would be, each and every morning. Funny how a person could fetishize just about anything, she thought, her mind wandering back over the complex world of fetish she had witnessed at the Castle last night.

SATURDAY NIGHT, Robbie had gone to the Castle for one of the regular "play parties." She went alone, which usually meant she'd only watch. When she arrived, she found her buddy Kathleen sitting on the couch, deep in conversation with a rather hirsute man who was wearing the most beautiful red leather corset, with heels to match. She remembered the first time she'd seen a man in a corset—a tall slender queen—and just how incredible he had looked.

Kathleen spied Robbie from across the room and motioned with that irresistible come-hither curl of an index finger. As soon as Robbie was within reach, Kathleen pulled her down into her ample lap. Robbie snuggled into the fleshy soft warmth of Kathleen's bosom and let her legs settle into the lap of the corseted man.

"Well, look who's here. How are you, darling?" Kathleen cooed.

"I'm good. How's the party?"

"Not bad so far. Are you alone?" Kathleen furrowed her brow, looking a bit concerned.

"Yeah, I couldn't round up anyone for this evening. Didn't quite have the energy, but I figured I'd at least come down and watch a bit." Robbie tried to slide off of Kathleen's lap and onto the couch beside her but Kathleen would have none of that.

"Hey, let me go!" Robbie said in mock-resistance.

"Not until you promise me something." Kathleen smiled her wicked smile, looking over the top of her glasses. "Promise you'll come find me later, and don't you dare sneak out of here without doing so. There're some knots I might need some help with . . ."

"Yes, ma'am," Robbie saluted and Kathleen released her.

It was relatively early in the night so the action was only just starting to heat up. Upstairs, one couple was preparing for what looked to be a pretty elaborate bondage scene. Right now, though, they were just unloading ropes and carefully laying them out beneath the pulley system than hung from the ceiling.

Over in the other corner, two cute radical faerie boys were chatting with a beautiful young hippie girl who was sporting wings and a blindfold and very little else. They caressed her gently with long strokes while whispering into her ears, one on each side. She squirmed slightly. Her hands were cuffed and affixed to an eye-bolt on the wall so she wasn't going anywhere anytime soon. Her laugh, though, showed that their ministrations were ticklish and delightful, at least now.

Robbie headed down the steel stairs, pausing halfway to take in the aerial view of the dungeon below. Things were a bit livelier down there. In the far corner, there was what looked to be a puppy pile, bodies all intertwined in a giant cuddle-fest. Nearer, along the right side, a beautiful straight couple had locked themselves into a cage and were busy attaching themselves to each other using a variety of mechanical devices.

The woman had taken a compression hanger, the kind with the two strips of wood intended to hold pants legs, and pinned her own lovely dark nipples inside of it. With the man's help, she'd tied a rope from the hanger to a collar around his neck. Clothespins arced down the sides of his torso like the seams on a tailored shirt. The clothespins were strung together with twine and the woman held the loose end in her teeth as she affixed the last of the pins to the tender flesh of his lower belly. Robbie could tell this was just the beginning and wondered what they'd do next.

Just then, the dungeon monitor paused beside her on the stairs and said, "While I agree it is a great view from here, we like to keep the stairs clear."

"Oh, yeah, sorry." Robbie smiled sheepishly, taking the hint, and continued down.

Couples and triads of all combinations were scattered throughout the room. An equal number of folks were quietly moving through the space, simply watching. That's one of the things she loved most about these parties—voyeurs and players were both essential. As long as you weren't putting out a lecherous vibe, your gaze was a gift to the actors. You too could dip your toes into the energetic flow.

The creak of the chains that supported the sling nearest to the stairs drew Robbie's attention. A mere slip of a woman was suspended in the black leather, hands loosely cuffed over her head, feet lifted by stirrups attached to the chains. She looked perfectly relaxed. If only my gynecologist could come up with something that comfortable, Robbie thought.

The woman on the sling was clearly a butch. Her buzz cut and tie looked oddly formal in contrast to the nakedness of the rest of her body. In fact, the only other thing she was wearing, aside from white gym socks, was a large, black and gray speckled, and fully erect silicone cock. The leather harness she wore was a near match to the leather of the sling. Nice touch, Robbie thought.

Between the butch's spread legs, a tall dark femme stood working up a sweat. She too had stripped off most of her clothes, leaving only a black lace push-up bra and garter belt to keep her warm. Of course, her stilettos had been retained as well. That was a given.

At first glance, Robbie thought the femme had also kept on her elbow-high silk opera gloves. Upon closer inspection, it was clear that these were actually long latex gloves, the kind that large animal vets use when delivering calves. The dark black rubber stretched just to her elbow. Robbie watched as the femme squeezed copious amounts of lube onto both her right arm and the entire length of the butch's crotch.

Forming her fingers into a tight snout, the way you might if you were trying to make shadow-puppets on the wall, she began to slide her hand towards its intended target. Slowly at first, she inserted one finger, then two fingers, then three. Pausing between each advance to breathe deeply in time with the butch, she modulated her decent. When she could fit in all four fingers, she twisted her hand slightly, moving just up to the knuckles and then retreating, up again, and then back in a corkscrew motion.

All the while she played with the hard nipples of the butch, stroked the vulnerable skin along the side of her torso, and took quick nips on her inner thigh. The butch closed her eyes and breathed deeply. No words flowed between them, everything was communicated through touch and intention. Robbie was getting wet just watching.

Once the femme was able to reach the knuckles without difficulty, she re-lubed and pushed again. Steady insistent pressure, waiting for the butch's cunt to surrender. Robbie knew that moment. Loved that visceral release that was part willful and part autonomic at its root. The pressure caused the butch to begin to swing slightly in the sling and the femme used that extra momentum to press home her point. Suddenly, with a slight sucking sound of latex and lube, vagina and fist, she was in. The butch arched her back in pleasure. The femme bent forward intently, inserting her wrist as deep as it could go. Robbie could see that the femme's legs were quivering like a thoroughbred's.

Having burrowed in as far as was possible, the femme bent fully over the butch and laid her body weight between her legs, her arm still buried within. With her free hand, she reached up and held tight behind the butch's neck leveraging against where their hips met to let the sling take both of

their weights. Her heels lifted off the floor and together they swung, embracing inside and out.

Robbie moved away, allowing them their dénouement in private. Idly, she surveyed the rest of the room. Over in one corner two women were taking their time dripping hot wax over a dark-skinned man. They'd built up quite a pool of the molten stuff over his belly, having constructed a wax dam that kept the fluid from spilling over his sides or running down towards his half stiff cock. When one of the women teased the candle nearer to his skin and let the wax drop from closer in, thus increasing the intensity of heat it delivered, his sudden intake of breath caused a little wave in the reservoir, making it spill over and run down his side. Robbie could see his struggle to remain still despite the intensity of the heat, and the mischievous glint in the women's eyes when he failed.

In the other corner, the distinctive sound of leather flogger tails catching bare skin called her gaze to a three-person scene at the St. Andrew's cross. A tall man, with slicked back silver hair, stood topping the whole scene while a pony-tailed man, wearing heavy boots, a tight leather vest, and an unusual black fur-covered codpiece worked hard on a lanky man tied spread-eagle to the cross. Black rope had been wrapped around both wrists and ankles, creating almost decorative bands that held him firm to the cross. He still wore his black Diesel briefs—the large letters of the label visible even in the dim light—but nothing else.

Both flogger and floggee wore well-tooled leather hoods. Pony-tail's hood was functional with holes for eyes, nose and mouth. But Cross-boy's hood was more complete, enveloping his whole head with only his lips visible through a small square hole across his mouth. She felt she could read his expression from just that one facial element and she was reading both pleasure and trepidation. Pony-tail had set down the flogger, donned a spiked glove, and moved in closer. He leaned into the boy from behind and reached to grab a handful of his close-cropped hair, pulling his head back. Reaching around, he drew the spikes slowly along the tender inside of Cross-boy's arm, across the bare skin of his chest, and up the other arm, leaving a trail of rapidly rising red welts.

The movement drew Robbie's eyes to the tattoos just visible on the inside of each of Cross-boy's forearms: a black heart over an American flag on one and a red heart over a blue-and-black striped flag on the other. A patriotic BDSMer, she wondered?

Taking one last look around, Robbie decided that she'd had enough for now. It was time to head home. She turned and went back up the stairs.

She had looked around for Kathleen to say her goodbyes but she had been nowhere to be found. Good for her, Robbie had thought, I hope she's having a great night.

BY THE light of late morning, Robbie savored these memories along with the final bite of her bagel. She washed it all down with a large swig of her coffee. Finally, taking the waxpaper the bagel had come wrapped in, she folded it in half then half again, and then twisted the paper into a tight rope. The sound of the paper crinkling, trying to unfurl itself, marked the last step in her morning ritual. Now it was time to get to work. She had a lot of writing ahead of her today.

THE MATTE BLACK DUCATI swung sharply onto the sidewalk in front of Maxfield's House of Caffeine. As an exclamation point, the biker brought the heavy machine to an abrupt stop, executing a little nose wheelie. The noise alone would have been enough to startle the two sweet labs tied up to the row of newspaper boxes on the edge of the sidewalk. But the fact that the Ducati driver seemed to aim right for the poor creatures was enough to send them scrambling to the full extent of their leashes.

The biker cut the motor, settled the machine onto its kickstand, and stepped off. He was stocky and his full leathers creaked with each movement. He pulled off his helmet, placed it atop the gas tank, then slicked back his startlingly silver hair. For just a moment, he stood still and regarded the tangle of distressed dogs. Panting slightly and still unsure, they looked back, hoping for reassurance. Without warning, he feigned a lunge in their directions, sending them back into a panic. He smiled at their discomfort and headed inside.

Maxfield's was rocking out as usual under Jackson's DJ/barista influence. This morning, he'd chosen a retro focus with some quiet Tears for Fears filling the space.

"Hey Jackson, what's with the oldies shit?"

"Oh, fuck off, Silverfox!" Jackson smiled. He was used to Silverfox's perpetually bitchy attitude.

"Missed me, did you?" Silverfox countered.

"As always, my dear." Most people were intimidated by Silverfox and his bullying style but Jackson just treated him like a curmudgeonly older uncle, all bluff and bluster. It probably came from their original point of connection, fashion. It's hard to intimidate when you're talking hemlines

and French seams.

They'd first met working on costumes for a Theater Rhino production. Then, through separate contacts, they'd been recruited into a stitch-and-bitch for the Sisters Who Reap What You Sow, the shadow splinter group from the Sisters of Perpetual Indulgence. They'd helped design an easy to embroider logo, an elegant X, that referenced the X from the old map marking Mission Dolores as the end of the line of the system of missions, kind of a "the buck stops here" idea. When their paths had finally crossed again at the Castle, they'd become friends. But it was clearly one of those friendships that existed at the margin of their regular social networks. It worked, but neither quite understood why.

Silverfox ordered a double espresso and leaned on the edge of the counter while Jackson let steam force its way through the dark grounds. "You look a little sunburned, Jackson. Were you at the beach?"

"Yeah, the grass one. I spent Sunday afternoon up at Dolores Park and even managed to sunburn my scalp." Jackson ran his fingers through his bleached blond buzz cut, cringing at the touch on the tender skin. "After the rains the last few days, though, it was a welcome change. The place was packed!"

Dolores Park was vibrant on the weekends with everything from family picnics and dog walks to soccer games. On a sunny day, it was one of the best places to hang out in the Mission. On weekends, the northwest corner had become the unofficial gay beach. Men would lay out their blankets or towels and strip practically naked. The excuse was to get a suntan but the real goal was to get something quite different.

"There was this one lithe young thing practicing his strip routine for his Daddy," Jackson continued as he finished the espresso pull and handed Silverfox the demitasse cup. "He brought a boombox with music and everything. If he hadn't been so good it would have been painful. I half expected him to bring out a portable pole from his backpack so he could really go to town." With this last comment, Jackson demonstrated the concept using the edge of the counter as an anchor for his pelvic gyrations.

"Sounds like I should have stopped by," Silverfox said, imagining what he'd missed. "I rode by there doing some errands. You should have seen the line at Bi-Rite Creamery. What is it with that place?" Silverfox shook his head pondering how this high-end ice cream shop, which had opened the year before just outside the southeast corner of the park, had so quickly acquired a cool factor far in excess of the quality of the ice cream.

"I know. It's always mobbed. And the strangest thing . . . it's always the absolutely straightest group of people I've ever seen around here. It's like the Creamery and the gay beach are on polar opposite sides of the park, geographically and culturally." They both chuckled, bemused by the way different worlds overlapped in this city.

Silverfox continued to lean on the counter and sip his espresso while surveying the crowd. The majority of folks were silent and stared intently at their laptops, tapping at the keys in staccato bursts. An atypically steady movement outside caught his eye as a large woman in an electric wheelchair rolled up and stopped next to his motorcycle. She reached out to the dogs, who had settled as far away from the bike as they could.

"God, that just turns my stomach!" he said to no one in particular.

"What?" Jackson said as he turned back from the sink where he'd been rinsing mugs.

"That," Silverfox said, pointing with the elbow of the arm that held the delicate espresso cup.

Jackson's gaze followed the gesture out the door, landing on the hulk that was Daisy and her dog friends. "What?" Jackson asked again.

"What is it with people who let themselves go like that? If they're going to be such sloths, couldn't they at least stay indoors and spare the rest of us the trauma of their visage?" Silverfox sneered.

"Ah, she's harmless," Jackson countered.

"Yeah, but she's ruining my view," Silverfox said.

Jackson, diplomatic instincts and skills honed from years behind the counter, changed the subject. "So did you make it to the Castle Saturday?" The song "Everybody Rules the World" came on and it was all Jackson could do to hold still. He did a little shimmy and winked at Silverfox, trying to get him to join in.

This pulled Silverfox's attention back inside. He raised an eyebrow and stared at Jackson, making it clear it would take more than that to get him to dance.

"I was there earlier in the evening," Jackson continued, "before much was happening. I ran into Allen and he said he was waiting on you. I was just wondering if you managed to connect up. He'd seemed eager to see you." Jackson noticed he was talking a mile a minute and he wasn't sure why. Maybe too much coffee? Or maybe something in Silverfox's demeanor set him on edge. As much as he'd found a way not to be intimidated by Silverfox, there were times when Silverfox's dark side made Jackson a bit anxious.

"Allen can be impatient sometimes. I got there later and found him but turned out to be a fairly uneventful evening. You know, some nights are like that at the Castle."

Jackson nodded and let the silence rest between them.

He turned back to the cups and dishes that had piled up in the sink, letting the dance rhythm feed into his manual rinse cycle. When he was done, he turned back to the counter.

"Another?" Jackson asked, choreographing his dance moves to include a gesture towards the empty espresso cup. Offering service always made him feel more grounded and whatever anxiety had been there before had now dissipated.

Silverfox just shook his head and shoved his cup back across the counter. Holding his palm up at arms length—the "talk to the hand" gesture—then turned and headed out. When he reached the door, he stopped and turned back. "Hey, if I don't see you . . . remember, Friday is the opening."

"Right. Can't wait!" Jackson said, slipping into the slow, contemplative drone of the next Tears for Fears song, "Woman in Chains." Dance club, coffee shop, it was pretty much the same thing in Jackson's world.

SKITTLES CURLED HIMSELF UP into a tight ball on the corner of Daisy's bed. She'd left some magazines there and he seemed to like the feel of crackling paper under his body as he settled in.

"You're a strange little beast," Daisy mused as she smoothed his tight fur. "Most dogs would go for the softest place they could find. But you, you found the most uncomfortable." She shook her head with wonder at the little creature.

It had been two days since she'd found Skittles cowering in the grass. Two days since the police had interviewed her. Two days since she'd taken the dog home. And still no one had called. Granted, she had gone out of her way to keep Animal Care and Control out of the picture but she'd figured the cops would have called by now. Certainly Skittles' dad must have had family. Didn't they want this precious pup?

The first day Skittles had eaten hungrily. Whatever she put down, he sucked up just as fast. It was like he never eaten before. He hadn't really stopped shaking until today; Daisy figured he'd probably been using lots of energy for that.

That first night, he'd paced across the apartment, whimpering quietly but persistently. It was too much work to get up and into her wheelchair so Daisy had tried calling to him to reassure him, but he was unwilling to be comforted.

Yesterday, he'd finally exhausted himself enough that he had to lie down. He'd parked himself directly in front of the door like a sphinx, just touching the space between the bottom of the door and the frame. Periodically, he would lean forward and press his wet black nose into the gap and snort. "No Allen yet!" he seemed to say as he pulled his head back

and let out a sigh.

Daisy knew dogs and she knew this one must be incredibly sad. She could only imagine how hard it would be for your master to disappear so suddenly, your leash-mate, the one at the other end. She wondered if dogs named their people, if they conversed amongst themselves about their people the same way people did about their dogs. Did they say "there's Skittles' snobby guy" or "here comes Rocco's patient lady?"

When she took Skittles out for walks these last two days she'd felt she could see him asking questions of each dog he met.

"Have you seen my person?" she imagined Skittles inquiring through a sniff.

"No man, sorry. Mine isn't acting strange, so I don't think she knows anything," the other dog might say sniffing back as he circled in that nose-to-tail, leash-tangling dance so familiar to dogs and so aggravating for owners.

This morning, when she'd taken Skittles out for a walk, they ran into Rich and his dog, G.M. She could tell that the bumbling adolescent energy of the big black shepherd scared Skittles, but she watched as Skittles still pushed himself forward, seeming to ask his same question of G.M., who seemed to have no new information to share.

"Who's your new friend?" Rich asked.

"This is Skittles. Didn't you hear what happened?" Daisy said, surprised.

"No, what?"

"I found Skittles' dad—murdered!" Daisy recounted the whole story again. She'd become familiar with how the tale unwound yet found herself curious to see which details she'd end up highlighting with each retelling. This time, for Rich, it was the body itself that became the focus—its lankiness, its dead-ness. She could tell it was making Rich squirm. She kind of enjoyed that.

"He was just lying there once they pulled him out, all peaceful. You could hardly tell anything was wrong with him aside from the fact that he was . . . dead." Daisy kept her voice even and watched Rich.

"That sounds horrible. I can't believe that happened right here!" Rich said, distressed by Daisy's lack of emotion. He looked over his shoulder at the familiar empty lot at the corner of Dolores and 15th. The side of the building that loomed over the lot was a patchwork of slightly varied swatches of gray paint that barely covered graffiti. The most recent paint job—which had covered up most of the sprayed tags but had already been freshly defaced with a large, black "R.J."—had neatly skirted the edge of a poster somebody else had pasted to the wall: a five-foot-tall image of Barack Obama in the stern, stylized, neo-communist propaganda style, with the word PROGRESS in block letters underneath. Obama's face stared impassively over the scene. It seemed an ironic juxtaposition, his genuine progress and the clear lack of it manifested in the empty lot.

Daisy continued, "The only wound I could actually see was on his arm. Someone had carved an X onto the inside of his arm, right on top of a tattoo."

"An artist's statement, perhaps?" Rich offered, unconvincingly mimicking Daisy's cavalier attitude. "Maybe they didn't like his ink."

"It looked kind of like the American flag, except it was blue-and-black stripes, and instead of stars it was a red heart. Kind of weird," Daisy offered.

Rich raised his eyebrows. He knew a Leather Pride flag when he heard one described. He decided not to share this info with Daisy; she was harmless enough but, over the years, he had gotten the sense that her Christian sensibilities would

be offended by this little piece of queer subculture. Granted, the city had put up the same flags on all the light posts along Market Street earlier in the summer, when Folsom Street Fair was on, but he doubted folks like Daisy took any notice. He certainly didn't feel like starting his morning by giving her an education on the politics of kink.

Luckily, he was rescued when Robbie came by, coffee cup in hand. Skittles and G.M. had grown bored and had been sitting patiently during the conversation but now they both sprang to life.

"Morning," Robbie said from behind dark glasses, unnecessary this early in the morning. She used her free hand to alternate pats between Skittles, who stood placing paws outstretched along her thigh, and G.M. who was pressing his head between her legs.

"What's up, sleepyhead?" Daisy said, laughing at Robbie. "Haven't had enough coffee yet?"

Robbie definitely was sleepy. "No, I just was up late. I'm doing this crazy thing called 'NaNoWriMo.' Stands for National Novel Writing Month. I'm trying to write a 50,000-word novel in 30 days and I've been glued to my computer."

"Oh, I've heard of that," Rich offered enthusiastically. "A friend of mine did it last year. He said it was great."

"It's an interesting process, that's for sure. Quantity over quality, that's the motto. Talk to me when it's done!" Robbie laughed.

"What's it going to be about?" Daisy asked.

"I think it's a murder mystery but I'm not sure yet," Robbie opined.

"Hardly original, considering. Inspired by your neighborhood?" Daisy asked. Robbie and Daisy had run into each other yesterday morning and Daisy had told Robbie all about the murder. It was one of those rough conversations that Robbie wished she didn't have to listen to but Daisy just went on and on. Robbie could see Daisy was unnerved by the experience, so she'd listened, all the while feeling the bagel in her jacket pocket getting colder and colder.

"Have you heard any more?" Robbie asked.

"No. Can you believe it? It's been two days and the cops haven't called. This poor little fella is still so stressed out." She patted her thigh, trying to get Skittles to come closer to her for some love. He stood his distance, stretched out to the end of the black leather leash.

Robbie kneeled down and put her hand on Skittles' back. He was shaking slightly and looked up at her with imploring eyes.

"Poor little guy. Don't worry, Daisy will take good care of you," Robbie said. She stood back up and waved goodbye to all of them.

Daisy yelled after her, "If the cops haven't called by tomorrow, I'm going right down to the Mission Street Station and find out what's going on!"

"I hear you," Robbie said over her shoulder. "I'm sorry but I've gotta go. I'm behind on my word count for this novel thing. I've got 3,000 words to crank out today!" Robbie moved quickly away, knowing that with Rich there Daisy would let her escape.

"See ya!" Daisy called, spinning her chair around to bring all her attention back onto Rich.

THEY WERE JUST THREE days away from Tintin's opening and Allen was nowhere to be found. J.B. was livid. This was just like him, she thought. Such a prima donna. He's probably decided that the stress is getting to be unbearable and, since everything is on track, that he needs—no, deserves—a little spa getaway.

She slid the virtual slider on her iPhone to check again, but nothing, not a single voicemail, email, text . . . not a word from him. She'd called and left messages. She'd emailed. She'd even direct–messaged him on Facebook and Twitter. He must know she was trying to reach him. She hated when he did this.

She couldn't concentrate so decided to take a break, leaving the confines of her cube in the Googleplex to wander downstairs to the cafeteria for her fourth double soy latte of the day. She was supposed to be working on setting the SEO metrics for the online strategy for the Android, the new Google phone. The FTC was requiring them to keep a long arm between business units lest the inside knowledge of the ranking algorithms give their own product an unfair advantage in search. She was going through the motions of at least creating the paper trail, just in case. In reality, they all knew it was a ruse. There was no way Google wouldn't use their insider knowledge to optimize the product launch.

Her Google task wasn't engaging enough to keep her from worrying about Tintin, despite Allen's promise that everything was right where it should be during their walkthrough of the restaurant on Saturday morning.

"See, didn't I tell you those fixtures would look fabulous?" J.B. had said. The handmade, snipped tin LCD lights over the bar were exactly what she'd envisioned; referential to the tin counters of French bistros with the green ethos of low-energy LCD bulbs. Perfect.

"The chairs came in yesterday." Allen had reached over and pulled one of the switchgrass, micro-caned chairs from the nearest table. "What do you think?"

J.B. had seen these on a trip to Santa Fe last year. She'd gone for the opera, like she did every year, with her friends Gary and Jim. Out for a drink one warm evening at this funky little bar, she'd been completely taken by these chairs. Completely green yet oddly reminiscent of those French café chairs with the black-and-white caned backs. Woven from locally grown switchgrass, assembled by an economic–empowerment business on the outskirts of Santa Fe, the backs and seats were hand-woven onto soy-glued bamboo frames. She had known they would be exactly the right thing for Tintin.

"They look great. I think they'll definitely complement and expand on the eco-theme I've been trying to create. Subtle but significant," J.B. had mused, experimenting with her high-style interior designer persona.

"I think we're good to go with pretty much everything else," Allen had said, surveying the mostly complete restaurant. "The linens are coming in on Monday. Pedro is going to do a tasting and review the menu with all the waitstaff on Wednesday. What else can go wrong?"

J.B. had felt reassured at the time, but now, sitting back in her cube sipping her latte, she didn't feel so confident. She'd found that "good to go" sometimes meant "I'm outta

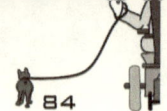

here" with Allen. He'd been through restaurant openings before but this was her first. She needed some comforting, some camaraderie, and she'd assumed Allen would to be there to provide it. She sighed and lamented—yet again—men and their inability to understand simple manners. He should have known that she'd need a little attention at this point; it shouldn't be her job to ask.

THIS MORNING'S PAPER HAD a long article on the latest food fad—leafy greens. It talked about the health benefits, how to cook them, different recipes, and described all the different kinds of leafy greens. The article raved, as if this was an amazing new food discovery.

Daisy could remember growing up on a steady diet of collard greens. The bitter, stringy vegetable would sit in a sodden pile on the corner of her dinner plate, always the last to go. On a good day she might be able to slide it surreptitiously into the waiting mouth of whatever mutt was around, but it didn't take long before even the dogs learned better. Greens. Black-eyed peas. Grits. The tastes made her homesick for good old Kentucky cooking—not something commonly found in the Bay Area.

Daisy wasn't much of a foodie, as the hipsters called it. She was just as happy to have some Kentucky Fried Chicken, or an onion/mushroom/cheese special at Burger Joint, as she was to have anything fancier. At home, she was most likely to prepare something frozen, maybe one of those Lean Cuisines that were easy on the palette, and the pocketbook. But with her ankles swelling so, she'd already been thinking she should start to eat just a bit better.

The article in the paper inspired her. That's how she found herself rolling down the produce aisle at Safeway just in time for the artificial storm—an electronic thunderclap, followed by a gentle rain as the misting system flipped on.

Daisy pulled back on the joystick of her chair, reversing away from the deluge, though she found the sound of thunder oddly comforting and familiar. That was something she missed in San Francisco. Yes, you might get a thunderstorm

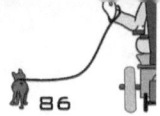

occasionally but it would kind of sneak up on you, blanketed in fog, going incognito.

Kentucky storms stood proud, in a broad-legged stance, hands on hips, announcing their presence before the show began. Tall, buttery cumulous clouds would rise up on the western horizon, their energy bubbling ever upwards until, having reached the ceiling of temperature inversion, an anvil top would form and the energy would channel sideways. If they hadn't been so masculine, she might imagine thunderclouds like a big old drag queen. A Sister-of-Perpetual-Indulgence kind. When they'd built themselves up to their full height, the flurry they released was all drag show, big lights and big moves. She could remember, as a kid, counting the seconds from the flash of lightening to when she finally heard the thunderclap, every five seconds representing a mile between her and the lightening strike.

The sound of thunder rolled through the produce section again. She hoped Safeway might flicker the lights as well.

After the supermarket storm had passed, Daisy picked out some rainbow chard. She'd never had it before but it was prettier than the collard greens, and she hoped it might be tastier as well. She detoured through the frozen food section to pick up some frozen horsemeat for Skittles, and waffles for herself, then headed straight to the checkout.

Daisy pulled up to the express checkout, in part because Robbie was second in the long line.

"Hey Robbie, fancy meeting you here," Daisy called over the heads of the others in line.

Robbie turned and waved back. "Whatcha getting?"

"Greens—the paper said they're good for you so I figured I'd give it a try. How 'bout you?"

"Oh just some stuff to keep me awake," Robbie said as she pushed a pile that included peppermint Altoids tins,

Reese's peanut butter cups, coffee, and half-and-half down the conveyer belt. "Have you heard anything more about Skittles?"

"Nope," Daisy frowned. "Did you drive up here?"

"I walked," Robbie offered cautiously, not sure where Daisy's question was going.

"Are you heading back home now?"

Robbie hesitated. Last week Daisy had gone off on a diatribe about capital punishment. Normally that would have been something on which they could have found common ground, but the context in which Daisy had framed the discussion—her wayward nephew on death row, the details of his crimes, how she was sure he'd done nothing wrong—made the argument more personal than Robbie could handle.

"Ah, I've got to run a couple more errands," Robbie lied. She wanted to go pick up a video, or maybe some porn, at Superstar but she really just needed to get home and keep writing. The last thing she needed was a long-winded walk back to 15th Street with Daisy.

Robbie handed her cash to the checker, waiting as the change ran down the metal slide. That always pleased her— a little amusement park ride for her pennies.

"I'll see you!" Robbie called back to Daisy as she hurried out of the store.

"She's my neighbor," Daisy explained loudly to the man just in front of her.

"Hmm, I see," he said, feigning sudden interest in the small red basket of groceries.

"AND THAT'S all the time we have for the California news. Now back to *All Things Considered.*"

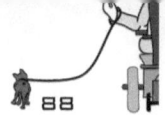

Daisy paused for a moment, knife poised above the chard. "I've always wondered whether that's all the California news there is or if they just ran out of time. Don't you think that's a funny way to run a radio station?" she asked Skittles. The dog sat quietly, looking up from the black-and-white linoleum. He licked his lips, his little pink tongue wiping across his flat nose then coming to rest, still visible on the left side of his mouth. Daisy tried not to laugh.

"Why're you sticking your tongue out, boy?"

Skittles maintained steady eye contact with the food, not falling for any attempt at distraction.

"You look ridiculous. And what are you waiting for, it's only chard up here." At the mention of the word "chard" Skittles stood and looked excited. He bent down, stretching his front paws forward, and then bounced right back up, panting.

"Are you looking for chard?" Daisy asked, incredulous.

Skittles yipped a quick yes in response.

"Well, I'll be." She took a small leaf off the cutting board and held it out for the dog. Skittles snatched it from her hand and snarfed it down with barely a chew.

"I don't know how good that's going to be for your digestion. Did your daddy used to feed you that?" This made Daisy wonder again about the tall man who'd been attached to Skittles. She couldn't quite imagine him cooking at home, let alone cooking greens and feeding them to his dog, but clearly she'd underestimated him.

"I'm going to feed you something you'll really like." Daisy chipped half of the frozen horsemeat out of its flimsy paper box. It looked like frozen spinach, only brown. But as it sizzled in the frying pan, it pinked nicely.

She finished chopping the chard and placed it into the steamer. She figured this was the best way to go, just steam the hell out of it, then dump a bit of vinegar on top to give it some punch while her skillet was busy dealing with the horsemeat.

Daisy rested for moment while their meals cooked. She adjusted the tilt on her chair, back and then a little bit forward. It was almost like a nervous tic, playing with the level like that, but it helped to shift her weight even that much. Being in the chair all day could do a number on her body. Her butt would get numb and she could feel the circulation in her calves slowing. They said the tingling in her feet was normal but it did bother her. She found that if she changed the tilt, sometimes it would get the blood flowing again to her legs.

Skittles had settled into a patient stance. Alert but at ease, he was keeping one eye on the food. "In good time, little buddy," she said quietly. She could reach the skillet from where she sat so she gave it a bit of a stir, breaking up the chunks of meat with the spoon, flipping the red sides down and the gray sides up.

"What are we going to do with you?" She could feel her shoulders tightening at the memory of finding Skittles on Sunday morning. Sure she felt bad for the guy who'd been killed, but what pissed her off more was that someone had left the dog like that, maybe out all night. People could fend for themselves—they usually were the source of their own problems, after all. Dogs were helpless.

She turned off the two burners and let the meat sit. Poking at it with a fork and blowing on it to hurry the cooling process along, she figured it was almost ready for Skittles. Skittles wholeheartedly agreed. Meanwhile, she pulled the steamy chard from the pot, placed it in a bowl, and sprinkled white vinegar across the top.

Wheeling back across the small kitchen, she put her plate on the table and Skittles' bowl on the floor. She dug into her

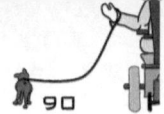

lunch just as eagerly as Skittles did into his. "Not bad," she said, pleased with her foodie effort. "How's yours?" she asked the dog.

A wet snorting pushing the bowl across the floor said it all.

"You know, I think we better find out if the police have any leads on your dad yet. Plus," Daisy chuckled, "after all this weird, rich food, I bet you're going to need to go out."

"DO YOU EVER DO this? Pop these things near your ear?" the first barista asked the other as she played with the bubble wrap from the packing box of wooden stirrers.

"Why? So you can make yourself deaf?" the second barista said, clearly skeptical.

"No, it feels great. It's like a kiss of air into your ear. Try it."

She did. "Ouch! Asshole, now I can't hear!"

They both laughed even as the second barista rubbed her ear in pain.

J.B. waited and wondered when they would be done with their antics. She didn't need another latte, the fifth of the day, but she wanted one desperately. The bus had dropped her at the corner and without thinking she'd gone straight into Dolores Park Café. "Maybe I should have gone for ice cream instead," she mumbled, thinking of the salted caramel at Bi-Rite Creamery across the street.

"Oh, sorry. Can I help you?"

"I'll have a—" J.B. replied grumpily, but just then her phone rang. A blocked number. "Just a minute," she said to the barista as she turned and moved towards the door.

"Hello. To whom am I speaking?" she held one hand over her other ear to block out the cacophony of the cafe.

"Detective Rendell, ma'am. I need to talk to you about Allen Pontarlier."

"What about him?" J.B. said cautiously. She was immediately worried that this had something to do with the restaurant. Had he bribed someone, taken off with the investors' cash, or—more likely—simply pissed someone off?

"We're wondering if you might be able to come down to

the station to talk. The Mission Station on Valencia and 17th."

"Can you tell me what this is about?"

"I'd prefer not to over the phone, ma'am. Could you come down please?" he asked again, his voice calm but insistent.

"Very well, then. I'm just around the corner. Should I come now?"

"We'd appreciate that. Just ask for Detective Rendell."

J.B. looked down at the face of her iPhone and watched the red "end call" button disappear before she could tap it. The detective had hung up first. "What on earth?" she wondered. She took a deep breath then shrugged. "I knew I should have gotten the ice cream."

THE ONE-story, tan brick building held the corner like an annoying squatter. Perhaps the architect had visions of softening the building by claiming an elementary school aesthetic—linoleum floors, bright overhead fluorescents, narrow floor-to-ceiling windows that offered a glimpse to the inside but no real access—but there was pretty much no way to disguise a Police Station. The abundant security cameras would have been a dead giveaway even without the fleet of police cruisers parked outside.

J.B. reached for the handle, preparing to pull the glass, chicken-wire reinforced door open. Just as she reached, though, the door swung out automatically.

"I got it!" A woman in a wheelchair had rolled up behind J.B. and was pressing the big round silver ADA button on the wall. "After you," she said graciously.

It took a moment for J.B. to register the connection between the door and this woman, but she quickly regained her composure. "No, after you," she said stepping back to allow the woman to roll through the door.

Daisy assessed J.B.'s slender, taut frame, then said, "I guess anyone would be nervous walking into this place."

"I'm fine," J.B. said coolly.

Once inside, they both paused. Silence echoed through the empty room. Not a single chair or piece of artwork provided comfort. This foyer was not designed to be welcoming. The duty officer's station was to the left and was completely walled off from the lobby by thick bullet-proof glass.

J.B. stepped forward at the same moment that Daisy shifted into gear.

"Oops!" They both stuttered, unsure who should go first.

"After you," Daisy indicated with a generous sweep of her hand.

J.B. stepped up to the glass, putting her hands on the narrow wooden shelf that stretched the length of the window, and leaned forward towards the circular microphone embedded at her eye height.

"Can I help you?" a tinny voice inquired.

"Yes, I got a call from a detective—Detective Rendell, I think? He asked me to come down."

"Your name?"

"J.B., I mean, Jennifer . . . Bellows."

"What is this regarding?"

J.B. wondered if the man behind the glass was actually speaking or if this was a canned recording and he was just lip-synching.

"To be honest, I don't know. He just called me, something about my friend Allen."

"All right. If you'll just wait, I'll let him know you're here."

Stepping back from the glass, J.B. tried to find a discrete place to stand. The room was like a boxing ring, and she wasn't sure which was the neutral corner. There was no place to hide.

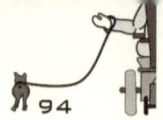

Now, it was Daisy's turn. She maneuvered up to the window. Since she was well below the microphone she tapped on the glass to get the officer's attention.

"Can I help you?" said the same bored voice.

"You bet you can. I need to talk to someone about the murder the other day. I'm the one that found Skittles." As if to make her point, Daisy opened her jacket to reveal the bright eyes of the pup.

J.B. had gone back to her iPhone, checking her Facebook news feed to distract herself. She was shifting her weight from one foot to the other, the rhythm of the slight movement calming her. It took her a few seconds to register what she had just heard. "Skittles?" she asked, startled.

Daisy rotated the joystick and revealed the small dog to J.B. "Isn't he the cutest?"

J.B.'s eyes opened as wide as Skittles'. The little dog's tail revved into motion, vibrating at Daisy's side.

"He likes you. Must be love at first sight!" Daisy laughed.

"Skittles?" J.B. repeated reaching her hand towards the little dog. "What are you doing here?" and, looking up at Daisy, "Why do you have Skittles?"

"You know him?" Daisy asked, eager to hear the answer.

"Yes, he's my friend Allen's dog. I'd recognize that collar anywhere."

"Is Allen a tall, skinny fellow?"

"Yeah, do you know him? I don't get it."

At that moment the door that led into the back—another school-like design, heavy wood with a narrow vertical window running top to bottom—opened. "Ms. Bellows?" the detective asked, trying to decide which woman to address.

"That's me." J.B. said. "What's is going on here? Why did you call me and why is Allen's dog here?"

"If you'll come with me, I'll explain everything," he said,

leading her back into the squad room.

"Hey!" Daisy called, "what about Skittles?" But they couldn't hear her through the thick door.

The small dog was getting restless under her coat. Daisy couldn't tell if it was from the encounter with this woman or if the combo of greens and horsemeat was finally moving through his system. "Let's go for a walk, little buddy."

Daisy tapped on the glass of the duty officer's station one more time. "Tell that lady that we'll be right outside. I want to talk to her." The man behind the glass nodded silently.

LIKE A sentinel, Daisy rolled back and forth in front of the station. Skittles had indeed been in some distress, but having relieved himself on the roots of one of the scrawny trees that lined the sidewalk, he was now trotting proudly alongside Daisy. His presence was attracting some attention. She was usually the one reaching out to dogs, so it amused her to be on the receiving end for a change.

A young man, passing by, was immediately smitten. His jeans were so tight Daisy could see he was carrying two keys not one. "Oh, he's so cute!" he said, squatting down to scratch under the dog's chest. Skittles put his front paws up on the young man's thigh (thinner than Daisy's calf by half, she noted) and begged for more touch. "I used to have one just like this when I was a kid." He pushed his large, bug-eyed sunglasses back on his head and leaned in for some canine kisses. When he'd had his fill, he stood and said, "Bye, cutie!" blowing a kiss to the dog—not Daisy—as he walked away.

Now a young woman—pierced nose, brow, and lip with eyeliner so thick Daisy could barely see into her eyes—walked a pit-mix that shied away from Skittles at first, only

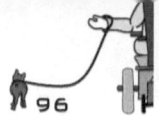

to try to sneak back around for sniff. "Come on, Lulu!" the woman urged as she pulled on the leash with both hands, the pressure of the collar barely registering on the dog's thick, muscled neck.

Even a serious young man, so focused in his Blackberry that he almost ran into Daisy, shifted his attention long enough to make little clicking noises towards Skittles.

Some of course paid no attention to Daisy or the dog, but they were the rare exceptions. Daisy decided that those few weren't fully human.

Daisy and Skittles had now done so many laps back and forth in front of the building, that Skittles was panting. Daisy pulled over near the front door of the station and patted her lap. Skittles jumped up and settled into the familiar place in the crook of Daisy's arm.

A flash of reflected sunlight slid across Daisy's face as the door swung open. J.B. emerged, looking shell-shocked.

"Ms. Bellows?" Daisy called. It took J.B. a moment to register the sound. "Ms. Bellows, can I talk to you?"

"J.B." she said flatly.

"Oh, right. J.B., how do you know Skittles?"

"He's my friend Allen's dog. Allen and I are . . . I mean were . . ." J.B. stopped talking or moving, as if unsure what to do next. Her shift of weight from foot to foot was just barely visible.

Daisy opened up her coat so J.B. and Skittles could see each other again. Skittles immediately sat up in Daisy's lap and strained forward. J.B. reached in and scooped him up, hugged him tightly and pressed her face into the dog's short scruff. "Oh, Skittles," she said sadly.

"J.B., did they tell you it was me who found Skittles?" Daisy asked gingerly.

"Yes. They told me they found Allen's—body—on the

street. That he'd been murdered. They said you found the body . . . and Skittles . . . you and another woman."

"I'm so sorry for your loss," Daisy said, her voice as warm as the dog's fur. "I took Skittles home with me because I didn't want him to end up at the shelter. I figured I would hear from his family when they were ready to take him back." Daisy moved carefully. Skittles, although in J.B.'s arms, was still tethered to Daisy by the black leather leash.

"I don't think Allen had any family, at least not any here," J.B. said weakly.

Daisy looked at how tightly J.B. was clinging to the dog. "Would you like to take him? Looks like you two might need each other."

"Oh, Skittles. I would . . ." J.B. gave him another tight squeeze and whispered ". . . but I can't."

"Excuse me?" Daisy squinted, as if that would improve her hearing. "You'll have to forgive me, my hearing isn't what it used to be."

"I can't take him." J.B. explained. "No dogs allowed where I live." Reluctantly, she handed Skittles back over to Daisy.

"Do you know if the police have any leads, are any closer to solving this . . . thing?"

"The detective said they're following up on leads, but right now they're stumped." J.B. wiped her hands along her sides, folded her arms, then unfolded them again. She stared at her palms, as if uncertain where they belonged. "Allen only moved to the city recently so they're having trouble tracking down his connections. It took them till today to find me."

"You two were good friends then?" Sometimes Daisy found that it helped people just to be able to talk, even if it was only about the simplest details of their person.

"Yeah, friends, but we were also in business together.

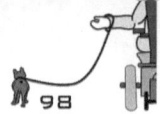
We're opening a restaurant together just around the corner. Tintin."

Daisy brightened. "Oh, yeah, I read about that in the Chronicle."

"We're scheduled to open this Friday. Day after tomorrow!" J.B. looked startled by the thought. "I don't even know if they know yet at the restaurant."

She dug into her bag for her phone. She looked down at it for a moment and then back up. Her gaze was pointing towards Daisy but she was looking right through her. "I don't even have Pedro's phone number. Allen dealt with all that." After a moment she seemed to reach a decision. Not a strong one but, in this situation, even a weak one was better than nothing. "I guess I'd better go over to the restaurant, I think Allen said Pedro was doing a training today . . . or tomorrow . . . ." She started to move off but then paused and turned back to Daisy.

"I'm sorry, that's so rude of me. I guess I'm not quite thinking straight." She said with a small humorless chuckle. "We'll figure something out about Skittles eventually, but in the meantime can you take care of him?"

"Sure, I'll take care of Skittles as long as necessary. Don't you worry about that. It makes me mad though that someone killed his owner and left him there all night long. Skittles that is. It's just not right! If the police won't get to the bottom of this, I will. You can count on that!"

J.B. was confused by Daisy's passion.

"Let me give you my phone number. I'm just over on 15th and Dolores. In the high-rise. You can come by any time if you want to see the little critter," Daisy said stroking Skittles.

J.B. punched in the numbers into her phone and hit the "save" button. "Got it," she said, and "I'll call you."

And like that, J.B. was gone.

Daisy paused for a moment, thinking. The little dog's big saucer eyes were staring at her. "I guess it's just you and me kid, at least for now."

She realized she had forgotten to get J.B.'s number. "Damn, how am I going to reach her?"

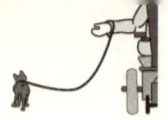

A HELICOPTER CIRCLED SLOWLY overhead. It had been hovering in the same spot for the last twenty minutes.

"I wonder if they know just how annoying that is!" Rich yelled to his partner over the noise. Dominic was in the kitchen doing the dishes. Rich was parked at the computer. G.M., their black shepherd, was asleep on her back on the couch, feet stretched out fully like an Olympic swimmer mid-backstroke. One paw flapped gently, the only evidence of her doggy dreams.

"Is there another protest in the Castro tonight?" Rich clicked on the bookmark for SFGate.com, checking to see if there was any news. Nothing. If they were going to scale back the print edition of the Chronicle, the least they could do was make sure the online version was updated once in a while.

Ever since the defeat of Prop 8 last week there had been protests almost every night. Of course, sometimes the protests were interrupted by a party or, like yesterday, the premiere of the movie "Milk" at the Castro Theatre. Queers knew how to keep their protests festive. They would never be accused of all work and no play.

Rich toggled through the open windows in his browser, bringing Craigslist to the front. He scrolled through the list of Men Seeking Men personals. His eyes scanned the predictable titles: "cum and get it," "sucking job," "hunting for a bear." He chuckled at "looking for a guy who shoots like a fire hose" but there was no picture, so he moved on. He wasn't sure exactly what he was searching for tonight. He clicked through to a few more with the yellow "pic" icons next to the titles just to get an idea of what his body wanted.

"Damn, that guy is thick!" Dominic said, coming up

from behind and placing his cool, damp hands on Rich's shoulders.

"Yeah, thick and thick. Can you believe the grammar in this ad? I suppose if he keeps his mouth shut it'll be OK." Rich was a bit of a stickler: the dirtier the better when it came to content but the person had to be able to write an intelligible sentence. "I can only infer what he wants but I can't actually figure it out with this sentence structure."

"Well, you're not looking for an intellectual conversation are you?"

"No, but I don't want him to be a moron. It makes the post-scene after-care such a bore."

"Poor baby," Dominic mocked playfully.

"Jerk!" Rich tilted his head back and smiled at his lover's upside-down face.

Dominic gave Rich's shoulders an affectionate squeeze. "I'm going to go read. You won't be long will you?" He pulled gently on Rich's dark ponytail, letting the hair slide through his fingers.

"I'll be *coming* any minute now," Rich winked.

"Well, just make sure you use a rag. I have to use that keyboard too."

Rich smiled as he turned back to the computer screen. He and Dominic had been together for twelve years. Part of their longevity was due to the fact that they learned long ago that they couldn't be everything to each other. Their sex life was good but Dominic was truly "vanilla," with little interest in anything beyond the lightest kink. He didn't begrudge Rich his desire for more serious BDSM play but he didn't want to go there. Instead, with Dominic's blessing, Rich found his outlets at play parties, at the Loading Dock, and, on nights like this, on Craigslist.

He clicked on another "pic." Yet another hard dick

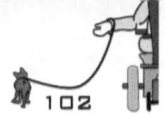

appeared, this one stroked by a strong tattooed forearm. The tattoo reminded him of something that had been nagging just outside his consciousness since this morning when he'd run into Daisy. She had told him about the murder and described a tattoo on the body's arm that sounded very much like a leather pride flag. All day, he'd had the feeling that he'd seen a tattoo like that somewhere but he couldn't quite place it.

"Help me unload before bed," the ad read.

"I hear you brother," Rich commiserated. With only half attention, he started to gently stroke his crotch through the denim barrier. His mind started to empty better than any yoga class made possible. He was just reaching to unzip his fly when he sat bolt upright. Suddenly, he remembered where he had seen that that tattoo.

It had been at the Castle last weekend. That boy Rich had flogged this past weekend. The boy had that tattoo and a mirror image one, only red and white, on the other arm. Rich remembered how he'd found the symmetry of the tattoos pleasing as he'd played with him. Now he wondered if that boy and the dead guy were one and the same. Rich thought back over the evening.

HE'D GONE to the Castle play party alone, figuring he'd run into some friends or at least some hot guy he could play with and, indeed, there had been several.

The early part of the party had been spent in the company of a bear, who was very much into caning. Rich remembered how the rebound of the cane kept getting caught up in the thick hair on the guy's ass. The guy was sweet though, and they'd laughed a lot afterwards and cuddled upstairs. With the bear fully recovered and off to his next adventure, Rich had been sitting on the couch when Silverfox had approached.

Rich didn't know Silverfox well. They'd met at several Society of Janus trainings and Rich had been drawn to Silverfox's quiet dominance. So when Silverfox sat down and asked if Rich would be willing to flog his boy downstairs, Rich readily agreed. They'd negotiated how the scene would go down and what the boy was and was not allowed to do. There was nothing too complicated about the scene and Rich figured it would be fun. For his own pleasure, Silverfox had asked Rich to wear a leather hood. It seemed a small enough thing, and it had fit comfortably over his ponytail, so he'd agreed. Besides, the rich dark leather was a nice match to the furry black codpiece Rich wore—a final memento he'd hand crafted to honor his favorite four-legged friends, Sodom and Gomorrah.

Silverfox and Rich had headed back downstairs to where Silverfox's "boy"—a lanky man, actually—had been left waiting, squatting in front of the cross, in an obedient "sit-stay." He was also wearing a black leather hood, but his had only one hole revealing some very sweet, pouty lips.

As he'd stretched the man's arms across the cross, Rich had noticed the complementary tattoos: a leather flag out along one forearm and an American flag on the other.

Rich had played with the boy using a variety of tools, building the tension, fear, and desire, finally leading up to a dramatic flogging finish. Rich prided himself on his technical skills and precision with the flogger. But he was a little off that night, his shoulder a little tight. He'd mishit with the flogger once, striking the boy too low across the back just under his ribs and above the waistband of his Diesel briefs. The boy had flinched so hard that it rocked the cross. Rich had placed a warm hand across the spot, soothing the welt, tacitly assuring the boy that he knew his mistake and that it wouldn't happen again. He'd held his hand still and, after a moment, he felt the

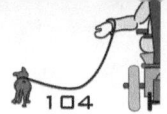

boy relax, the tension ebbing out of his body.

When they'd finished, Silverfox had taken the boy upstairs for after-care. That'd been part of their negotiation: Rich would take care the scene space, Silverfox would take care of the boy.

Rich sprayed down the cross and mat with disinfectant, coiled the ropes and placed them, along with the leather hood and the other toys, into a duffle bag. He took it upstairs and placed it on the floor next to the couch. Silverfox nodded to him in acknowledgement of the completion of their scene. As he walked away, he could still see Silverfox stroking the leather hood and holding the boy in the warmth of his body. Rich headed home into Dominic's safe arms. That was the after-care he always longed for at the end of the night.

RICH CLOSED the Craigslist window on his browser and snapped the laptop shut.

"Well, I'll be damned!" he said aloud, startling G.M. awake from her slumber on the couch. She sat upright, lips parted and panting slightly, trying anxiously to shake the sleep from her doggy brain. Rich stood and tapped G.M. on the back of her big head, urging her off the couch.

She sniffed at his hand, trying to measure his stress level. Moderate, she thought.

"Hurry, girl, we've got to tell Dominic about this!" he said as they both ran upstairs to join him in the "family bed."

SKITTLES HAD SETTLED IN at the foot of Daisy's bed and was dreaming of an exciting chase. Periodically, he barked a muffled doggie bark in his sleep. She wondered if he was gaining on the prey.

Having hefted herself out of the chair and onto the bed, Daisy reached over and pushed the joystick to back it up just a little further away from the side of bed. She always found it odd to see the chair moving on its own without her in it. Although she could use her legs, it had been years since she'd been able to walk. First it had been the fibromyalgia, exacerbated by the Type II diabetes. In the beginning, the chair had been liberating, allowing her to stay active in ways she never would have otherwise, but surrendering into the chair had also hastened her physical decline. Lack of work had made her muscles weak and flaccid, atrophying her body into the chair's particular curve, tightening tendons that should have been loose—and loosening ones that should have been tight. As a result, her body was now more comfortable in the S-curve of the chair than in any other position. Stretching out in bed each night required an extended period of adjustment.

As she lay there trying to unfold, she listened to NPR. The voices soothed her towards sleep. At this hour it was a rebroadcast of the evening's *All Things Considered*, so it was the news but just slightly out of date. She had a pillow under her knees, helping ease the strain on her low back from hips made too tight from a day in the chair. Her feet felt warm and slightly itchy. They'd definitely been swelling more lately and her skin felt taut and injured. Her legs were restless, despite their heaviness. She lifted her shoulders towards her ears and then down and back, trying to untie the knot between

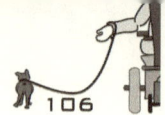

her shoulder blades. She clenched and unclenched her fists, the pressure rippling up her arms. Finally, she took one long breath and held it, pausing for just a second before releasing it in one long sigh, her entire body deflating like a big rubber balloon.

Relaxation flowed back into her tired body, creating space for the memory of a younger body, a body once visible to all but now only existing inside her imagination. An image of Russ fluttered through her mind to join it. Tall and lanky, he stood cocky with one foot up on the bumper of his Dodge pickup, fingers hooked behind his large silver belt buckle. His cowboy hat slipped back on his head and a cigarette dangled from his wicked grin.

Russ had been Daisy's second husband out of the three and by far the best of the lot. He was mischievous and good-hearted and they'd laughed a lot together. To this day, just thinking about him could set her to chuckling.

They'd met at the local Win-Dixie where Daisy worked behind the cash register. She'd rung up his six-pack of Schlitz and peanuts and wisecracked, "On a diet like that, you're going to waste away." His leanness intrigued her.

Taking one look at her curves he winked and said, "Well, maybe you'd like to give me some good home cooking, see if we might not remedy that problem."

Daisy was feeling feistier than usual that day. "Well why don't you come pick me up at six, and I'll do just that," she said, raising one penciled eyebrow in challenge.

"Deal!" he'd said, nodding slightly as he fingered the wide brim of his cowboy hat then boot-scooted his way out the door.

She hadn't really expected him to show up but he had, standing outside by his truck just like she pictured him now. From that moment on they had been inseparable. Twelve years of fights and frolics, a daughter together, before the throat cancer got him.

She thought back to the way Russ had touched her that first night. She'd been big, even back then, but he seemed to worship her mass. She could still feel the way he'd held a single breast in both hands, marveling at its heft before lifting it gently towards his lips.

Skittles snored quietly at the foot of the bed as Daisy traced the outside edge of her breast where it sagged over her rib cage, and tumbled down towards the mattress beside her.

Their lovemaking had been a revelation, a grace. He'd levitate himself over her body, only his hips touching hers. She could see the veins popping and snaking beneath the thin skin on his forearms as he held himself aloft. Once inside her, he'd pause for a moment. His eyes would narrow and his tongue would pass slowly across his lips. To her, he looked like a self-satisfied puppy just about to fall off its mother's teat. She often wondered what he thought about at that moment. Perhaps he was just feeling, bringing all of his being to the place where his dick nestled inside her warm, wet folds.

At the memory, Daisy slid a hand down along her abundant torso, catching the curve at her thigh like a toboggan run and accelerating towards her crotch.

Once Russ snapped out of his reverie, he'd get to humping and things would move pretty quickly from there. Like the cowboy he was, he'd whoop and holler, sweating and trembling to hold on, crying out a high-pitched "yippie ki-yay" as he came. Finished, he'd roll off, turn his back towards Daisy then spoon back into her softness, seeking warmth. They'd stay like that for the rest of the night. Her Pentecostal upbringing had rooted in Daisy's psyche a fear that sex might suck the life out of him, the very heat. She

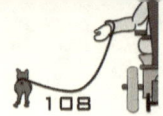

hoped that if she held on tight enough all through the night, he would be restored. And he *had* been, until the very end.

Daisy pressed the flat length of all five fingers against the lips of her cunt. She didn't move at all, just held the pressure. Slowly she could begin to feel a timid pulse build beneath her palm. The pulse rose upwards, then slipped away. Rose again. Veered off. Then rose once more. She pressed harder trapping it between her fingers. With nowhere to hide, the pulse focused and surrendered, shivering throughout the empty cavern of her pelvis, dissipating as quickly as it came.

Daisy flopped over half onto her side, finished but not satisfied. She reached out and hit the sleep button and turned off the light, hoping the soft voices would snuggle up to her in the dark, ease the longing she always felt for Russ's touch, lull her into forgetful sleep.

Skittles was stretched out on his back, still snoring. She reached out and pulled the little dog closer for comfort. "Tomorrow is another day," she said quietly, "and tomorrow, by gum, we are going to find out who killed your dad."

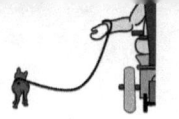

THE FLOOD OF MORNING commuter traffic was in full flow along Dolores. Daisy had often thought they should rename the corner at 15th the "impatient piazza." It was the only intersection in the six blocks between Dolores Park and Market Street that didn't have a traffic light. Drivers viewed the stop sign as a minor impediment to their morning commute, barely coming to a rolling stop. This morning, the traffic noise was so loud that the flock of pigeons feeding on the sidewalk didn't even hear Daisy as she approached. "I feel like I'm in Rome!" she said, as the birds scattered up and around her just like in an old Audrey Hepburn movie she'd seen on TV late one night.

Skittles poked his head out from under her coat and they both craned their heads to the left. No dogs visible down Dolores and Joe didn't seem to be outside yet either. Even so, she decided to turn and roll in that direction: today would be a Maxfield's day for coffee. Skittles tucked himself back in and returned to his cozy nap.

She rolled past the Holy Family Day Home, one of San Francisco's oldest early childhood education centers for working families. Hard to believe that just a year ago this had been a decrepit, one-story building with trailers parked on the playground to handle the overflow of students. Now it was a substantial, yellow stucco, two-storied building occupying the entire lot. It looked like it had been there forever. Parents double-parked along the street and hurriedly escorted their kids inside. Most kids were so excited to be there that it was all the parents could do to keep up with them.

This was in contrast to the upscale Children's Day School just on the next block. There, the anonymous parade of black-

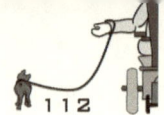

windowed SUVs rolled slowly into the driveway where, set back from the street and safely away from view, they dropped off their little charges. The parents, once unburdened of their precious cargo and back out on the street, practically drag-raced down the remainder of Dolores. Daisy hoped these kids were just as excited as the ones across the street but somehow she felt they were already feeling the pressure.

Daisy crossed over Dolores at 17th and rolled into Maxfield's, skirting the power cords that stretched from various tables and laptops to the few overloaded outlets along the wall. One day, someone was going to come up with a better, laptop-friendly seating design because their ubiquitous presence was changing everything. Instead of a coffee shop filled with cheery conversation and the soft crinkle of newspaper pages, there was a sea of blank faces illuminated blue by the screens and the dry rough click of keyboard strokes.

Funhouse, Pink's latest CD, was cranked up on the stereo and Jackson was grooving behind the counter, solidifying his reputation as the best DJ/Barista in the city. He moved right, only his blond buzz cut visible above the espresso machine, then moved left again in a series of shimmy-shakes. Daisy wasn't sure how he found the energy this early in the morning. The Asian-American woman and her Chihuahua were ahead in line. The dog sat quivering, staring up at Jackson who was leaning across the counter dangling a treat temptingly over his head.

"Are you ready, Paco?" Jackson asked the little dog.

Paco shimmied just a few inches closer and then resumed his anchored sit. His little tongue flashed across his lips.

"Here you go!" and Jackson let slip the day-old chunk of pumpkin bread.

Paco timed it perfectly, lifting up onto his hind legs to

meet the treat just as it reached his outstretched nose, not a millisecond wasted on the decent. A wet snap of canine mouth and it was gone. He resumed sitting and stared back at Jackson.

"No, don't be greedy. That's all for today."

Paco's woman bent down and scooped up the small dog who, if he had his way, would have sat there all day waiting for the next morsel.

"Hey Daisy," Jackson said, throwing in a few side steps and a quick 360-degree twirl while waiting for her to move to the front of the line.

"Hi Jackson. I'll have a large coffee."

He turned back to the coffee urn, flipped a large cup off the stack, and filled it shy of the brim. "Room for cream, right?"

"Yes. The doctor said I shouldn't have so much sugar so I'm putting in lots of cream instead." Daisy was a little sad over this change but what could you do. At least the doctor hadn't told her to give up on the caffeine altogether.

Jackson put the paper coffee cup on the front edge of the counter so Daisy could reach it, rang her up, and then asked "Would Skittles like his usual?"

"You know Skittles?" Daisy asked, completely surprised.

"Sure, it's Allen's dog. How come he's with you?" Jackson said, smiling and tossing a morsel of biscotti to the waiting dog.

"You haven't heard?"

"Heard what?" Jackson head-bobbed, dipped one shoulder, and slid left, then repeated the same move to the right, jiving with the music.

"About Allen," Daisy hesitated, then continued softly, "he was murdered."

Jackson froze mid-spin. "What?"

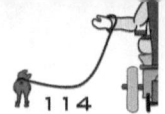

"I found him on Sunday morning, just up the street, with Skittles right beside him." Daisy was concerned. Jackson still had not moved. "I'm sorry to have to be the one to tell you."

"But I just saw him on Saturday. We were at the same party." Jackson leaned heavily on the counter. "Do they know who did it?"

"I don't think so. I ran into his friend J.B. yesterday at the police station and she said they had no idea yet."

"That's . . . strange." Jackson looked pale.

"What is?"

"When I saw Allen on Saturday night he was having fun. He was bragging about Tintin opening soon, how it was gonna be the hottest place in the Mission, gonna kick Delfina's ass."

"I read about it in the paper, then J.B. told me that was his place." Daisy said.

Jackson stepped around the counter and reached out for Skittles. He held the little creature tight to his chest. "I just can't believe he's gone."

"Do you know where he might have been going that night?" Daisy didn't really mean to be nosy but when there were questions to be asked, there were questions to be asked. Jackson would understand.

"Well, when I talked to him we were at this party at the Castle near MICU."

"Me Coo?" Daisy queried. The city was informally divided into so many neighborhoods, each with its own name: Excelsior, SOMA, Sunset, The Avenues, Inner and Outer Richmond, Castro, Mission, Dogpatch . . . she knew a lot of them but it seemed like every day the city was being divided into more and smaller regions, each wanting the cachet of a moniker.

"Yeah, Mission Curve. MICU. You know that part

between 9th and 14th and Mission and South Van Ness, where Mission curves south."

"I didn't know it had a name of its own."

"There's a bunch of clubs and art spaces that have sprung up along there. I guess MICU might be just my little name for it." Jackson continued to stroke Skittles, whose eyes thinned into little slits of pleasure.

"Anyway," Jackson said, "we were just talking, shooting the shit. He was waiting on another friend of his who hadn't showed yet. We were just talking . . ." he paused again in disbelief. "I ended up going off with someone else. I think he was still waiting when I left." Jackson gave Skittles one last squeeze and placed him back down in Daisy's lap.

"When I found Skittles, it seemed like he'd been out there all night. He was pretty damp from the fog and drizzle." Daisy remembered how the dog was so wet that she couldn't tell why he was shaking so badly—fear, cold, or both.

"If you find anything out, will you let me know?" Jackson asked.

"Absolutely!" said Daisy, and she squeezed her chair through the tables over to where she could pour a good half-cup of cream into her coffee. She pressed the lid carefully onto the brown paper cup, making sure that the plastic sealed all the way around. She'd had the "drippy cup" lid experience once too often. She waved a solemn goodbye to Jackson and headed back outside the coffee shop. What now, she wondered.

PEDRO PLACED THE MENUS and wine lists along the middle of the big family-style table that ran down the middle of Tintin. He put out the place settings exactly as he and Allen had designed them, trying to draw on the reporter theme from the Tintin comics. He put the spoon and knife at the top rather than to the right, a 2-B pencil and notepad where the knife and spoon should be. He even went through the trouble of folding the napkins like the hats pressmen used to fold out of newsprint to keep the ink misting from the presses from getting in their hair. Everything looked great!

Back in the kitchen, several of the signature dishes were in preparation. The cassoulet and the mini escargot were done. The flummery had just come out of the oven and would be cooled to the right temperature by the time they were ready for dessert.

Pedro was fully prepped for this final staff training. Like a full dress rehearsal, the staff would sit at the table like customers and have the full experience from that point of view. He hoped that giving the waitstaff this first-hand experience would make all the difference in the quality of service they could provide.

He set out the twelve major wines he wanted the staff to taste.

Now, the only thing missing was Allen.

Yesterday, Pedro and his staff had taken the day off. The opening was this Friday and they'd been working overtime for weeks trying to get the place ready to go. Once they opened, there'd be little time to rest, so Pedro had decided they should all get one last break before the deluge. At this point, everything was pretty much in his hands so it didn't really surprise him that Allen had been so out of touch over the last few days—it disappointed him a little, maybe, but he wasn't surprised. Allen was the face of the restaurant but Pedro was its legs. This was his first opening as head chef and he wanted it to go well. One thing that would have helped was a little bit more support from his boss. At the very least, he expected him to show up for this final dry run with the staff but the closer they had gotten to the opening, the less reliable Allen had become. It seemed lately Allen spent as much time pissing people off as he did getting things done. So maybe it was just as well he hadn't been around this week, Pedro sighed.

"Allen's can be such a prick!" Pedro found himself saying out loud as he placed one last wine bottle into the array. He pulled out his tire-bouchon, the antique one he'd found in the Marias during the wine-buying tour he and Allen had taken over the summer. He flipped open the little knife and sliced through the lead foil around the cork. Snapping the knife back in place, he pulled out the corkscrew and lever and made quick work of twisting it deep into the cork and pulling it free. Now this bottle could breathe, too.

A knock on the door. The first of the staff arriving for the training, no doubt. Everything was in place. Fuck Allen, we'll just do this without him. Pedro took one long last look at the table and around the restaurant—they were ready. He walked to the heavy oak door, unlocked the deadbolt, and pulled, ready to welcome the staff into his gem.

J.B. KNOCKED on the thick oak doors and waited. Nothing. Yesterday, when she'd come by, the place had been locked tight. No one around. Since she didn't have Pedro's number she'd had no choice but to come back here again

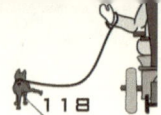

today hoping to find him.

She'd spent the night both stunned and agitated. She couldn't believe that Allen was gone. He was such a force, such a pain-in-the-ass too, but he was her pain-in-the-ass force. It just didn't seem right that he could be snuffed out so easily. She'd also realized that as much as he'd involved her and made her feel like a partner in the restaurant, he'd actually kept her very much in the dark. She didn't have Pedro's number, she didn't have the wine buyer's name, she didn't know which construction crew had done all the outfitting. Other than Pedro, she really didn't know much of anything at all. Allen had been the conduit, all information flowing through him. She'd looked, rooting through all her papers last night and finding nothing. The more she dug, the more she'd been surprised by how little she actually knew, about the business, about Allen.

J.B. knocked again, harder this time, and finally got a response.

"What are you doing here?" Pedro said with surprise, pulling the door open. "Did you come for the training? Allen's not here yet." He scowled.

"Pedro, we need to talk." J.B. stepped into the foyer of the restaurant.

"What's up?"

"I think we'd better sit down," she said, heading towards the big table at the center of the room.

"Uh . . . the staff will be here pretty soon. Can we make it quick?" he said, trailing after her.

"It's so horrible!" she said, sinking sideways into the nearest chair. "Allen has been murdered."

"What?" Pedro looked shocked.

"I got a call yesterday from the police. They found his body Sunday, over on Dolores, in some bushes." She paused there, the weight of it just beginning to sink in, poking little needle-like jabs through her steely façade.

"Sunday? Why didn't they call sooner? Why are we just finding out now? Damn it, he's supposed to be here today." Pedro was all restaurant all the time and even now, even in the midst of this, he couldn't quite pull himself out.

"Apparently it took them a while to figure out who he was. He didn't have any ID on him."

"What an ass!" Pedro frowned. "This is totally going to mess up the opening."

"Pedro!"

"What? Allen's a selfish bastard and this is just one more example."

J.B. knew Allen was difficult but she was surprised by Pedro's animosity. She couldn't let them sink down to such a base level.

"Pedro, we need to figure how we're going to handle this. We don't even know who did it."

"That's for the police to figure out, not us. We've got to get this restaurant open in just two days and this will really screw things up."

For a moment, they sat silent, at an impasse. Allen's presence hung in the air, both necessary and annoying.

"OK, here's what we're going to have to do," Pedro said, slapping his palm against the table. "You're going to have to take his place at the opening. We need a face out front, and it's going to have to be yours."

"Are you kidding?" The idea seemed ridiculous. "I'm not that gregarious. I don't know enough about 'selling' the place like he does . . . did."

"But there's no one else. I can't do it. I'm in the kitchen. You have to." Pedro was emphatic. "This restaurant is opening, with Allen or without, and we've got to make a show of it. The press is coming, the reviewers. Shit, even Gavin said he'd try and make it, and when our handsome Mayor comes, someone has to play hostess."

"But . . . ."

"And someone has *got* to tell the staff. They have to know, but we can't spook them. This is a very delicate time and spirits need to be high."

Pedro started to take on a slightly crazed look. If he looses it, J.B. thought, we're really sunk. J.B. contemplated her next move. Secretly, she'd envied Allen the limelight. That was one of the reasons she'd gotten involved in this project to start. But she had been planning on just riding on his coattails. She didn't feel at all ready to be front and center. As Pedro stared at her, waiting for her answer, she could feel something shift inside and slowly take form.

A knock at the door interrupted the moment.

"Well?" Pedro said, "What's it going to be?"

She steeled her nerve. "I'll do it."

And with that, Pedro arose and opened the door to the staff, J.B. at his side.

DAISY'S THICK WHEELS MADE that familiar squishing squeak as she rounded the corner just in time to see Joe's garage door swing open. By the time Daisy arrived, he was just reaching up to catch the pull-rope and cushion the collision of the door's rollers hitting the end of the tracks. The stretch upwards had untucked his shirt from his belt, revealing his slight paunch.

"Afternoon, Joe! Catchin' a little air there?" Daisy said with a laugh.

Joe immediately checked his fly and, finding it zipped, noticed the shirt and tucked it back in self-consciously. "Hey Daisy, what's happening? How are you feeling?" They hadn't seen each other since the morning when she'd found the body. That was three days ago.

"I'm on the prowl!" Daisy said.

"What do you mean?" One of the many reasons Joe liked Daisy was that she had her finger on the pulse of the neighborhood. Every day she had stories to tell, one way or another.

"They still haven't found out anything more about who killed his dad," she said, stroking Skittles' head. He had settled into the corner of her lap again, his new favorite spot, and was drifting off to sleep. His eyes closed softly at the warmth of her touch.

"The police? Well, I guess these things take time. It's kind of unnerving though to have something happen so close to home—right across the street—and not have them have any better sense of what happened."

"I know. I must say it's made it a little harder to sleep at night. You'd think I'd be used to it by now. I've seen so

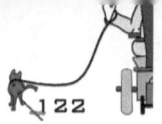

much in the time I've lived here. Remember that guy who jumped from the top balcony of my building? I think that was the worst one, till this." So much blood had flowed from the jumper's body that rainy day that it had created a steady river of red all the way down to Guerrero. Daisy shivered, remembering it all too clearly.

"Yeah, that was the worst," Joe hooked his thumbs in his front pockets, letting his shoulders slump forward, and nodded in agreement.

"It just pisses me off that they're taking so long with this," Daisy frowned. "So I've been doing a little investigating on my own."

"Hey, I'm going to make some coffee. Want any?" Joe asked. He'd been relegated to the garage again, like he was every day, and he could use the company.

"Nah, I'm good on the coffee."

Joe turned and walked back into the garage, rinsed the stale coffee from the carafe, and then filled it to the little 6 on the side. He figured it was going to be a long, cold afternoon in the garage. "So what have you found out so far?"

"Well, I talked to the police. They were no help at all." Daisy gave a quick jerk on the joystick, twisting her chair left and right in frustration. "But I did run into this woman named J.B. at the police station. Turns out she was Allen's business partner. Oh, and 'Allen,' that's his name. I also talked with Jackson, down at Maxfield's. Turns out he knew Allen and he saw him the night he was killed. They were at a party at someplace called the Castle."

"Hmm, can't say that I've heard of it." Joe poured the ground coffee into the filter, eyeballing the pile for a rough measurement.

"It's down on Mission somewhere, near Van Ness."

Mr. Coffee started to sputter and hiss as the steamy

water forced its way through the grounds. Another reason Joe liked Daisy was that she made his world seem just a little bit bigger. "So what's next then?" Joe asked.

Daisy paused, thinking. Truth be told, she wasn't sure exactly what to do next.

Joe found the silence awkward. He worried about Daisy, wanted to help her out but frankly, he was concerned about how involved she was getting in this. "You know, I was thinking of going to the afternoon service down at Mission Dolores later. Do you want to come?" Not only was it a good excuse to get out of the garage but he also hoped that Daisy might enjoy his company, or at least that it would be something of a distraction. She'd been so upset the morning she'd found the body, and now here she was trying to solve a murder. Maybe he could take her mind off it, at least for an hour or two.

"I'm not sure. I was thinking I might go over to Tintin— that's the restaurant he was opening—and see if I can learn anything else."

"Daisy, you ought to be careful. This is no time to be playing detective." He had an impulse to reach out, to put a hand on her shoulder and hold her in place, to get her to think before acting. The contact would comfort him every bit as much as it would her, though that thought was barely on the edge of his awareness. As his hand reached out across the divide, she spun her chair away.

"Hey Robbie!" she yelled out, that piercing twang echoing all the way down the block.

Joe dropped his hand back to his side and smiled. That was his Daisy.

Robbie waved silently. She was just crossing over Dolores and came over to join them on the sidewalk in front of Joe's garage.

"Hey Daisy. How are you feeling? I see you and Skittles are still hanging out." Robbie took a sip from her green travel mug, clutching it tightly between both hands.

"I'm doing OK," Daisy granted, "but I'm frustrated. They still haven't figured out anything about who killed Skittles' dad." Daisy brought Robbie up to speed on all that she'd learned thus far. During the whole recitation, Robbie nodded and sipped her coffee, trying to pull the warmth into the core of her body.

". . . and Jackson told me he saw him at some place called the Castle . . ."

"Hold on!" Robbie said.

Daisy stopped mid-sentence, startled by Robbie's animation.

"Did you say 'the Castle'?"

"Yeah. Jackson said he saw him there at a party on Saturday night. The night he was killed."

"What did you say he looked like again?"

"Jackson?" Daisy looked puzzled.

"No, the guy who was killed."

"Oh, Allen, he was tall and lanky, dark hair."

"Hmm. I was at that party too. I wonder if I saw him?" Robbie pondered aloud.

"Well that would be quite a coincidence," Joe offered, trying to find a foothold in the conversation.

"There were a lot of people at the party, and more than a few of them fit the 'tall and lanky' bill," Robbie said.

"He also had a tattoo on his arm, some sort of blue and black flag with a red heart," Daisy offered hopefully.

Jeez, Robbie thought. I remember that—the guy on the cross. "Shit, I do think I saw him." Robbie bit her tongue about the exact circumstances, figuring that might be a bit too much for Daisy and Joe. "I didn't really get a good look at his face," she said, recalling the leather hood, "but I do remember that tattoo."

"Oh, that's great!" Daisy said. "Did you see who he was with?"

Robbie thought back, remembering the hoods. "Not really. He was with a skinny guy with a dark ponytail—built kind of like Rich—and then another stockier guy with silvery hair. I didn't get a good look at any of them."

Daisy thought for a moment. "Jackson said Allen was waiting for a friend. Maybe it was one of those two."

"Did you see Allen leaving?" Joe asked, wanting to play a somewhat useful role in the conversation.

"No, I left pretty early. I think he was still there when I left."

"Now at least we're getting somewhere. Somewhere that the cops haven't managed to get to!" Daisy said triumphantly, only fueling her desire to continue her detective work.

They all stood silently, pondering this advance, and what, if anything, to do next.

"Well, I should probably get going," Robbie said. She was coming back to her senses and wanted to escape before Daisy drew her in any further. "I'm still really behind on my word count."

Daisy turned back towards Joe and was about to speak.

"Daisy, I want you to be careful with this stuff!" he said sternly, pointing a warning finger at Daisy, cutting her off before she could start.

"What do you mean? I'm just asking questions," Daisy said. She pulled the joystick back and forth, shifting herself into a more upright posture.

"But this isn't just being nosy-nellie-of-the-neighborhood. This is serious stuff. Someone was murdered." Joe was genuinely concerned for her safety.

"Nosy-nellie. Is that what you think I am?"

"I'm just saying . . ."

But Daisy cut him off. "You know, I don't need your advice, Joe. I can take care of myself."

"Alright, already," Joe said, trying to calm her down, but she was not going to be calmed right now. Daisy was like one of those big tankers out on the bay—once she got up a head of steam, there was no turning her around.

"I'll see you later, Joe," Daisy said, pushing the wheelchair into fast-forward.

"Ah Daisy, don't go like that." But she was already gone.

As Daisy headed back towards her apartment, she nudged Skittles out of her lap so he could get a little bit more exercise before they went in. She thought about all the people she'd seen come and go through this neighborhood. Most of them had been young and up-and-coming. They'd moved in and then out as their lives unfolded, growing fuller and richer with each year. These were the ones who gave the fabric of the city its vibrancy.

But a substantial number who came and went were gone for good. They were the old, the invisible, the ones who life had finally worn down. She had long since lost count of all the folks who fell in this latter category, but their passing made her sad. They were the warp threads of the city, barely visible but essential to the whole.

Allen should have been one the former but he'd suddenly become up one the latter. This offended Daisy profoundly, even though she hadn't really known him well, and she'd be damned if his murder would go unsolved.

J.B. SENT A DIRECT tweet to her boss, telling him she would be working from home for the rest of the day. At this rate, she'd probably have to call in sick for the rest of the week, there was so much left to be done. While she knew it made no sense to be mad at Allen—certainly he hadn't planned on getting murdered—she was furious. She couldn't believe how much he'd left until the last minute.

After the staff training, she and Pedro retreated to the tiny office at the back of the restaurant to see what papers they could unearth. They'd found a majority of the contact info, and some of the PR plan Allen had formulated. But they hadn't found the guest list for the opening night party, and they hadn't found any of the financials or bank information. The cash register had already been set up with credit-card processing, so Pedro was all set from the point of view of daily operations, but anything beyond that remained a mystery.

As soon as she got home, J.B. called the police station.

"Detective Rendell, please," she said, and was immediately put on hold, exiled into a realm of annoying "world" music.

"Detective Rendell. Yes?" he'd said impatiently, as if he was the one who'd been waiting on hold.

J.B. explained her predicament with the opening and her need for more of the restaurant information. "If I could just get into Allen's apartment, I should be able to find the stuff I need. At least I hope I'll find it," J.B. groaned, exasperated at Allen's thoughtlessness.

"No can do. Until we notify next of kin, no one gets access to the apartment."

"But why haven't you reached them yet? It's been days since he was killed," J.B. asked, surprised.

"Apparently, his parents are on the road. Neighbors said they took off in their Winnebago sometime last week, said they have some theory about cell phones causing brain cancer and refuse to use them. They call their neighbors every week or so to check that things are OK on the homefront, but so far no word." Detective Rendell paused there, weighing whether he'd already said too much. In fact, he kind of appreciated that the parents were MIA as it put the case on hold for the time being. There'd been a rash of gang-related shootings over on Capp Street on Monday and top brass was all over his case to show some results on those as soon as possible.

J.B. was getting panicky. "But it's essential I get in there. I need to see his cell phone and laptop. We open in two days!"

"I'm sorry, ma'am, but my hands are tied."

J.B. hated to be called "ma'am." It made her feel old.

"Well, will you call me as soon as I might be able to get in? It's really important." She tried to coo that last sentence, tried to leverage her feminine wiles to get in under the detective's resistance, but the "ma'am" had thrown her off her game.

"Yes, ma'am," he said, clicking off.

"Fuck you!" she replied to the dead line.

The afternoon sun was streaming through the front windows of her apartment. She watched as a dust mote floated slowly down and came to rest on the smooth brown surface of the Italian chrome and leather couch. Absentmindedly, she licked her fingertip and swiped it across the offending lint, annoyed when that motion left a damp streak. With the flat of her palm, she slapped the spot in frustration.

Her apartment was pristine. The couch, a knotted white wool rug, and a glass topped Noguchi coffee table with the latest copy of Elle Decor and a stack of recycled glass coasters the only items gracing its surface. She had just one piece of art on the wall, a large 1930s travel poster she'd bought in Paris. J.B. was not used to things being out of order.

"OK, J.B., buck up!" she said aloud, pulling herself into a stiff upright posture. "You had better come up with a plan."

She moved over to one of the stools tucked under the amber granite counter adjacent to the kitchen. Pulling out a pad of paper, she started to make a list:

1. *Call PR firm—see if they have guest list.*
2. *Call cash register company—see which bank linked with account.*
3. *Call bank.*
4. *Plan outfit for Friday night.*
5. *Make mani-pedi appointment w/ Lin-Su.*

J.B. paused, pen hovering above the yellow pad. Pedro had said that everything with the restaurant was on track. The food, the wine, the staff . . . everything was in place for the immediate future. The concern was longer term. Plus they didn't know what Allen had left hanging that might suddenly come up.

J.B. relaxed as she felt some semblance of control return with the listmaking. She felt sure she'd gotten the important items down. Others would flow from these but she hoped that before too long she'd get into Allen's files and access the rest of the information she needed.

She placed the small Bang & Olufsen bluetooth headset into her ear and began the calls.

J.B. explained the situation to Emily, the woman at the PR firm, breaking the news of Allen's death. They realized that since Allen's next of kin hadn't been notified, there'd been no publicity, no connecting the body found on Dolores to Allen. Emily was shocked, of course, but immediately concerned about the PR implications. J.B. explained what she needed

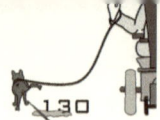

and Emily took only a moment to produce the guest list.

"OK, so here it is. I've just emailed it to you. It's really important that you pay attention to the color scheme. The ones in red are the folks Allen had really pissed off during the build-out phase."

J.B. opened the document on her laptop and noted that red made up the largest category of guests.

"I think it's pretty likely that a lot of them won't show." Emily said. "But we needed to at least go through the motions of making peace offerings, trying to rebuild bridges Allen had happily torched. If you don't mind my saying, he was a trifle difficult when something got in his way,"

"Don't worry, I've known—knew—Allen a long time. I know what a prick he could be," J.B. offered.

Emily laughed with relief.

"The ones in green are the 'influencers,'" Emily continued.

"The what?" J.B. asked.

"Influencers—the seed planters, the ones we've identified as having broad networks. We really want to impress them to get kickass word-of-mouth."

J.B. scrolled through the list, trying to commit these names to memory. Luckily, it was a relatively small group.

Emily continued, "And then, the blues are the 'hangers-on.' These are the ones that Allen felt he needed to invite—whether from past associations, or in return for favors already collected, or what-have-you—but they are definitely ones to receive the least attention. Get it? Blue is for iced out," she laughed.

"What are the ones in yellow?" J.B. asked. There were just a two of these.

"I'm not really sure to tell you the truth. Allen marked them that way. I think they might be some of his friends."

J.B. looked at the names: Jackson and Silverfox. No last

names. J.B. puzzled over this, then said, "So how will I know who's who? Allen's the one who knew all these people, I've been in the background . . . do you have any suggestions for how to pretend to fill his shoes? I'm a product marketer, not an ambassador."

"Well, this is a bit delicate, isn't it. It's not like you want to lead with Allen's death."

"True," J.B. acknowledged.

"Unless the news comes out beforehand, I think we should just keep it low-key. Maybe just say Allen was called out of town unexpectedly. But then again you don't want to outright lie. Maybe just say that you're sure he'd be there if he could and that you really hope he'll turn up soon."

"OK, I'll work on that, something that excuses him without coming back to haunt us." J.B. wrote another item on her list: *6. Plan lie about Allen's absence.*

"I'd suggest you use nametags. I know that seems lame but maybe we could create something that looks like a reporter's credential, something in keeping with the Tintin journalistic theme. It might be a nice souvenir of the opening." Emily was getting excited about this idea. J.B. was just pissed that Allen hadn't already thought of it.

"OK, I have some production contacts from Google. I'll see if I can get them to do me a favor and whip something up . . . in two days." J.B. let out a sigh. There was a lot to be done.

"Thanks for your help, Emily. I'll be in touch if I need anything else."

J.B. clicked the red "end call" button on her iPhone and immediately tapped in the next number.

LIKE A TRUFFLE HOUND, Skittles rooted around the apartment, finally focusing his attention on the gap at the bottom of the front door.

Daisy sat at the kitchen table, working the Sudoku from this morning's paper. The bright overhead fluorescents made her squint as she studied the newsprint spread out before her. Somewhere she'd read that doing puzzles like this kept one's mind sharp. She figured she could use some sharpening.

The dog's blunt nose snorted once more at the door. He spun quickly and came into the kitchen alcove, whining and restless. Back out to the door and then back to the kitchen. Finally, he sat before Daisy and stared longingly. She reached down and stroked the top of his head giving him only half of her attention. Skittles pawed at her leg, insisting she give it all.

"What's up little buddy?" Daisy asked, his anxiety finally registering fully on her Sudoku-sharpened brain.

Skittles did just what his name suggested, skittling his still seated butt across the floor to get just a little closer to Daisy. A small whimper escaped his doggy lips.

"Do you need to go out?"

Duh! Skittles was incredulous that the increased vibrational frequency of his body hadn't already communicated this clearly. Sometimes, it was a drag not being able to talk.

"OK, let's go take a walk. Let's swing by Tintin and see if anyone is around." She'd hoped that someone at the restaurant might be able to give her something, anything, that could lead to Allen's killer.

Daisy slipped on her blue fleece jacket, clipped the

soft leather leash to Skittles' collar, and grabbed her keys. Shutting the door behind them, she slipped the key ring over the joystick and pressed forward.

Once outside, Skittles relaxed. He peed on the usual spots, adding his scent to the complex story at the base of each tree. This neighborhood had such a rich perfume, he thought to himself, it was almost too much to bear. The smells let him know who'd had kibble for dinner last night and who'd gotten table scraps. Even, in one small wet patch, who'd managed to steal a whole roasted chicken off the kitchen countertop. Nice prize!

In some places he could even smell remnants of his old self, Skittles-with-Allen, that was different from Skittles-with-Daisy, and not just because his food had changed. There was something stressed out in his old smell and now it was lighter. As he pondered this, he stumbled across yet another smell—a fresh one. It was from a female dog, a big one, and she too seemed stressed. Skittles had just pressed in for a closer sniff just when his collar snapped him back.

"Oh, sorry Skittles!" Daisy said. She hadn't noticed that he'd stopped. She'd been distracted by the closed garage door as they rolled past Joe's. Maybe he's napping, she thought to herself, the old fart. She was still angry with him for his warnings to her earlier in the day. All along Dolores, she was keenly aware of the closed doors and blank face each Marina-style building presented to the street. No yards, no porches, no invitations, not a single hint about what went on inside. This was one of the ironies of this peculiar city: blank facades almost like a counterbalance to the very public whimsy so often on display.

Passing by the entry of one building, though, what caught her eye was a wild vine escaping through the gaps in the metal gate, fighting for purchase on the course brick

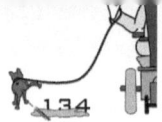

outer wall. Its tendrils and green leaves trembled a little in the ever-present San Francisco breeze, but what really drew her attention was its delicate, red flowers. The open ones were flat and fragile and broad but the closed ones were rolled up into tight red cones no bigger than the pad of her thumb. She chuckled to herself as she connected to what made them seem familiar in her imagination. How many dogs had she watched lick themselves with great focus and then look up with an innocent gaze, unaware that their little pink doggy penis was still protruding out of the furry folds of their belly. She laughed at how everything could have a dog theme in her mind's eye.

Daisy and Skittles continued along Dolores to the end of the block. They waited for the light, then crossed, and headed east along 16th. As they approached Tintin she could see that the lights inside were on. The brightwork and broad glass windows stood in stark contrast to the dirty stucco of the buildings on either side. The place sparkled.

Daisy knocked on the thick wooden door. No answer. She rolled back around to where she could see through the window and spied one of the waiters inside, setting tables. She tapped on the glass and waved. The staffer looked up, perplexed, and shrugged his shoulders while lifting his palms upwards. Daisy gestured towards the door. He shook his head no. Daisy gestured again. Reluctantly, he dropped his hands to his sides and both he and Daisy headed for their rendezvous.

As soon as the door had opened a crack, "Hey there, my name's Daisy," she offered, hoping her politeness could lever it open more.

The staffer's double-breasted white tunic was stiff with starch. *"No estamos abiertos!"* he said, starting to pull the door closed again.

"I know!" Daisy hurried. "I'm here about Allen. This is Skittles, his dog."

The man looked at Daisy and then at the dog in her lap and then back at Daisy again. "Señor Allen not here. Señor *Pendejo*," he muttered as he started to pull the door again.

"I know that," Daisy said, stating what was obvious to her. "I want to talk with someone about him. Is there someone here I can talk to?"

The man took one more look at the familiar dog and decided to pass the problem on to Pedro.

"*Un momento por favor*. Come, come . . . ," he said pushing the heavy oak door wider.

He left her sitting just inside the door while he went off in search of Pedro. Daisy took a quick survey of the décor. It seemed to be French-themed, nice lighting, and kind of quirky. Not quite as stiff as what she'd seen from peeking in the windows of places like Delfina or Foreign Cinema. Those weren't places she had ever eaten so it was interesting to finally see one from the inside. She especially liked the white dog standing guard at the end of the bar. "Any place with a dog—stuffed or not—is my kind of place," she smiled.

Two men appeared from the back: the one who'd opened the door was following behind another, taller man, also wearing a stiff tunic. Despite the similar attire, this new one was definitely in charge. The shorter man's deference made that clear.

"Isandro, finish getting those place settings out." the taller man commanded. "We've got tons to do and I don't want this hanging over us tomorrow." The shorter man went back to what he'd been doing when Daisy had knocked on the window.

"I'm Pedro, what can I do for you?" he said impatiently. Only when he turned his full attention towards Daisy did he

notice the small dog in her lap. "Is that Skittles?" He reached out towards the damp nose. Skittles responded immediately, licking the outstretched human paw. Pedro assessed Daisy with slightly more interest.

"Are you the woman who found Allen?" he asked, startled that she had found her way to Tintin. J.B. had described Daisy to him and, from what he understood of her, it had seemed unlikely that she would have ventured into this kind of place.

"Unfortunately, I am."

"J.B. told me this morning. We were all so shocked!" Pedro said, allowing an appropriate moment of silence. "That must have been horrible for you. It certainly is for us. It couldn't have come at a worse time, as we open on Friday."

Daisy was a little surprised by Pedro's calm. "Have the police talked to you?" she asked, "They won't tell me anything, and they seem to be getting nowhere fast."

"No, J.B. has been dealing with them. We're actually trying to keep it kind of quiet. I know this sounds callous, but we don't want it to distract from the opening." He continued to scratch behind Skittles' ears. Skittles, eyes dreamy and distant, seemed content to let this go on as long as Pedro was willing.

"Do you have any idea who might have done it? I can't stand having this unresolved . . . for Skittles' sake as much as my own." Daisy noticed that Isandro had moved to a table slightly closer to them and had one ear cocked towards their conversation.

"Allen was a good guy. Sure, trying to get over all the hurdles of opening a new restaurant, you can step on a few toes sometimes but Allen was a pretty stand-up guy. It just doesn't make any sense to me." Pedro shook his head.

Daisy was puzzled. She didn't mince words: "I'd only

met him and Skittles twice before—before I found him, that is—and to tell you the truth, he seemed like the kind of guy who might rub people the wrong way." She paused. "Are you sure you can't think of anyone who might have had a particular grudge?"

"No, not really, I'm at a loss." Pedro gave Skittles' ear one final pull and stepped back. "You'll have to excuse me but I really need to get back to work. We're really getting down to the wire here."

Daisy absentmindedly adjusted the tilt angle of her seat using the small toggle switch just in front of the joystick, working off nervous energy. She stared at Pedro, still thinking.

"So if you wouldn't mind . . . ." Pedro gestured towards the door. "I'll have Isandro show you out."

Daisy was still a bit at a loss for words. She'd expected some clear sense from him of who had a beef with Allen. But how he described Allen just didn't jibe with everything she'd seen or heard thus far.

Pedro nodded, as if acknowledging something Daisy had said, and turned, disappearing through the kitchen doors just past the bar.

Isandro set a pile of silverware carefully on the table and led Daisy toward the door. As he fiddled with the lock, he leaned towards Daisy and said in a hushed voice, "Señor Allen, not a good man. Not good to us. You should talk to MUA."

"Moo-Ah?" Daisy asked in her always-penetrating voice.

"Shh!" Isandro gestured flat palmed, as if he was trying to push her sound waves into the floor. "Mujeres Unidas y Activas, at the Women's Building. They help us." And with that he gestured frantically through the open door, hoping that might encourage her to leave.

Daisy, catching this now more obvious cue, complied.

Out on the sidewalk, she and Skittles considered their good fortune: maybe not a strong lead, but a lead nonetheless.

THE RADIANT faces of women stared defiantly from the "Maestra Peace" mural that guarded the middle of 18th street. The image on the building-sized mural was a siren call to strong women everywhere and beacon to women in need. The Women's Building itself was well-known and iconic throughout the city, but the inner workings were a mystery to most.

Although the building, the organization, and the mural had been there for years, Daisy—like most people—had never been inside. She pressed the handicapped button by the door and was ushered into a new world.

"Hola!" a young woman cried out from inside a windowed reception area just to the left of the entrance. "Can I help you?"

"Well, I hope so." Daisy was comforted by the eagerness of the woman who leaned over the counter towards Daisy but distracted by her new surroundings. Flyers and postcards were spread on the nearby table and taped to the wall, everything from yoga, to a radical women's conference, to a transgender stitch-and-bitch sewing session. It was a beehive of activity, with women of all shapes, sizes, and colors coming and going—working class Latina women with small children in tow heading for the elevator crossing paths with blonde, pony-tailed, lululemon-wearing dancers heading towards the Rhythm and Motion class in the auditorium.

"Someone told me I should talk to the folks at Moo—I mean, Em-You-Ay—said they might help me."

"Sure, if you take the elevator up to the third floor, their offices are just inside on the left."

Daisy followed her instructions, rolling into the creaky old wooden elevator for the trip upstairs. She located the MUA office on the third floor. It was bustling too. A dozen women sat around a large table in the windowed conference room in animated discussion. Daisy couldn't hear them but she could see big gestures, papers being waved, and the woman leading the meeting standing in a futile effort to reign in their energy.

A woman who'd been sitting at a desk at the back of the large space stood up and approached Daisy. "Can I help you?"

"I hope so but, I'm not sure exactly how . . . ." Daisy hesitated. Even though Isandro had sent her here, she wasn't sure why. "This guy at Tintin suggested I come here and ask . . . that you might have some information about Allen, the owner . . . ." She really wasn't sure how MUA could help. She waited for the woman to reply, hoping she might have some idea.

"Tintin?" she asked.

"Yeah, it's a restaurant on 16th. They haven't opened yet but they're getting ready."

"And you are?" The dark-haired woman looked carefully at this large white woman sitting in a wheelchair. While she was willing to be helpful, all the women at MUA had learned to be cautious. So many of her colleagues were in close contact with, or were themselves, undocumented immigrants, and the folks at Immigration and Customs Enforcement had become pretty devious and mean-spirited of late. This just might be the latest I.C.E. decoy.

Daisy paused, thinking how to continue. "My name's Daisy. It's a bit of a long story." Daisy explained the murder, the restaurant, the slow police investigation, and her desire to get to the bottom of it all, especially for the sake of poor Skittles, who she revealed as he napped under her coat.

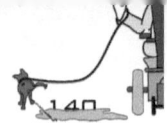

"*O, qué perro tan mono,*" the woman said as she reached out and patted the drowsy dog. "Let me check the computer and see what I can find." She moved behind a nearby desk and started typing. "We have a database of where our people are working. It helps us keep in touch with them, but it also helps us to know where work opportunities might be." She clicked a few more keys and then leaned forward, pointing at the screen. "It appears that three of our people have worked at Tintin."

"Do you know how I could get in touch with them?" Daisy asked.

"Well, I can't give out any of their contact information. That is definitely against policy." The woman paused, thinking. "But if you will leave me your information, I can tell them your situation and ask them to call you."

It was at moments like this that Daisy wished she could afford a cell phone. It would be so much easier than having to go home to check messages. "Alright. If you could just tell them I'm trying to find out who might have had a grudge against Allen. That's all. I'm just so frustrated that no one's been able to find out who killed him. Tell them it's a matter of safety for this neighborhood."

The woman was sympathetic. She assured Daisy that her message would be passed along. Daisy, though, was beginning to feel like this was a bit of a dead end. Frustrated, she backed her chair out of the office, the little beeping backup warning barely audible over a cacophony of voices as the women in the meeting spilled out of the conference room.

OUTSIDE THE Women's Building, Daisy paused. The mural loomed large overhead, topped by the massive image of the indigenous activist and Nobel Prize–winner, Rigoberta

Menchú, spreading her arms wide to welcome all. Daisy didn't recognize the woman, but could feel her embrace, so she made a plea for guidance. "Now where do I go? We're not making much progress here."

Skittles hopped down and lifted a leg towards the colorful "Community Resource Room" sandwich board on the sidewalk outside the front door. He hadn't had any water recently, so his pee was more gestural than actual.

Daisy looked across the street in surprise. Where was Anna's Danish Cookies, one of her favorites stores? Now there was another upscale trendy restaurant, barking its presence with the large red letters spelling *FARINA* across the front facade. "When did that change?"

Two young guys dressed in matching black windbreakers were standing outside the restaurant. Valet parkers, she figured, and her mind started working. They were in the restaurant biz too, you never know who might have something interesting to say. Daisy picked up Skittles, rolled to the sidewalk cut through on the corner, and pushed her way out across traffic on 18th.

"Hey there, fellas!"

They both stared at her without response.

"Can I talk to you for a second? I'm wondering if you know that new restaurant over on 16th?" Daisy paused.

Dead silence.

"You know, Tintin?" Daisy offered.

A black Audi TT pulled up in front and an elegant couple, worthy of a glamour magazine cover, emerged. One of the silent windbreakers hurried to first hold the door for the woman, and then to exchange the keys and $20 with the man. Windbreak tied a ticket to the key ring and handed over the stub. The couple slipped past Daisy into the restaurant, skirting around her as if she might be infectious. Skittles let out a low growl.

"Listen lady . . . ," the remaining windbreaker said.

"Oh, you can speak!" Daisy exclaimed, sarcastically.

He scowled and continued, "Listen lady, we're busy here, you gotta keep moving."

"But I just wanted to ask . . ."

"Get lost, you old hag!"

"No need to be rude," Daisy said indignantly. "Maybe I'm coming for dinner here later."

"You? Have a reservation?" he mocked her. "I don't think so. Now get moving. Vámonos!"

Daisy had had enough. "Alright, already," she said as she pushed the joystick forward, brushing his shin with the wide back end of the chair.

"Hey!" he yelled, hopping on one foot, holding onto his leg.

"Sorry!" Daisy said with feigned concern. If this was how all these restaurant people were, then it was no wonder Allen had some enemies. They behaved as if they were in a parallel universe, separate and unequal from the neighborhood in which they operated. "These people have no manners," Daisy muttered to Skittles as they headed home.

"HAVE YOU SEEN MY vest?" Rich yelled as he rooted through the messy pile at the bottom of the closet.

"What, honey? I can barely hear you," Dominic yelled back from the couch where he'd just collapsed, pulling the knot of his paisley tie loose from the collar of his cornflower Charles Tyrwhitt shirt.

"Have you seen my CCOP vest? You know the orange one." Rich was like a dog digging a hole; all Dominic could see from the couch was the backside of Rich's blue jeans and things flying out between his legs. A single shoe flew airborne followed by a slightly moldy rain jacket.

"It's my patrol night and I'm late!" Last year, Rich had joined CCOP—Castro Community On Patrol—after a good friend was attacked leaving Badlands. Three teenagers had pummeled him pretty hard before some other guys leaving the bar had chased them off. It turned out to have been a bunch of young kids who had BARTed in from Hayward, looking for trouble. Rich was so pissed that even in the Castro—the gayest neighborhood on earth—there could be gay bashing. He'd called the CCOP immediately, taken their safety and defense training, and joined a unit. Wednesday was his patrol night.

"Here it is!" He emerged from the closet triumphant. Dominic half expected him to be holding it in his teeth, panting.

Rich pulled the vest on over his tight-fitting hoodie. The big black CCOP letters, set off nicely by the reflective orange of the vest, matched the black of his sweatshirt. Where was it written that one couldn't be stylish and tough at the same time?

He walked over to where Dominic continued to melt into the couch. "So I'll be done at eleven o'clock, but I think we are going to go out for a drink afterwards. Are you good for dinner? I think we've got some Lean Cuisines in the freezer, if you're totally desperate, or La Med's takeout menu is in the drawer."

"Yeah, I'm good. I'm so beat I think I'll just watch Rachel Maddow and call it a night." Dominic had just started a new position that operated in sync with the markets on the East Coast. He was still adjusting to a workday that started at 5 a.m.

Rich bent down and took hold of Dominic's tie, sitting him upright and letting his head loll back, suspended from the fabric. Rich smiled down at the vision of Dominic hanging, waiting, longing. Without releasing the tension, he leaned far enough in to bridge the gap and take hold of Dominic's lower lip between his teeth. Dominic moaned slightly and tried to lift his jaw closer. Rich responded by releasing some of the tension on the tie, allowing more of Dominic's weight to be taken by his teeth. Dominic gasped with a mixture of surprise and delight. Then Rich released his "kiss" and the tie simultaneously, allowing Dominic to slump back into the couch.

Dominic smiled up at Rich. "Don't be too late or I might have to punish you!" he said in mock threat. Rich and Dominic switched easily between top and bottom, in their psychological play at any rate, their years together having built flexibility rather than rigidity into their relationship.

Rich laughed at the mock threat, knowing that Dominic would be sound asleep by the time he got home. He patted him gently on one cheek, squeezing the flesh gently between his fingers. "See you later, baby."

Dominic reached out to spank Rich's tight ass but caught

only air as he danced out of range before Dominic could make contact. "Be safe out there!" he called, finally surrendering to the couch completely.

RICH HURRIED to the corner of 18th and Castro to meet with his patrol. He hoped that it would be another quiet Wednesday night. His buddies Jackson and Lou were already there waiting.

"Sorry," Rich said, catching his breath, "I couldn't find my vest."

"Oh, and here I thought you were working on your makeup, you big queen!" Jackson laughed.

"Takes one to know one!" Rich laughed too. He loved being queer.

"Well, let's get started," Lou said seriously. She was a tough dyke, short and squat but filled with power. A heavy flashlight hung from her webbed belt, which also held her cell phone and a LeatherMan tool. She was training for the police academy and Rich thought crooks weren't going to stand a chance against her.

"All right, after you," he said, gesturing grandly and bowing slightly in mock chivalry.

She looked him straight in the eye, arching one eyebrow to question his assumptions—she was certainly no one's damsel in distress—then laughed at Rich's camp, curtsied, and led off on their patrol. Rich and Jackson fell in behind, flying wing.

Rich watched Lou's spring-loaded sneakers silently absorb the impact on the cement. He wondered if those shoes really made much of a difference. He could see her calf muscles rippling beneath her cargo shorts and figured maybe they did.

Jackson, never one to stay still or silent for long, started chattering beside him. "Trannyshack was fantastic last night! Heklina was in fine form—they even did a little preview of a Golden Girls Christmas show."

"Where do you get your energy?" Rich marveled. He knew Jackson had to be at Maxfield's in time to open at 7 a.m. and that Trannyshack didn't even get started until after 10 p.m. Jackson could certainly burn the candle at both ends.

"It's my clean living!" he said, laying a delicate hand across his heart in feigned piousness.

They passed by The Edge, the deep bass of the dance music vibrating through the sidewalk, then turned right onto Collingwood. Their route would weave between the bars and the darkened corners of the Castro. In another simpler time, these dark spots had been filled with passion. They were the spots you stumbled towards when you left the bar with the latest nameless hottie, the desire of hard bodies surpassing all caution. They were the spots where quick gropes and a quick fuck could happen unmolested. Now those quickies—if they happened at all—were safe quickies, sheathed in latex, a three-way of hard bodies and medical fear. More recently, these spots had become the ones where people were as likely to get beaten up as beaten off. Times certainly change.

They turned right onto Market and headed down towards Twin Peaks, or "God's Waiting Room," as some of the younger twinks liked to call it. Through the floor-to-ceiling windows, they could see the space filled with gray-haired men. Back in the day, gay bars had been secretive and dark, one plain door marking the guarded entrance. Twin Peaks had been the first gay bar in the country, if not the world, with windows, open and visible for all to see. The youngsters who mocked the place couldn't appreciate the radicalness of what they now took for granted. One day, if they were lucky, their own world would be just as quaint to the next generation.

As Jackson, Rich, and Lou reached the corner, an elegant older man emerged from Twin Peaks across the street and bent down, placing his Boston Terrier gently back on the ground. The dog shook, settling himself onto the sidewalk, reawakening his senses after a long nap at the bar.

"That reminds me . . . ," Jackson and Rich said almost simultaneously.

"What?" Rich asked.

"That's weird," Jackson said, still pondering their stereophonic remarks. They had stopped at the corner and were waiting for the light to change. "Ah, let's see, oh yeah, I was going to say . . . did you know a guy named Allen? He had a dog like that one."

"That's what I was going to say too!" Rich exclaimed.

"So you did know him," Jackson continued.

"Yes, I'd seen him out walking dogs," Rich explained. "And you?"

"All roads lead to Maxfield's, don't you know. I'd met him there and then seen him around. This morning, Daisy told me he'd been murdered." Jackson said, growing pale again as he recalled the news.

"Daisy told me too," Rich said.

"You also know Daisy?" Jackson's eyes opened wide at the mounting coincidences.

"Doesn't everyone?" Rich said. They laughed at the truth of that. After a moment's pause he continued, "I didn't really know him well, I'd just seen him around the 'hood. But you know the weird part?" Rich lowered his voice at this and leaned in towards Jackson conspiratorially, touching his shoulder as they followed Lou down Market Street, "I think I was playing with him at the Castle on Saturday."

"Really?!" Jackson looked surprised. "That was the night he was killed."

"I know. I mean he was still there when I left but it's just a little too close for comfort."

"Who was he with? Have the cops talked to you yet? Are you sure?" Jackson's mind was running a mile a minute.

"No, they haven't. I don't think they even know he was there. At least no one has talked to me about it."

Their patrol passed by The Lookout and turned down 16th. Mostly, it was a normal night in the queer neighborhood. A few straight couples out for dinner at Catch—new Castro residents swimming in the strange flow of gentrification—but otherwise, just regular flamboyant gayness. There was no sense trouble in the air, but Lou stayed vigilant out in front as the men chatted one step behind her.

"I'm pretty sure it was him. The guy I was playing with was wearing a hood so I didn't get a look at his face. But he had a leather pride flag tattoo on his forearm, and Daisy mentioned that the guy she found—Allen—had that too."

"Oh that's just too weird," Jackson said. "It's not like that many people have that tattoo. It's just a little too, how shall I say, obvious." Jackson's arms were covered with tattoos: a full sleeve on one and a collection of miscellaneous inks on the other. To him, there was something unimaginative about a simple flag, even if it was a kinky one.

"So who was he with when you left? Maybe that's a clue." Jackson's curiosity was growing.

"You know, in my imagination, I can almost see you pulling on your Sherlock Holmes hat right now," Rich laughed.

"Well, you know me—any excuse for being in drag!" Jackson smiled, pretending to bring a pipe up to his lips for a long puff.

They turned to the right as they approached the Harvey Milk branch of the public library, then headed down the darkened side street.

"When I left, he was with this guy Silverfox. He's the one who asked me to flog him. I just assumed the masked guy, Allen, I guess, was his boy. We'd agreed that he would take care of the boy's after-care by himself, which was fine with me." Rich shrugged his shoulders at what he felt had been a slight deviation from protocol.

As they continued along the narrow street, a group of three young kids dressed in baggy black jeans and sweatshirts rounded the corner at the other end of Pond Street.

"Psst!" Lou said quietly over her shoulder, drawing Jackson's and Rich's attention forward.

"It's probably just a bunch of Mission High kids," Jackson said. The Mission High School's students were among the regulars at Maxfield's House of Caffeine, often stopping on their way to school in the morning. Typically, they were dressed in black hoodies, baggy black pants, and oversized white gang-neutral T-shirts hanging down almost to their knees. Everything was so baggy that it often took forever for them to fish their money from the depths of their pockets to pay for their drinks at the counter.

The youth seemed harmless enough as the two groups approached each other mid-block; one flagging black, the other flagging orange.

"How ya doin'?" Lou said as they passed, acknowledging their presence with that urban protocol that requires no answer.

A silent nod from the kids, heads hung toward the ground. It was only after the last had passed that Rich heard, clear as a bell, "Faggot!"

Rich swung around. Jackson, the agile dancer that he

was, swinging right with him. "What did you say?"

"I said you're a bunch of faggots." The kids turned and faced them, arrogance and bravery beaming from their white, suburban faces. In the dim light, Rich thought he noticed an X tattooed on neck of the one who spoke. Funny what your mind fixates on in moments like these.

Lou, Jackson, and Rich were stunned by the kids' boldness. In the moment of silence that stood between them, the sound of a switchblade clicking open rang out clear as a bell.

"Why you little punks!" Lou yelled, diving forward, wielding her flashlight like a club. This was not how the safety training had suggested they proceed. That was all about de-escalation. Lou just followed her butch-dyke, PMS-ing heart. Jackson and Rich were just a split-nellie-second behind her.

The kids were clearly caught off guard by this aggression.

"That's Mr. Faggot to you!" Jackson yelled like a battle cry.

In the chaos, the loose clothing on the punks made it hard for the patrol to get a firm grasp. Their bluster, once put to the test, quickly evaporated. The punks turned and ran, CCOP in hot pursuit. The patrol put up a good chase but by the time they'd reached the corner of Market and 16th, they'd lost sight of the kids.

Breathing heavily, Lou, Rich and Jackson retraced their steps back to Pond Street. As they walked down the dark street, Rich was the first to see the knife lying in the middle of the pavement. He picked it up.

"Aren't you supposed to worry about fingerprints or something?" Jackson said, looking at the weapon with horror.

"Oh well, too late for that." Rich looked chagrined. The mother-of-pearl handle glowed in the dim light. He weighed the heft of the knife in his palm. "This is quite a piece," he said as Lou and Jackson peered in with curiosity.

"Let me see that," Lou said, reaching to take it from Rich. She ran her finger slowly and lightly along the open blade. "Shit, this thing is sharp!" she cried, pulling back to reveal a small line of red growing along the pad of her index finger.

"Damn, Lou, that's like a needle stick. You don't know where that blade has been!" Jackson said. "Are you up-to-date on all your Hepatitis and Tetanus vaccinations?"

"Yeah, I have to be. For the academy." Still, Lou looked pale at the thought of the blood-borne risk.

"Tell you what. Let's take you over to the CPMC Emergency Room right now, just to be safe, and then we can take this knife in to the police and file a report. I think we've had enough for tonight, don't you?"

"Definitely!" they confirmed in unison. With Jackson on one side, Rich on the other, the three linked arms and headed back to the bright lights and enveloping gay energy of the Castro.

MOTHER NATURE HAD TURNED off the air conditioning, that persistent cool foggy breeze that chilled San Franciscans to the bone and seemed always to be set on high. This morning it was clear, quiet and warm.

Daisy made her usual rounds after getting a coffee at Maxfield's.

She saw Marty walking with Tim and Stubs. It had been several days since their paths had crossed so Tim was especially happy to see Daisy. He pressed his big Great Dane head into her lap with twice his usual enthusiasm.

Lisa and Rocco meandered by, Rocco as doddering as ever. He almost ran into Daisy's chair before noticing her, then couldn't seem to hold to the idea that to keep getting her delicious pats and rubs, he need to stay within reach. Mid-caress, he lifted his head, cocked his shepherd ears, and just wandered off.

"Sometimes, I think he hears voices," Lisa said. "Things seem to be calling him that I can't see or hear." She shrugged her shoulders. "At least he's happy in his own little world." Lisa waved as she headed off in hot pursuit of her slow-moving dog.

Rich was out with G.M. on the Dolores median, about a block up. Daisy waved at them too but didn't feel like waiting for them to cross back over. In her chair, she couldn't join them on the grassy, curbed strip.

She was about to give up for the morning when she noted Robbie coming down 15th, coffee in hand, so lost in thought she took no notice of Daisy's gesticulations.

"Hey there!" Daisy yelled.

"Oh, sorry, I didn't see you," Robbie said as she dodged

yet another SUV rushing through the stop sign on Dolores. "I've been kind of spacey lately. It's all this writing."

"What's your word count?" Daisy asked. When Robbie had explained her NaNoWriMo project, she had suggested that it would be "supportive" for others to ask this question. Daisy figured it was the least she could do.

"Just crossed over 39K!" Robbie said. "I still have no idea where it's going. In fact, I was just trying to figure out what should happen next."

"Well I have a little story for you."

"What's that?" Robbie asked, only half paying attention.

"I talked to Jackson, you know him? Down at Maxfield's?"

"Yep," Robbie said.

"Remember how I told you that Jackson saw Allen the night he was killed, at that same party you mentioned, the one at the Castle?"

"You still trying to figure that out? I guess that means the cops haven't gotten anywhere?" She was surprised that Daisy was still thinking so much about Allen's murder but, then again, Robbie probably would be obsessing too if she'd been the one who had found the body.

"No, the cops won't tell me a thing. Anyway, this morning Jackson told me that a friend of his had told him that he saw Allen, too. With some guy named Silverfox!" Daisy was triumphant. "Didn't you say you saw Allen with some silvery-haired guy that night too?"

"Yeah, I did." Robbie felt more than a little weird discussing an SM play party with Daisy. She wondered if Daisy had any idea of what kind of things went on at the Castle.

"I was thinking we could track this Silverfox down. If he was with Allen that night then he might have some idea of what happened."

Just then Joe's garage door swung up. He stepped out and stretched, scenting the air, taking the measure of the neighborhood. Maybe that's why I like him, Daisy thought, he's got a little bit of the hound dog in him.

"Let's go over and run this by Joe," Daisy said, spinning her chair and whirring off to close the short distance.

"Uh, I've got to get back to my writing . . ." Robbie protested to the fast-moving Daisy.

"Come on, it'll only take a minute!" she called back over her shoulder. Robbie was in no hurry to get back to the quagmire of her plot problems and, anyway, there was no arguing with Daisy.

"OK, sure," she said, jogging to catch up. She followed obediently on Daisy's left while Skittles trotted along on the right. They exchanged glances, Robbie and Skittles, a slight nod to their shared fates, powerless over being towed in the wake of Daisy's chair.

"Mornin' Joe, what's shakin'?" Daisy and Joe shared this old greeting, a remnant of having both grown up in the '50s.

"Hey there, not much," Joe replied smiling.

"Robbie and I were just talking. I think I have a lead about Allen." Joe noted that Daisy was even more enthusiastic than usual, if that was possible, and that made him cautious. "Jackson told me that there's this guy named Silverfox who was with Allen that night. I want to see if we can talk with him."

"Silverfox? That's an odd name. But how are you ever going to find him?" Joe asked. He hoped that pointing out some of the logistical hurdles might defuse her passion.

"Well, that's where Robbie comes in!"

"Huh?" Robbie raised her head, wondering when she had she had volunteered to have any part of this.

"There must be some way we can talk to this guy.

Jackson said he comes into Maxfield's but not on any regular schedule. I can't just hang out there all day waiting and hoping he might show. He also said that this guy works at Mr. Something-or-other, a clothing store. Can't we just go find him there?" Daisy looked directly at Robbie.

"Daisy, um, there's something you should know about the Castle. These aren't exactly your average parties. There's kind of a rule of confidentiality about them. Do you know what BDSM is?" Robbie ventured carefully. She knew Daisy's churchgoing nature and figured this side of life in San Francisco, a normal sub-culture for her, would be completely foreign to Daisy. Robbie braced herself for Daisy's brimstone.

"Of course I do, silly. You can't live near the Castro for as many years I have and not have some sense of what goes on around here. Do you think I haven't seen all the naked butts in chaps heading down to Folsom Street Fair?" Daisy replied evenly.

"Really? But I thought you'd be more . . ."

"Judgmental?" Daisy offered.

"Well, honestly, yes. I know you go to church and all so I figured that if you even knew what it was that you'd have, uh . . . an opinion."

Joe and Robbie stared at Daisy, both surprised at the dialogue that was unfolding. Skittles simply stood, nose lifted, sniffing scents on the gentle breeze.

"I am a Christian woman, to be sure. But the God I know now has a bit more of a sense of humor than the one I grew up with. He saw all the horrors of AIDS, how it ravaged this beautiful community. He figured he'd come up with some fun things to keep those boys alive. As near as I can tell, BDSM is sort of like God's little gift, a way to help people have safe sex, or I guess now they say safer sex, don't they?"

Robbie leaned back on her heels, almost literally bowled

over by Daisy's response. For a moment, she didn't know what to say. Joe finally broke the silence.

"OK, I see where you're coming from on this. The thing I've never understood is the SM part. B and D—bondage and discipline, right? That just seems like a little bit of theater, I mean, who hasn't done a little bit of slap and tickle." Joe thought back, far back, to when there had been passion between himself and Janet. He could easily remember the powerful gleam in her eyes as she'd sat astride him, pinning his wrists over his head, while he feigned struggle. "But the SM part—sadism and masochism? That just seems so . . . mean. I've never understood that."

Robbie was still in shock that Daisy, or Joe for that matter, had ever even thought about this stuff, let alone that she was now talking to them about it. "I think it's a little complicated. It has to do with power and pain, intense sensation, taking and surrendering . . ." Robbie started to explain but found she was at a loss as to where to begin describing the subtleties of psychological power dynamics in S/M play. She hadn't even had a full cup of coffee yet this morning and her brain was not firing on all cylinders.

"Actually, I think it's kind of simple," Daisy interrupted. "The Bible says: 'Each man should give what he has decided in his heart to give, not reluctantly or under compulsion, for God loves a cheerful giver.' That's from Corinthians. Seems like that pretty much covers it." Daisy shrugged her shoulders as if stating the obvious.

Joe nodded as if that did it for him too.

Robbie, perplexed, decided to leave well enough alone and turned the conversation in another direction. "OK then, sounds like you understand the world you're poking around in. You say you want to try and find Silverfox. You still want to do that?"

Daisy nodded. Joe still looked concerned.

"Well, you could wait for the next play party at the Castle and go and see if he's there. But that doesn't seem any better than hanging out at Maxfield's. The next party probably wouldn't be until the weekend."

"I don't want to wait any longer." Daisy shifted her chair more upright to match her energy. "The body's getting cold and so is the trail, and we might have a killer roaming our neighborhood."

Robbie kneeled down to pat Skittles and tried to think of where to begin. As her fingers worried the silver studs on the dog's black leather collar, an idea came to her. She placed her coffee on the sidewalk and twisted Skittles' collar enough to see the inside surface. Burned into the dark leather was a distinctive and familiar brand.

"The guy I saw at the party—the one you think was Allen—and the guy he was playing with, they were both wearing similar leather hoods. Really nice ones. I would guess the hoods belonged to the silver-haired guy since he was running the scene. This collar was made at a shop called Mr. S, I can tell by the brand on the inside." Robbie twisted the collar so Daisy could see. Skittles remained patient even as he struggled to breathe.

"I'd bet that's the Mr. Something store Jackson mentioned! It's the best leather and play shop in town. I figure that's as good a place to start as any!" Robbie was getting jazzed by the idea of having a clue to follow, or maybe just jazzed at having a distraction to lead her away from her writing.

"So when do we go?" Daisy asked.

"We?" she and Joe said in unison.

"Not you, Joe," Daisy said firmly. "I know you never leave your garage."

She said this without rancor but the remark still stung.

Joe studied his shoelaces. "Well, I wouldn't go *that* far," he mumbled.

"It's just that I meant Robbie and me. You know, two's company, three's a crowd—"

Now it was Robbie's turn to be stunned. "Me? I've really got a lot of writing to do today."

"Come on, it's our neighborhood I'm trying to keep safe. If we don't do this, who knows who might be next?!" Daisy urged.

Robbie was pretty sure it wasn't going to be her, but Daisy's concern planted a seed of doubt in her mind that started to germinate. Why had Allen been killed? Could she really dismiss it so easily? What if it was related to the Castle? Or something in this neighborhood? Maybe she did owe something to her overlapping communities.

A young professional woman clicked down the sidewalk heading towards them, spiked heels thundering off the cement. As she passed, she pulled just enough of her attention away from her bluetooth conversation to cast a disgusted glance their way. Daisy barely noticed. She'd seen it so many times before it splashed off her thick skin. But Robbie was disturbed to bear witness to how easily people judged Daisy based on nothing more than appearance and the volume of her voice.

"Alright," Robbie said, the noisy heels cementing her own resolve. "How 'bout I meet you at three o'clock. We can go down to Mr. S together and see if they can help us track down this Silverfox guy."

"Good enough!" Daisy joysticked her chair into a quick left-right shimmy.

"I hope you two will be careful. Remember, someone was murdered. This isn't a game," Joe warned, choke-chaining against Daisy's enthusiasm, trying to bring it down to the level with which he felt comfortable.

"Ah, Joe, you gotta get out and live a little!" Friend or foe, it was impossible to stifle Daisy's energy.

"Later then!" Robbie said, heading back home to eat her now cold bagel and get in some morning writing. When she reached the corner, she paused to look back at Joe and Daisy, who remained deep in conversation. Robbie could see something shimmer between them, some tether, but she could also see Skittles pulling Daisy in a different direction and with a force somewhere beyond that of his simple Boston Terrier strength.

J.B. SKIRTED A CROWD of high school students on a late lunch break who were blocking most of the sidewalk outside Maxfield's. Their black and white outfits gave a false sense of unity to their chaotic energy, bustling with sexual tension and self-doubt, bravado outrunning vulnerability. The girls trash talked each other in escalating voices while the boys played out their drama physically, mock-wrestling each other so as to accidentally bump into the girls they favored. The boys' pants were so baggy that they had to hold them up with their hands as they moved. The girls' shirts were so tight and revealing that they embraced every curve—the curves of the emerging woman and left-over curves of baby fat—with equal passion.

Continuing down 17th towards Mission, J.B. was so busy checking text messages and tweets on her iPhone that she almost walked right by Pied à Terre, the new eco-green mani-pedi salon that had taken over the old Saraha Buddhist Center building. She pushed open the door into an oasis of bamboo flooring, thriving plants, and hemp-covered recliners. Enya's lilting voice played gently in the background, slightly muffled by the umber-colored earth plaster walls.

Now this is a find, she thought. And so much nicer than those cookie-cutter nail salons that seem to spring up overnight anytime there's a small vacant storefront. Strange thing was that this place, like the others, appeared to be staffed by the same group of deferential, recent Asian immigrants. J.B. remembered reading an exposé on Salon.com about how these women were often trapped into indentured servitude, trying in vain to work off the up front cost of their immigration. Before she could give it much more thought, her phone vibrated in her palm.

Looking down at the screen, she saw the Twitterific notification. She had a feed going to track any tweets that referenced Tintin. The PR firm had launched a viral campaign this morning and it seemed to be catching fire. In the last hour, there had been twenty-three tweets using the #tintin hashtag.

"May I help you?" asked the woman who had waited patiently while J.B. negotiated her phone's demands.

"Oh, I'm sorry. I have an appointment. J.B. Bellows," she said, finally looking up.

The woman traced her finger down the flat screen embedded in the counter, "Yes, here we are. Welcome, Ms. Bellows. I see this is your first time with us."

"Indeed," J.B. said, fully taking in the surroundings.

"Welcome, then. Why don't you come right back here and we'll get started. Can I get you some green tea? Or rooibos red, perhaps?"

J.B. settled into the familiar rhythm of the treatment. Once you got down to it, other than cleanliness, there was little difference between a mani-pedi at this place and one at one of the more questionable spots down on Mission Street. In either case, it was soaking, cleaning, clipping, trimming, buffing, oiling, and painting. J.B. didn't like to dwell on the details of the process—especially the cuticle trimmings that piled up in the crevasse of the clippers—preferring to simply relax into the experience of the whole. Mostly, she was grateful that providing this service to others was not her job.

The woman worked quickly and efficiently; J.B., unable to use her phone since her hands were soaking, spent the time doing some positive visualization about tomorrow's opening. She imagined the crowds flowing in, the energy and excitement, the warmth of the décor (especially the fixtures she'd chosen), and the good cheer the food and wine would generate. She pictured herself at the center of it all, basking in the fabulous reviews of Tintin, appropriately humble in response. Pretty soon it was all going to be real.

"Color?" the question pulled her out of her reverie. The woman was holding a palette of enamel colors for J.B.'s review.

"Oh, let's see. I'm going to be wearing a smoke blue-gray outfit, so I want something bold to offset it. How about this . . ." she said pointing out a bold orange-red called Uber-Cantelope.

"Perfect, Ms. Bellows," the woman concurred, knowing better than to disagree with even the most ill-advised choice of the client.

It was going to be strange to have all this happen without Allen. J.B. still hadn't heard anything from the police, and still no access to his apartment and files. When she'd called Detective Rendell for an update he said he was busy with some gang shootings. Why that would take precedence she couldn't quite understand. Weren't there enough police in this town to deal with all of it?

After her nails were painted and finished drying under the ultraviolet light, she held her hands up for inspection and was pleased with the result. Just the right bold contrast. "Nice!"

She leaned against the front counter as she swiped her Working Assets credit card, adding a five percent tip to the total before scribbling her electronic signature. That seemed appropriate, she thought, as the woman had done an excellent job.

J.B. turned and paused before the full-length mirror adjacent to the front door. She scanned herself from head to toe. The nails did look great but the rest . . . a little bit of doubt bloomed in her imagination. Was that a tiny muffin top folding over the edge of her belt? Why was the skin under her eyes looking so sallow? And her hair . . . where was the usual luster, and it wasn't getting thin on top, was it? J.B. could feel the voices take possession of her. Like the fog that rolled over the city, the damp thoughts dipped and curled, relentlessly seeking out low spots in her psyche. She knew it was just that—a fog, an illusion—but it chilled her nonetheless. "Come on J.B., snap out of it!" she said under her breath. And, just as quickly as it had come, the fog lifted.

"Thanks again!" she called, and hurried out and away from the mirror before the fog could roll back in. The woman stood silently behind the counter, frowning at the receipt.

Out on the sidewalk, a plaintive voice sang out from inside J.B.'s cavernous Big Buddha purse. "I need you, just a little . . . ," Edie Carey crooned, announcing the incoming call. Last night, J.B. had picked this song from her iTunes library as her new ringtone. She wasn't sure why the twangy tune and the singer's bright voice had resonated with her so. There was something simple and vulnerable but also hopeful in the song, and she couldn't stop tapping her toe whenever she heard it. Curious how music could do that—animate the body without ever explaining exactly why.

She dug out the phone and looked at the screen as Edie kept right on singing. Although she didn't recognize the number, she hit the green "answer" button anyway.

"Hello, this is J.B.," she said with a tone that implied, *and who are you?*

"Honey, we need to talk," an epicene voice said.

"I'm sorry, do you have the right number? Who is this?" Mrs. Bellows had raised her daughter to be polite above all else. Even in the face of another's rudeness, she couldn't let go of that.

"If you want your precious restaurant opening to go

well, we better talk."

"Excuse me?" an edge of fear crept into J.B.'s voice.

"Allen and us, we had a deal, sweetie!" the voice pressed. The high-register, Southern lilt incongruous with the seriousness of the message.

Clearly this was about the restaurant but, beyond that, she had no idea what he was talking about. "Perhaps if you could give me just a little more information about your, uh, arrangement?" she tried to remain calm and businesslike.

"We know all about the code violations. If you don't want everyone else to know too then you better deliver what Allen promised."

"How did you get my number?" J.B. was beginning to feel like a broken record, asking question after unanswered question.

"Never mind! You better pay up and it better be today."

J.B. decided on another tactic. "I'm happy to follow up on whatever agreement Allen had with you but I need a little bit more detail. If you spell it out, then I can make this an actionable item." Her old marketing lingo had crept into the negotiation. Pretty soon she'd be talking about deliverables and arguing ROI with him.

"Fifty K, my dear, you know the deal." He was growing impatient.

Despite trying to think on her feet, she felt her mind wandering, thrown off by the phrase "fifty K." Her wayward mind scanned back through the filed images stored in her memory, finally pulling out the image of a Team In Training poster for a cross-country skiing event. The Anchorage 50km Race, she remembered. She was pretty sure his fifty K was from a different world of fundraising.

"Are you still there?" the voice hissed.

"Yes, yes. Sorry. Clearly you know about what happened

to Allen"—she figured he wouldn't be talking to her if he didn't—"but what you don't know is that the police haven't given me access to the bank accounts yet."

"That's not our problem. $50K," he repeated, his voice breaking into a lower register, "Or we go to the media."

"But I don't have access—"

"Again, not our problem. Just get it. I'll call you later tonight. If you don't pay up today, your fancy opening is going to be one big bust."

She heard three quick beeps indicating that the call had was over. Lowering the phone, she watched as the "Call Ended" pleasantly faded to gray.

OK, well at least I didn't just imagine that, but how did he get my number? J.B. was immobilized, disbelief struggling against the call to action.

All the time she'd been talking, J.B. had been walking without paying attention so that now she found herself standing at the corner of Valencia and 17th. She stared across the street, trying to think about what to do next. On one corner, the new loft/storefront building rose three oddly pristine stories with T-Mobile leaning up against Good Vibrations on the ground floor. Cell phones next to sex toys . . . at least they both vibrated. On the other corner, Harrington's—the old used furniture store that had been there forever—had windows as dusty as T-Mobile's were gleaming. Despite the steady flow of people on the sidewalk, J.B. stood stock still, running her eyes back and forth between the two buildings.

"Street Sheet?" a gap-toothed man with a twinkle in his eye rattled the homeless-fundraising paper in her line of sight, one nonprofit's answer to panhandling.

J.B. jumped, but the shock crystallized her thinking. "No thank you," she shook her head. Clearly it was time to talk with Pedro. J.B. brushed past him and hurried towards Tintin.

"OK, I'M ALL CHARGED up and ready to go!" Daisy said enthusiastically, "My brain *and* my chair!" She and Robbie were on the sidewalk in front Daisy's high-rise. It was a nice afternoon so, even though it was a bit far to their destination, they had decided to walk it, or roll it, as the case might be.

"I'm going to leave Skittles at home for this one. I think he's a little tired from our big morning."

"You still sure you want to go?" Robbie felt compelled to double-check that Daisy was still up for a visit to Mr. S, the bastion of SM equipment and fetishwear. Despite Daisy's assurances, Robbie was worried that the place would freak her out. Daisy's voice in a *good* mood was loud enough; Robbie didn't really want to find out what a freaked-out Daisy might sound like.

"I wanna track down this silver-haired guy and this seems like our only lead. Don't worry about me, I'm a tough old bird."

"All right then, let's get going."

Their route took them through slice after slice of San Francisco life. Past Mission Beach Café, the new upscale eatery, which cozied up to Bleeding Heart, one of about five medical marijuana clinics along their route. Past the new Laundry Mat, that had replaced the old Socialist Bookstore. Past the massive brick Armory, now home to a thriving porn film business. Past the Day Laborer Center and the City Permits Office, an urban lumber yard keeping the peace between them. Past the Voice Factory, a home to experimental theater. Past the busy Bike Kitchen, the DIY bike shop where hipsters cared for their beloved fixed-gear rides. Turning right at The Stud, they arrived at their final destination—Mr. S, San Francisco's biggest fetish/leather store near 8th and Folsom. All the while Daisy had told story after story of her time in San Francisco while Robbie listened intently, taking mental notes for her novel.

"Ready?" Robbie asked again, still not convinced Daisy understood what she'd find in *this* store.

"Yup," Daisy replied. If Daisy felt any trepidation, Robbie couldn't read it in her voice or body language. Daisy had to be one of the most resolute people Robbie had ever encountered. She silently rebuked herself for underestimating Daisy as she held the doors wide enough for Daisy to roll inside.

Although it was mid-afternoon the place was full, customers mixing easily with bare-chested staff. Some customers slinked about, trying to go unnoticed, while others moved confidently towards their intended purchase.

"Wow, you'd never know we're in an economic crisis by the looks of this place," Daisy observed.

They passed by the front counter, around the spiral staircase that lead upstairs, and into the main part of the shop. Robbie said a silent "thank you" that the upstairs wasn't wheelchair accessible. She'd only gone up there once. It was where the hardcore stuff was housed; even *she* had been a little bit shocked.

"So what's the big deal?" Daisy said. At first glance the placed appeared little different from any small clothing store, save for a decided preference for black and a focus on one particular fabric. On the clothing rack to her left were a variety of vests and shirts, all leather. Straight ahead, pants—some of which were missing the backside—all leather. To the right, a wide variety of accessories—combinations of leather and metal—hung on the wall. It was the accessories that drew Daisy's attention. She rolled over for closer inspection.

"What's this?" Daisy asked Robbie, holding up what looked like a stiff leather paint stirrer with a few extra flaps attached.

"Uh, I guess you'd call that a thumper," Robbie said quietly. Daisy was talking in her usual booming voice, drawing a bit of attention. Robbie hoped her own hushed tones might encourage Daisy to speak more quietly. She reached out and took the thumper and, against her palm, demonstrated how—depending upon which way you held it—the extra flaps could add sound or momentum to the impact. Daisy nodded, satisfied with the demo. Robbie hung the thumper back on the wall.

"Now this looks kind of like the one Skittles has, only for a much bigger dog," Daisy said, inspecting a lovely studded black collar.

They continued to explore, Daisy asking and Robbie explaining the myriad toys on display. Robbie admired Daisy's equanimity about it all. They wheeled past the dildo display, past the latex pants and full body suits, and paused in the tight space next to the dressing rooms. A tall, exquisitely muscled man had thrown back the curtain of one of the rooms and stepped out to get a full view in the mirror. His skin, smooth and hairless, was like caramel. He turned and looked back over his shoulder toward the mirror trying to get a better view of the tight-fitting chaps. "Do you think these make my butt cheeks look fat?"

Daisy and Robbie raised a collective eyebrow. "Uh, not really!" they chimed, laughing at the absurdity of the question. His ass was perfectly chiseled and set off to full advantage by the curve of the leather chaps. Surprisingly, Robbie felt herself get a little hot as she admired his masculine form.

"Sweetie, you look sublime," Daisy said encouragingly.

"You think so?" he asked, still insanely unsure. Directing

his attention back into the dressing room he said, "Well, if *they* say it's OK then it must be so."

From inside the dressing room the voice of the fitter replied. "I agree, I think we've got the waist and inseam just right. Let me just mark the cuff and I'll finish them up," he said, stepping out of the dressing room to join his client.

Daisy and Robbie did a double-take. They looked at him, then looked at each other, and then back at the silver-haired man who had emerged, a long fabric measuring tape draped over his shoulders and sliver of white tailor's chalk in hand. The spotlights shimmered off his slick hair: not gray, not white, but a pure polished silver.

Robbie cocked her head to the side, indicating to Daisy that they should retreat back over into the dildo section. Daisy, reluctantly, reversed her chair.

"I think that's him," Robbie whispered.

"Excellent!" Daisy replied, not quite taking the volume-control hint from Robbie's tone. "He's beautiful," she finally whispered.

Daisy wasn't sure exactly why but this silver-haired man pulled at her imagination. It was like there was some sort of shimmer coming off his body, a metallic glint, impermeable yet seductive.

"What are we going to do now?" Robbie asked. She'd agreed to go with Daisy on this adventure but she hadn't really thought through what they would do if they actually found the guy.

"Well, why don't I just ask him when he last saw Allen?" Daisy said as she peered around Robbie, hard-pressed to take her eyes off of him.

"Ah, I think we have to be a little subtler than that. Plus, there's a little bit of protocol here that we have to follow," Robbie paused.

Daisy cocked her head to the side, perplexed. "But he's almost done."

"I know, it's not just that. It's like church: you don't talk while the sermon is going on, the priest doesn't tell what he hears in confession, and you don't chew the wafer. You know, things like that."

"I don't get it."

"This guy, he's kind of like a priest in a certain community. We've got to pay him his due."

"OK, if you say so, but however we do it, we've got to talk with him today." Daisy kept trying to maneuver around Robbie who held her ground.

"Let me talk to him. OK?" Robbie insisted.

Daisy nodded her assent, as her eyes and chair turning to follow the object of her infatuation as he disappeared into the back room.

They waited until Silverfox had reemerged, the neatly hemmed chaps draped over his forearm. He handed them to the very excited customer. "Here you go," he said, bestowing them like a sacramental vestment.

"Thank you so much!" the man said, shaking Silverfox's hand and adding a little curtsy. "I really appreciate all your help." Turning, he said, "And thanks to you two as well!" and blew a kiss towards Daisy and Robbie.

"Excuse me, could we have a moment of your time?" Robbie drew Silverfox's attention.

"How can I help you?" he asked, assuming they were shopping together. He had seen every possible pairing in this place so this combo (what he read as younger butch boi and older, disabled dyke) hardly drew his notice.

"I don't mean to be out of line, but I'm wondering if I could ask you something about something that happened at the Castle this past weekend?" Robbie asked deferentially.

Robbie saw him flinch—subtle but perceptible. Where was this conversation was going to go, she wondered. Taking a deep breath, she plowed on, hoping Daisy would continue to bite her tongue.

HURRYING UP 16TH, J.B. tried to figure out how to approach the whole mess with Pedro. Did Pedro know that Allen was being blackmailed? Could he be in on it? One thing her training had taught her was to always question assumptions. When you weren't sure which way to proceed, it always paid to step back and look at where you thought you were. Sometimes, you'd find you were nowhere near where you first imagined. So question number one: were there actually any code violations? No point in allowing yourself to be blackmailed over nothing.

She reached Tintin's big door and stopped dead in her tracks. Across the full width of the beautiful oak surface someone had spray-painted YUPPYIES DINE, PEOPLE STARVE! and a big fancy X as a signature below that. Spelling mistakes aside, they'd made their point. Pedro was going to have to find someone to refinish the door immediately. She knocked loudly on the door. One of the waitstaff—she couldn't remember his name—came and opened the door.

"Hola!" he said quietly.

"Is Pedro in the kitchen?" she said as she swept past.

"Sí," he said, relocking the door.

Pedro came out of the kitchen and around the corner of the bar before J.B. could make it halfway across the dining room.

"Have you seen that?" she said, pointing back towards the entrance.

"What?"

"The graffiti!" They stepped back outside to inspect the damage.

"That must have just happened. It wasn't there when

I came in this morning," he said, running his fingers over the fresh paint.

"Well, we're going to have to get that fixed today!"

"Not to worry. We anticipated that this kind of thing might happen. We had the door finished with a special anti-tagging coating. They developed it for all the murals around town to cut down on maintenance costs. A little soap and water and we're good as new."

The two of them stepped back into the quiet restaurant. Pedro turned and clicked the deadbolt shut. "Hey, Isandro!" he called across the room, "Can you take care of the door when you finish up with that?"

Isandro's head popped up from behind the bar and he nodded in quiet assent.

That crisis resolved, J.B. got down to business. "Pedro, I need to talk to you. Right now. Let's go back into the office."

The two of them walked to the back of the restaurant. J.B. closed the door behind her.

"I got a call this morning. Someone who says there are code violations and he's going to call the authorities unless—"

"Unless what?" Pedro said dismissively.

"Unless we pay fifty thousand dollars!" J.B. said, still horrified by the amount.

"They're bluffing." Pedro was clearly not taking this seriously.

"I don't think so. They said they'd already talked with Allen and he'd agreed to pay up," J.B. pushed back.

This thing, the blackmail, sat between them like a holiday fruitcake—an unwanted gift that they were both too polite to decline.

"Well, if Allen agreed, then I guess we have to." Pedro was the first to blink. J.B. was suspicious of how easily he had changed his mind.

"But do you know of any code violations? You were here during all the build-out." J.B. was hoping Pedro might be able to dismiss the blackmailer's claim, convince her that there was nothing but bluff and bluster behind it.

"Well, I was mostly focused on the kitchen space, not the main area. I do remember that there was a small problem with the electrical, something about those fixtures over the bar, but I'm pretty sure they resolved that."

J.B. could tell that was an intentional dig. Pedro knew full well that those fixtures were her pride and joy, custom ones she'd commissioned.

"If this guy's telling the truth and we don't pay, we're screwed. If he's bluffing and we pay, we're out $50K for nothing."

"But I'll tell you, if we open and everything goes according to plan, we'll make back that $50K in the first few weeks. I don't think we really have any choice but to pay up," Pedro concluded. He seemed so assured in his reasoning. That should have reassured J.B. but it didn't. Instead, she felt more and more alone in her dilemma.

"I guess that logic makes some sense but even if we wanted to pay, where are we going to come up with that cash?" J.B. certainly didn't have access to that amount in her own bank account. What savings she'd had she'd put into Tintin long ago. Access to the business account was still closed off by the police and would remain so until they'd contacted his next of kin.

"Allen had given me access to the petty cash account, we could check that," Pedro suggested.

"How much is going to be in there?" J.B. said skeptically. She doubted that there'd be more than a few thousand dollars in that account.

"I'm not sure. No harm in checking." Pedro hit the space

bar on the computer's keyboard and the screen came to life. He logged into the Wells Fargo account and clicked on the "account balances" tab.

"Wow!" Pedro hadn't looked at the account in over a week because everything had already been brought in for the opening and he hadn't needed to make any additional purchases.

"What?" J.B. said, coming around the desk to peer over his shoulder.

The balance on the screen was stunning: $51,833.

"Do you think . . . ?" J.B. tried to work it all out in her head. Did this mean Allen really *had* been getting ready to pay? But why out this account, the only one to which Pedro had access? Why shift the money? Did Pedro already know about this?

They looked at each other, a moment of mutual questioning.

Pedro's words seemed to gently tip the balance, "Looks like he was going to pay."

J.B. stood upright and clenched her fists by her side, barely able to contain her frustration. "Allen is dead and who knows what the hell he was thinking!" She was still so mad at him for getting himself killed. "We are just going to have to make the decision ourselves."

"Well, I'd say we have everything to lose and nothing to gain . . . let's pay." Pedro looked J.B. directly in the eye, almost daring her to say no. This time, she blinked first.

"OK. The guy said he'd call me later today. I suspect he's not going take a regular check. You hurry to the bank and get a cashier's check. As soon as I get the instructions from him, I'll call you."

"Good enough," Pedro assented, offering a mock military salute.

As J.B. left Tintin, she had an uneasy feeling that she was still missing something. She didn't trust Pedro, he'd been so quick to lean towards paying. She wished she hadn't let Allen keep her in the dark about so much of the operations, but she had to hold herself accountable for that too. If only the cops had already solved the murder—already knew why Allen had been killed, already knew if it was in any way connected to this blackmail—then she'd know whether or not to take this seriously. But she couldn't exactly waltz into the police station and say "I'm being blackmailed for some alleged illegal activities at our restaurant. I'm wondering if that information would help you solve Allen's murder. Oh, and can you give me advice on whether or not I should pay?"

She thought back to her first conversation with Detective Rendell and remembered the woman she'd met outside the station, the one with Skittles. That woman had promised that she would get to the bottom of the murder and seemed like just the busybody type who might. Maybe she had learned something that the cops hadn't yet?

J.B. rooted around in her purse for the piece of paper the woman had given her. Duh! I put it directly into my phone, she said to herself, slapping a palm against her forehead. This blackmail business was making her into a space cadet, a state of mind she definitely did not enjoy.

As Daisy approached her apartment, she saw that the two jade plants next to her door had been pushed to the outside railing and the potted lavender had been knocked over onto its side. She knew it hadn't been that way when she left. As she rolled closer she could hear the plaintive sound of claws scratching on the other side of the door.

"All right, Skittles. Just hold your horses!" she said as she fumbled with her keys.

The trip to Mr. S had taken longer than she'd expected. By the time they'd gotten back, what with non–daylight savings and everything, it was almost dark. Skittles had been inside for a long time.

She pushed the door open and before she could even get inside, Skittles was airborne, launching himself into her lap. The little dog shook violently in her arms.

"What's the matter, little buddy?" He burrowed deeper into her embrace in response. "Do you need to go out, is that it?" She knew he must but he didn't respond with any of the usual affirmations—a bark, a jump down, a wagging tail. It was at moments like this that she really wished dogs had better language skills.

"Well let's go anyway, maybe it'll calm you down."

She clipped the leash onto the little dog and encouraged him out the door. His nails tick-tacked across the cement of the balcony. When they rolled into the elevator for the ride down, just two floors, Skittles jumped into her lap again.

"What is it, baby?" Daisy hated to see a dog in such distress. She couldn't imagine what had spooked him so. They headed up to Dolores and rolled halfway across the street to a spot where Daisy could stop in the crosswalk, protected by the median, and hold the leash for Skittles as he climbed onto the grassy strip and looked for a place to pee.

"Oh, that's a good boy," she said as the dog squatted slightly, lifting one leg. "Don't you feel better now?" *She* always did after she'd had herself a good pee but the dog still seemed anxious. He paced back and forth at the end of the leash, testing the outer boundaries of his space attached to Daisy. As he did, he started to whimper.

"What is up with you boy?" Paws-to-grass was definitely not calming him down. Deciding that perhaps a little more movement would do the trick, she led the dog across the second half of Dolores and turned left towards 16th. As they passed the spot where she'd found Allen's body Skittles darted sideways in front of her chair and away from the empty lot, so fast that Daisy had to pull back on the joystick to keep from running him over.

"I'm sorry, Skittles, of course you're freaked out here—how thoughtless of me." She realized they hadn't walked directly past this spot since she'd found him. She'd made a point of staying on the opposite side of the street until now.

"Let's keep going." She shifted the joystick into fast forward. Despite the traffic on the street, the sidewalk was relatively quiet, but also dark. They were just passing by the historic twin Tanforan cottages with their matching front porches when Skittles jumped sideways again. Three young kids—in that all-black baggy clothing that seemed to be the style of the day—were coming down the narrow alley that ran beside the southern side of the cottages. In the dim light, they'd surprised Daisy too.

"Oh dear, you scared me! I didn't see you kids there." Daisy pressed her hand to her enormous breasts and took a deep breath. Usually, Daisy connected with kids as easily as she did with dogs. They were all from similar intuitive camps, barely socialized into the adult human world. But teenagers, those liminal creatures, were more of a challenge. The three continued to approach, offering no response to her greeting.

Skittles stood still, shivering, eyes wide. Daisy could feel his anxiety vibrating up the length of the leash. A low growl began to rumble from deep in his belly.

"Cute dog," one of the kids said as they drew closer. "Can I pat him?" he asked, pulling back the hood of his black sweatshirt and crouching down to get closer to Skittles. As he did, Daisy noticed the top of what looked like a big X tattoo poking out from his collar. Oddly, it made her think of Lurch from *The Addams Family*, her favorite childhood TV show.

The poor dog was practically shaking his head "no," but Daisy urged him closer. "Come on, Skittles. Say hello to the young man."

The youth scratched Skittles roughly behind the ears. Skittles stood still, suffering the attention.

"Come on, R.J.," one of the others said. "Let's go!" They seemed to be getting a little edgy.

"No, I think I know this dog," R.J. replied. "Do I know this dog?" he asked slowly, looking up at Daisy. His eyes sparkled, deep and startlingly dark. His gaze was compelling.

"Maybe you've met him before, with his owner? I'm just taking care of him while—" Daisy started to explain.

"Oh, I know. And you live just around the corner, don't you?" he interrupted.

Daisy was surprised that he knew where she lived. Before she could ask how, he spoke again.

"Are you one of those special P.A.W.S. walkers?"

P.A.W.S. stood for Pets Are Wonderful Support, an organization that helped people with AIDS and other conditions to keep their pets at home even when they couldn't care for them themselves. R.J. continued to run his hand over

Skittles body, head to tail and then back again, standing the dog's fur on end. Skittles was not thrilled with this.

Daisy's natural inclination to be friendly was at war with some internal voice that was encouraging caution. Friendliness won. "No, not P.A.W.S., just taking care of Skittles here until we can find him a home. His owner was murdered real near here last Saturday. I found him." Daisy spoke rapidly even as her mind went back to that horrible moment when the leash had come loose, and the sight of Allen's dead hand.

"Yeah, I thought he looked familiar. I've seen that guy out walking him around here. I'd recognize that collar anywhere." R.J. stood, scooping up Skittles in his arms as he did so. He held the dog awkwardly without support under his rump.

"R.J.!" his friends said, a plea rather than a question.

"He's a gay dog, isn't he?" Skittles was squirming in his grasp.

A Chavez Distributors truck rumbled by, heavy with tortillas.

"See, he's shivering like the little faggot dog that he is!" As R.J. said this, he unclipped the leash from the collar and tossed the loose end to the ground.

"Hey!" Daisy said, as deep inside, friendliness started calling out to caution for help.

"I bet he is too much of a sissy dog to even fend for himself. Let's see . . ." and with that R.J. tossed Skittles out onto Dolores, into the path of oncoming traffic.

Daisy snapped! She slammed the joystick into full-throttle forward, driving the footrests of the chair directly into R.J.'s shin. He screamed out and hopped on one leg, bent over and clasping the other one in both arms. Daisy spun rapidly to the left, swinging the battery pack rack that extended off the back of her chair directly into the knees of another one of the punks.

"Bitch!" he grunted as he too bent over in pain.

Out on the road, Skittles had bounced twice and then slid to a halt exactly on the white line. He'd scrambled back to his feet just in time to narrowly avoid being sliced in half by the unlit cyclist who'd come flying down the hill on Dolores, blowing through the stop sign. Gathering all his energy, Skittles charged back towards Daisy. In his little doggy brain a sense of purpose found expression as he sank his teeth into the calf of the third of the trio of trouble. Who is the sissy dog now, he thought, as he bit harder.

The scuffle was raising quite a ruckus and drawing attention. The unlit cyclist circled back; someone came out onto the porch of the nearest cottage and flipped on the porchlight, flooding the sidewalk with light.

"Hey, what's going on out there?" a voice called out from the cottage.

"Are you OK?" from the cyclist, coming fast back down the sidewalk.

"Let's get out of here!" The third punk had managed to shake Skittles loose but blood was seeping through his baggy pant leg. Skittles was growling with a strange but pronounced lisp, threatening another attack.

"Fuckin' queer-lovers!" R.J. growled. The three turned and limped back up the alley as fast as they could go.

Daisy clapped both her hands to break the spell that held Skittles frozen. He shook himself head to tail and then leapt back into her lap just as the cyclist pulled to a halt in front of her.

"Is everything alright? I think I almost ran over your dog!" the cyclist straddled the top tube of his bike, breathing hard and looking quite pale.

Daisy felt all over Skittles body for injury. He didn't flinch under her touch. She heaved a sigh of relief.

"Yeah, I think so."

Skittles took a deep breath and sighed too.

"Those kids . . . ." Daisy wasn't sure what to say, "They seem to have some issues."

The cyclist frowned, trying to catch her drift. He looked up the alley and then back at Daisy and began to understand that this had been more than just a dog running into the street. "Well, in that case, I'm extra glad I stopped."

"Me too!" Daisy said, clipping the leash back onto Skittles' collar. "Thanks," she smiled genuinely at him.

He nodded, tipping the visor of his helmet, and rode off.

"You should get a light!" she called after him, long after he was out of earshot, vanishing into the night.

As soon as Daisy returned to her apartment, the phone started ringing. She set Skittles down and unclipped the leash from his collar. Immediately, he headed to the bathroom to drink long and hard from the toilet. For just a second, Daisy wondered if she had flushed last time. Too late now, she thought, picking the phone.

"Hello?" she inquired.

"Hello. Is this Ms. Cat . . . sim . . . ," the voice stumbled over the long name. "Is this Daisy?"

"Yes, indeed."

"Oh, I'm so glad you're finally home!" the voice said with much relief. "This is J.B., do you remember me? We met outside the police station. I'm Allen's friend."

"Oh, honey, how are you doing?" Daisy was glad to finally hear from her. She hoped J.B. might have some news about Allen's murder.

"Well, as you can imagine, it's been a tough week. We open tomorrow and without Allen it's been hard to get on top of everything. How's Skittles?" J.B. tried to calm herself down. She'd been calling Daisy all afternoon but hadn't wanted to leave a message. Now that she had her on the line, J.B. took a deep breath and tried to feign nonchalance.

"Drinking out of the toilet right now, so I suspect he's thinking life is pretty good," Daisy chuckled.

"I'm wondering if you've heard from anyone about Skittles or anything?" J.B. asked innocently.

"I was wondering the same thing, wondering if you've heard anything from the police?" Daisy countered.

"Well, then, good thing we're talking," J.B. said, allowing for a pause as they staked out this new territory of dueling questions.

Daisy was the first to dive in. "No one has contacted me about Skittles but I have to say that he and I have had some weird encounters. Not half an hour ago these punks terrorized him. They called him a 'gay dog'! Can you believe that? He actually bit one and scared them off."

"How awful! Why would they say something like that?" J.B. queried, stumped why someone would see a little neutered dog as gay.

"They apparently recognized the dog from having seen him with Allen. Guess they were assuming guilt by association." Daisy pondered the absurdity of determining a dog's sexual orientation based on his human's. Her first thought was always about the dog and only after that did she give much attention to the other end of the leash. "I wonder . . . do you think those punks had anything to do with Allen's death? They were awfully mean." She let the question hang.

J.B. was thinking. If it was punks who had murdered

Allen, maybe this blackmail thing was a hoax. She didn't want to leap to conclusions. "Doesn't that seem a bit far-fetched? I know people can be homophobic but nobody gets killed anymore just for being gay, do they?"

Daisy thought back to her conversations with G.M.'s dad Rich about Prop 8 (or 'Prop Hate,' as he called it). He'd talked about how all the TV ads promoting the ballot measure had made him feel less than human, and that the vote meant that a majority of Californians seemed to agree with those hateful messages. Some of those folks might just be crazy enough to take it too far. Daisy broke the silence with, "I don't know but maybe I should tell Detective Rendell what happened."

"That's probably a good idea," J.B. said, trying to be reassuring but sensing that Daisy had no need for encouragement. She was obviously a tough broad, surprisingly calm in the face of all this.

"The funny thing is, ever since I've been out and about with Skittles, I've found all these people who knew Allen. In fact, today I went to this store down on Folsom and talked with a guy who was with Allen on the same night he was killed."

"Really?" J.B. was truly startled by this development. Someone who was with Allen that night might get the police motivated, and motivated police might solve the case, and solving the case would get her access to the bank accounts, and access to the bank accounts . . . but all that would be way too late—she needed to make the decision about the blackmail today.

"Yeah, this guy named Silverfox," Daisy said, her energy rising as she recalled the silver-haired man and their conversation at Mr. S. "He told us he'd been with Allen until late that night but they'd parted company after Allen had gotten a phone call, something about the restaurant. He thought it was kind of weird to be getting business calls so late but Allen told him that was par for the course for restaurant openings. He said Allen had been pissed off after the call, mumbling something about where was he going to get that much at that hour, and then had left to go meet someone. He was really quite handsome." Daisy finally wound down and paused.

J.B. was having a hard time tracking Daisy's rush of words. "Allen was handsome?"

"No, Silverfox. You should see his hair. Like polished chrome on '65 Impala," Daisy said dreamily.

J.B. pulled the phone away from her ear and stared at it in disbelief. She recognized the name Silverfox from the guest list: a friend of Allen's.

"Did he say anything more about who Allen was going to meet? If it was about the restaurant maybe it's something I should follow up on," J.B. said evenly, trying not to press— but she really needed to know if it was the same guy who was now blackmailing her.

"No, I don't think so. Just what I've told you." Daisy was running out of steam. It had been a long day.

"OK, well if I hear anything from the police, I'll let you know." J.B. replied, then added, "And I do think you should tell them about what happened today. It might be related." J.B. really wanted the police to get on top of this case.

"Right now, I think Skittles and I just need dinner and little TV. Dog's night!" she laughed, "Guess that's what my social life has come to. It still pisses me off that this stuff is happening in my neighborhood. First thing tomorrow, I'll call Detective Rendell."

"Good!" J.B. said feigning sisterly solidarity and clicked off.

MINUTES AFTER she'd hung up with Daisy, her phone vibrated across the surface of her glass coffee table. "Caller Unknown," the iPhone gods offered, but she knew it was the call that she'd been waiting for and dreading all day.

The voice had been brief and to the point.

"Do you have the money, sweet pea?" asked the now familiar lilting voice.

"Yes." She fingered the envelope with the bank draft—made out to "cash"—that she had picked from Pedro late that afternoon. "But how do I know you're not going to just come back asking for more money in a week or a month from now?"

"We're an honorable bunch," he giggled. "I'm going to give you all the documentation we have, the false inspection reports, the whole paper trail. After that, you'll just have to trust us."

"Hardly a confidence booster, having to take the word of a blackmailer."

"Listen, do you want a smooth opening or not? It's entirely up to you. I'll tell you one thing, though, you people need to understand that you're part of a community now. A complex community, with a history, that requires a little give and take."

J.B. was a bit confused by where he was going with this. She'd been assuming he was a lone actor. Now he seemed to be claiming some sort of cultural angle, as if he was Robin Hood. "Are you trying to tell me that you're *not* just operating out of greed?"

"Just consider this your opportunity to be a good neighbor. Remember, you can't valet park your way through all of life, my dear."

J.B. could tell he was definitely enjoying this.

Taking her silence as an affirmative response, he continued.

"Good. Do you know the Hidalgo statue in the middle of Dolores Park?"

Miguel Hidalgo was called the "George Washington of Mexico." Nice historic touch, J.B. thought, as she accepted that the blackmailer was about to liberate her from a healthy chunk of her investment. "Yes," she said, feeling powerless at this point to do anything more than comply.

"Go there alone at 9 pm sharp. Tuck the envelope under the statue's left foot. Do this not a minute sooner or later. I'd bet you've got one of those fancy little phones to help you keep exact track of time. Then walk straight down the hill through the park, down the left side of 19th to Valencia. Cross and go into the falafel place on the far corner, the one with the green awning. Ask for Omar and tell him you want the Tintin delivery. If we get the money then the delivery will be there. If not . . . well, you're a smart woman, you can figure out what'll happen next."

J.B.'s mind raced. Couldn't she just call the police and tell them the whole story and have this accomplice Omar arrested? Only if she was also willing to risk having Tintin shut down. Damn, she wished she knew if Allen had really cut corners. She was so frustrated being in this in-between place. "Fuck you," she muttered to the memory of Allen.

"You got a problem with that?" the blackmailer screeched, his voice rising to soprano.

"No, sorry, I was just thinking out loud. I've got it: 9 pm, left foot, falafel. I'll do it."

"Wise choice!" he said, his voice returning to the now familiar Southern lilt, and he hung up.

J.B. stared out the window across the darkness into the relative quiet of Duboce Park. Even this small park had the same schizoid nature of many of San Francisco's other pocket parks. By day, a playground for puppies and perambulators.

After dark, a home for the underbelly of San Francisco's urban life. Through a thin veil of fog she often watched pinpricks of cigarettes glowing red—homeless settling in for the night and men cruising for action, others for drugs. J.B. had lived nearby long enough to know what the night kept hidden from most. She knew to skirt the perimeter of the park once darkness had fallen. That she now intended to do the opposite at the bigger, sketchier Dolores Park was only a partial explanation for her racing pulse.

J.B. TRACED her usual route towards the Mission for this most unusual errand: Noe Street, left onto quaint Henry Street, right onto Sanchez, across Market, and then downhill to 18th, left at Samovar Tea Lounge, then straight down towards the park. She paused at the corner of Church and 18th to contemplate her approach. The fog was rolling gently over Twin Peaks, not quite the tidal wave it often was but rather the gentle suggestion of the cool moist air that would soon blanket the city. The blue twilight had faded into urban inkiness—black overlaid with highlighter yellow from the sodium street lights. J.B. was anxious. She took a deep breath and tried to center herself. She asked herself if this could really be any more challenging than one of her senior management marketing presentations. "No," she said aloud, the sound of her own voice steeling her nerve and launching her into the park.

The park path parallel to the Church Street MUNI tracks was deserted. Antique street lamps spilled soft yellow light around their iron pedestals. J.B. moved carefully up the four steps that led to the statue, checking the pedestrian bridge to her right to make sure she was alone. She could see a few folks down lower in the park but, for now, it was just her and the statue of Miguel Hidalgo. Together, they gazed out over the lights of the city, towards Potrero Hill and the bay beyond. Everything seemed calm and completely manageable.

"Really?" she asked her new bronze friend, "Are we really going to do this?"

Miguel held his tongue.

"Easy for you to say," she complained, "you've got nothing to lose." She tapped on the hollow metal of his boots with her phone, the dull ring emphasizing her point. She took a final look around, saw no one, and took one last deep breath. She checked the world clock on her phone, watching as the digital second hand sweep up towards 12. The parallel digital time switched to "9:00 pm today."

"This is your fault, Allen!" she said angrily as she tucked the envelope in the groove just under Hidalgo's left heel.

She moved away quickly, heading down the main path of the park past the bathrooms. A few tourists with bulky cameras hanging from their necks hurried past her, having gotten off at the wrong J-Church stop at the top slope of the park. In the growing darkness she could sense men, some in small groups, others alone, scattered across the lawn. A chill ran up her spine and she kept her head down. That's why she almost collided with the fixed-gear biker struggling uphill on the path she was descending. "Ridiculous!" she said, venting some of her anxiety and anger towards the biker. Those bikes, with their single speed, seemed so foolish in such a hilly city but so popular among trendy hipsters.

She continued on her journey exactly as instructed, reaching the downhill corner of Valencia and 19th in no time, gravity being her friend. When the light changed she crossed towards the green awning proclaiming Ali Baba's Cave. She was almost to the other side when yet another fixie bike—this one carrying a passenger sidesaddle on the top crossbar—

flew by, cutting her off. The rider winked at her and didn't miss a pedal stroke while the passenger—a drag queen with flowing headdress à la *Priscilla, Queen of the Desert*—waved vigorously towards at the folks in Ali Baba's. "Watch where you're going!" she yelled after them, the trailing fabric snapping so near her face she had to arch backwards to keep from being whipped.

J.B. straightened up and continued. Entering through the corner doors, she found the proprietor smiling and chuckling to himself. J.B. frowned.

He cleared his throat and said seriously, "What will you have, ma'am? Falafel? Espresso?" and then averted his gaze downwards. J.B. could swear he was trying very hard not to laugh.

The furrow between her brows deepened. "Are you Omar? I'm here for the Tintin delivery," her voice rose at the end, a statement couched in a question.

"Yes indeed, we just got the OK . . . hmm . . . I mean, we just *finished* the order. Let me get it." He reached to the far side of the moist, steaming shawarma, pulled out a thick manila envelope and handed it across the counter to J.B.

"Uh, thank you," she mumbled. She nodded then stepping outside.

Turning right, J.B. walked rapidly along Valencia, hugging the envelope to her chest. The heft it nagged at her. She couldn't wait any longer to see what was inside of it, plus she sorely needed a drink and Luna Park beaconed just ahead. She accelerated fast towards this safe haven.

Sitting at a small table in the back corner, J.B. ordered a glass of Merlot and opened the package. All original documents, that was for sure, but clearly showing the shortcuts, the payoffs, and the corners cut by Allen. She felt both relief and frustration. If she and Pedro hadn't paid, they would definitely have been screwed. But why had Allen done this? Had it really been necessary? She hoped the blackmailers would be as good as their word, that this would really mark the end to the whole sordid affair.

Stuffing the thick pile back into the envelope, she rose, dropped a $20 on the table, and headed outside. She hailed a cab to take her home to her haven of order and to the waiting teeth of her award-winning Destroyit 2360C cross-cut shredder.

WITH SKITTLES TROTTING BESIDE her, Daisy cruised slowly down Dolores trying to decide where to go next. It had been five days and they still had no idea who had taken Skittles' dad away from him. She paused mid-block while Skittles sniffed the complex story spelled out on the damp pee-stained tree trunk. She was directly in front of Mission Dolores, the most northerly of the system of missions build by the Spanish settlers.

Daisy had once listened to a tour guide describe how, in classic missionary style, Father Palóu had planted himself on the banks of the Arroyo de los Dolores in the spot where the Native Americans had long gathered. Having usurped their natural center of community, the church flourished and pushed the older culture into the shadows. The creek itself had been buried underground as the city grew. But it couldn't be fully suppressed. Ironically, it still reasserted its name—Creek of Sorrows—by periodically rising to dampen basements of frustrated T.I.C. owners throughout the Mission district. Mission Dolores was still a vibrant and active church. She and Joe came to for the service sometimes, mostly when his wife was out of town visiting her family in Modesto.

It was early still. The tall wooden doors were closed tight, firmly holding the world at bay from the sacred space within. The first service wasn't until noon and the older part of the Mission wouldn't open for tours until nine o'clock. The only sign of life was a homeless man, curled up under a gray wool blanket in the alcove of the great big doors. He was sound asleep and snoring lightly, probably just having settled in. Daisy had noticed that the city's homeless seemed to sleep more during the day than at night. Maybe it was safer that way. She couldn't imagine what it must be like to be out on the street like that, plus so many of them were so young, it broke her heart.

She watched idly as Skittles added his own mark to the story on the tree. Suddenly, like an invisible tap on the shoulder, an idea came to her with startling clarity. If these homeless foks were asleep during the day and awake at night then maybe one of them saw something the night that Allen died. She doubted that the cops would have thought to interview any of the homeless.

More than once, she'd come out in the morning to see a cruiser pull up alongside a sleeping homeless person and startle them awake with a rude blast of the siren. It was almost sport for them. If the cops bothered to get out of their cruiser, they'd write the poor guy a citation and call the Department of Public Works to pick up their carts and possessions like so much trash. Daisy wasn't thrilled to have so many homeless in this city but she still thought they should be treated with some dignity.

She headed up Dolores to 15th. There was a green PG&E electrical box tucked under a tree on the corner. It often provided a little shelter and invisibility for street sleepers. More important, it was ten yards from where she had found Skittles and Allen's body.

During her morning walks she'd frequently noticed one particular guy camped out there. He was skinny, with a thick gray beard. She'd seen him other places around the neighborhood too: up at Muddy Waters, by the recycling center at Safeway, over at Dolores Park. One Veteran's Day she'd seen him up on the corner of Market standing tall and saluting the commuters rushing down into the MUNI station, periodically yelling out "Hey Man, slow down. It's a holiday!" He seemed less volatile to her than some of the other homeless; therefore, Daisy hoped that today she'd find him camped out in the usual spot and ready to talk.

Rounding the corner, she spied the sleeping lump she'd hoped for and rolled right up to him. Skittles sniffed tentatively at the form and then retreated quickly, leaping back into Daisy's lap.

"Hey, buddy!" Daisy prodded. "Are you awake?"

One sleepy eye peered out, eyebrow raised, "I am now." The body sat up on its elbows, the blanket falling down around its waist. The smell of a sleeping body, infrequently bathed, wafted out towards Daisy. She'd had her share of tough times but she couldn't imagine how tough this must be. I mean, even if you wanted to shower, where would you go?

"Sorry to bug you but can I ask you a question?"

"I do believe you already have," the gray blanket replied.

"Yeah, I guess you're right." Daisy was chagrined but she didn't let that stop her. "I'm wondering if you were sleeping here this past weekend, on Saturday night?"

"When was that?" he asked. "I don't exactly keep a day planner."

"Well, today is Friday so it would be . . ." Daisy counted backwards under her breath, keeping track on the fingers of her non-joystick hand, "I guess it would be six nights ago."

"Hmm, I'm not sure. That's a long time ago. My days tend to blend into each other."

"It was last weekend and, if I remember correctly, there was a heavy fog that night."

"Maybe," he said. "Why do you want to know?" Sitting up fully and crossing his legs, he ran his fingers through his gray hair, scratching at his scalp.

While Skittles approved of this gesture, Daisy cringed as her mind went involuntarily to images of head lice. She shifted her gaze and noticed a small pile of paperback books, tucked under one edge of the blanket. This included a dog-eared Mary Higgins Clarke mystery and another, with the unlikely title *Legends of Latvian Hockey*. She cocked her head, trying to get a better look at the latter until his voice brought her back. "Why do you want to know?" he prodded.

"Oh, see this little fella here? This is Skittles," Daisy said, lifting the little dog to sit upright in her lap. "I found him just over there on Sunday morning." She pointed towards the thin space between the building and the vacant lot just a few yards away. "The problem is, he was attached to a dead body."

"Well that must have sucked, for all three of you." He was up now, folding his blanket, and tucking it into a well-used baby stroller. A broom was tied along the length of the stroller's handle, acting like a main mast.

"Yeah, it did. Thanks. Turns out that the body was Skittles' dad, this guy named Allen. He was kind of new to the neighborhood. Anyway, I was hoping maybe you saw something."

The thin man, gray man, secured his books under the blanket into the seat of the stroller. A police cruiser rolled by, slowing slightly, the officer casting a glance that clearly said, "Get moving!"

"Let's see," the man continued. "Last Saturday night, you say. Six nights ago . . . I do believe I slept here. I almost always do unless it's pouring. Then I'm over along Dolores. There's a house mid-block with a good entranceway in the lee. Much better port in a storm."

Daisy wondered at his use of the words "lee" and "port." Perhaps this guy was a navy vet.

"What did this guy Allen look like?"

"Tall. Skinny. He was wearing a suit jacket. Skittles and he were attached by a nice black leather leash."

"Was he a prick?" blanket man asked.

Daisy laughed loudly. "Yeah, I think he was, or so I'm learning. But how would you know that?"

"I remember him from around. I'm invisible to people like him but that doesn't mean he was invisible to me. He tended to walk his dog—the one in your lap—late morning and very late at night. He'd be on his phone, completely self-absorbed. Most of the time, he never picked up after that thing!" he said, gesturing at Skittles with a vehemence that scared Daisy. "I remember once he actually stepped on me when I was right here. He was so wrapped up in his own little world that he didn't even see me. Does that sound like the same guy?"

"Indeed," Daisy said, not wanting to interrupt his flow.

"So, let's see . . . Saturday? I do remember it being a noisy night. Lots of action. Lots of people out and about. Hard to get any rest but entertaining. I remember hearing some kids, a bunch of thugs really . . . I usually keep my distance from that kind. But can't say I remember hearing somebody get killed. That seems like something I'd remember." He grinned sardonically at Daisy, revealing his yellowed teeth.

"Er, yeah. I guess I was hoping you might," Daisy replied, crestfallen.

"But then again, sometimes I don't remember things so well. Sometimes I'm a little loco," he said, casting an astonishingly piercing gaze her way.

Daisy was growing uneasy. The more the blanket man woke up the meaner he seemed to be getting. But maybe he just needed some coffee before being sociable. She, of all people, could certainly understand that.

"Tell you what, I'm sure I'll see you around. If you think of anything, will you let me know? My name's Daisy, by the way."

"Sam," he said, reaching a weathered but surprisingly

well-manicured hand her way.

"Pleased to meet you, Sam."

They nodded to each other across the handshake, with a subtle tilt of the head. Daisy couldn't say exactly where the gesture came from, just one of those things that emerges from some dark recess of socialization, unbidden and unknown, yet exactly right for the moment. She placed her hand back on the joystick, pirouetted, and rolled off.

THE LOW AFTERNOON LIGHT, yellowed slightly by the thin fog, streamed into the corners of Dominic and Rich's living room. The markets were closed on the East Coast, so Dominic's day was done. He was stretched out on the couch, absorbed in *Comfortable With Uncertainty*, the latest book from Pema Chödrön. His hand hung down and toyed with the thick shepherd fur on G.M.'s back as she snored quietly on the floor beside him.

Rich sat at the computer in the far corner, his mind wandering. The computer had been idle so long that the screen saver popped on, jolting him back from his reverie.

Things had been off for Rich all week long. Craigslist, his usual source of pleasure and distraction, was a barren wasteland. To his jaundiced eye, one Photoshopped dick after another wilted in his imagination. Yesterday, he'd gone to an Advanced Flogging workshop with Master Crocker. It had been skillfully done, as all Master Crocker's workshops were—technically precise, spiritual, and well presented. He had already taken other classes: How to Pick Your Flogger, How to Avoid Repetitive Stress While Flogging. Every class, even this advanced one, stressed the critical information about where you should and should not to hit on the body. Rich was always particularly interested in this, having once switched and gotten more than he bargained for with mishits over his kidneys and liver. He'd been amazed that the pain could be so intense and that it had lasted for so long. But despite the quality of the workshop, this time he couldn't get fully engaged. Between Allen's murder and the run-in with those punks while on patrol Wednesday night, he was a mess.

Rich pushed the keyboard back and stood. "Hey Babe,

I've got a question," he said, plopping himself down on the far end of the couch and lifting Dominic's feet into his lap.

Dominic laid the hardcover book face down on his broad chest and gazed at Rich over the top of his reading glasses. He knew things were bothering Rich but he'd been waiting patiently for him to bring it up.

Rich was quiet for a moment, kneading Dominic's big woolen feet, stretching their length and breadth. "You know that guy I was telling you about, Allen, the one from the Castle?"

"Yeeesss?" Dominic drew the word out long and low, an invitation and acknowledgment.

"Well, G.M. and I ran into Daisy earlier today. You know how she tells you everything that's going on?"

"To be sure," Dominic smiled. Daisy was a font of neighborhood gossip.

"Well she said they still haven't figured out how Allen died. The cops are getting nowhere so she's been asking around."

Rich paused. Dominic waited quietly, stretching his toes as wide apart as he could while Rich kneaded his arches.

"She said she'd talked to Silverfox. That he told her he was with Allen until late on the night he was killed. Weirder still, she sounded quite smitten with him." Rich shook his head in amazement. "Anyway, I started wondering if I should go talk to him myself. Maybe he knows something that he wouldn't tell Daisy, something that could help solve the murder." Rich kept his gaze glued to Dominic's socks.

"Like what?" Dominic probed.

"I don't know, like maybe the kind of play he and Allen were doing later that night, what state Allen was in when he left, why he left . . . you know the whole BDSM 411."

"What makes you think there's more to tell?"

"After I did that scene with them earlier in the evening, that boy—I mean, Allen—was pretty high on endorphins. He hardly seemed like he was ready to be done. In fact, I'd call him a bit of a pain slut." Rich thought back to that missed strike with the flogger and how Allen hadn't really seemed to want any comforting. "I mishit with the flogger once and it hardly fazed him when it probably hurt like hell. Anyway, I wouldn't be surprised if he and Silverfox did more play after I left, or even went somewhere else. I think I've heard that Silverfox has a dungeon in his loft. Oxymoronic, I know."

"Well first off, I don't think you need to worry about the missed strike." Dominic said, sitting upright and putting his hand on the back of Rich's neck. "You'd have to be pretty far off target to do any serious damage, and I know how attentive you are," he said, smiling.

Rich bent his head forward then pushed back into Dominic's hand, allowing himself to lean into the warmth of Dominic's broad Italian paw. Rich smiled at the complement.

"Do you know if the cops have talked to him?" Dominic asked.

"I doubt it. From what Daisy said, it seems like they're completely distracted. Allen's murder is already yesterday's news," Rich replied

"OK, so if you think Silverfox might tell you something that would help, I'd say by all means go for it. Just follow your gut . . . but be careful. I know you think he's pretty sane, but from the stories you tell, I get the feeling that some of the folks at the Castle are just a little off, if you know what I mean."

"Want to come with?" Rich brightened, falling back into the slang of his Philadelphia youth. "Keep me safe?"

"With you babe? I'd come anywhere." Dominic leaned forward, his last word smothered as their lips met, wet and wide.

RICH AND DOMINIC HEADED out down 16th with G.M. in the lead. She was pulling like the best Iditarod sled dog.

"We're really going to have to buckle down with her training," Rich said, releasing Dominic's hand and grabbing the leash with both of his.

They'd called down to Mr. S and talked with Silverfox. He was just about to get off work and had agreed to meet them at the Eagle for a drink. One of the oldest leather bars in the city, its back patio was a perfect place for G.M. to get some much-needed socialization. Bears and leather daddies had a soft spot for big dogs, so G.M. would receive lots of attention.

They passed by Tintin where they could see a bustle of activity through the plate glass windows of the still closed restaurant. Tonight was the grand opening. Across the street, a large banner hung from the second story windows. In big, bold, hand-drawn letters it proclaimed: "Yuppies suck the life from our community!" Tintin was sure in for an interesting evening.

At the Eagle, Dominic, Rich, and G.M. pushed single-file through the leather curtains into the dark interior. Even though it was still light out, not one photon penetrated into the inner space. Dominic veered towards the bar to order beers while Rich and G.M. headed out onto the bright patio in search of Silverfox. They found him on the far side, leaning up against the empty stage. Rich smiled as he approached, half at Silverfox and half at the memory of all the wild performances he'd witnessed on that stage over the years.

"Hey there. Thanks for coming out." Rich reached his

hand out. He felt like a peer with Silverfox but at the same time, he was a little intimidated by him. Silverfox had been a player for many years and, as a pure top, earned a certain deference.

"Who's this?" Silverfox said, ignoring Rich's hand and leaning down to take G.M.'s head in both of his, rubbing behind her ears in just the way she liked. G.M. responded by pressing her head into his knees.

"G.M., short for Gay Marriage. She seems to like you," Rich said, somewhat surprised by G.M.'s sudden shift of affection.

"She knows a master when she meets one," Silverfox stated matter-of-factly.

Rich nodded in agreement.

Dominic wound his way through the space that was rapidly filling with the after-work crowd. It was kind of fun to see them in their street clothes rather than full-dress leathers. Dominic handed one bottle to Rich and reached out to shake hands with Silverfox.

"Hey, I'm Dominic. We haven't met. Sorry, my hand is a bit cold from the beer."

"No problem." Silverfox shook his hand with warmth and just a bit more pressure than Dominic expected. A test, he guessed.

Rich explained the situation. He reminded Silverfox of the play session the past weekend, described their connection to Daisy, and how the police had done little to solve the crime. "So the thing is, I figured you were probably a little circumspect with Daisy. She's not exactly part of this community," he said, gesturing around the patio.

"No, you're right, but she does have a certain grotesque charm."

Rich thought it strange, this unlikely attraction that Daisy and Silverfox seemed to have.

"I was loath to give her too much detail, though," Silverfox continued.

"I'm wondering what went down after I left you guys at the Castle? Do you mind saying?"

"Not at all." Silverfox had the air of a professor delivering a well-worn lecture to eager but ignorant freshmen. "We stayed at the Castle long after you left. Allen was insatiable. I think the restaurant opening had stirred him up and it was taking a lot of action to counter that energy. We played together some and then I asked Kathleen to join us. We're old friends from back in the day—we actually did hospice work together."

Rich had forgotten that Silverfox had once been a nurse and worked with a lot of people with AIDS, before burning out and turning leather tailor.

"Anyway, you remember that Allen was hooded so it really freaked him out when Kathleen joined in. It took him a while to figure it out—he doesn't usually play with women. But she was just so mean and such a tease that he got over that pretty quickly. By then, he was starting to get pretty beat up but he was still hungry for more.

"What do you mean 'beat up'?" Rich was hoping Silverfox wouldn't mention the missed strike.

"Bruised mostly, and that endorphin stupor that sometimes happens when you've had too much intensity. He did say later that his back was bugging him, but he thought it was stress. He figured it would wear off as soon as Tintin opened."

Rich's anxiety rose at the mention of Allen's back pain, fearing that it indicated an injury from the off-target strike. He hoped Allen had been right and that it really was stress. "Did you two part company there?"

"We should have, but you know I'm a sucker for a begging bottom." He looked directly at Dominic as he spoke. All three paused, half a second too long for Rich's liking. Rich raised one eyebrow, warring for Dominic's attention. Rich wanted to say "Back off, big boy!" but he bit his tongue.

Just then, a particular fuzzy bear stopped and clicked his tongue trying to get G.M.'s attention. The shepherd just pressed herself closer to Silverfox, where she'd been leaning since the conversation began.

"She's a little shy sometimes," Rich explained, wondering what had become of his frisky, outgoing pup.

"So what happened?" Dominic asked, far too attentive now.

"Well, do you know Sketch?" Silverfox continued.

Rich and Dominic both shook their heads no.

"He's a handsome, dark-haired FTM. I think he's kind of new to town but I've met him at some of Ivor and Ursula's classes. Anyway, he was kind of in the same un-satisfied state as Allen. I thought it might be fun to play with the both of them, to kind of round out Allen's night, gender-wise. Since the Castle was closing, we decided to go back to my place." Silverfox reached down and patted G.M., raking a slow path with two fingers from G.M.'s brow back between her ears and then spreading down to squeeze her neck. She closed her eyes, immensely content.

"Sketch has a fabulous body . . . although he's not as buff as you." Silverfox reached out and squeezed Dominic's bicep. "I was looking forward to pummeling both of them but by the time we got to my place, it seemed like the moment had passed. Let's just say the mind was willing but the flesh was weak." Silverfox chuckled at his own cleverness. Dominic started to laugh as well, until Rich shifted his weight to step squarely on his partner's toe.

Dominic cocked his head in question at Rich. Rich glared back, lifting both eyebrows to reinforce his warning.

"So you all kind of ran out of steam. I hear they have little blue pills for that kind of thing." Rich's attempt at snide humor fell flat.

After a heavy pause, Silverfox continued, "Then it was like I told Daisy. Allen's phone rang, something related to the restaurant, and he decided he had to deal with it right then. Too much drama so I kicked them both out. Allen got dressed and left with Sketch right behind him. I was asleep about two seconds after they left." Silverfox paused, leaving the floor open to questions but clearly communicating that the story was full and complete.

"And that's the last time you saw him?" Rich asked. Something made him feel like he wasn't getting the full story.

"Yes," he said coolly. Silverfox ran one hand over his gleaming hair, pressing a stray strand that had floated free back into what was clearly a significant amount of product.

"Have you talked to Sketch since then?" Rich pressed, still feeling like there might be more. If Sketch had left at the same time as Allen, maybe he'd seen or heard something more.

"No, I haven't even seen him around, but then again, it's only been a few days. Maybe he'll be out this weekend. Shall I ask him to call you if I see him? Or maybe he should call Daisy," Silverfox mocked.

The more he talked the less Rich liked him. He pulled his wallet out of his pocket and withdrew a card, handing it over to Silverfox. "It would be great if you'd give this to him, if, of course, you see him." Rich was reverting to protocol, hoping that the deferential formality might politely end things. "I really appreciate your help," he added extending his hand.

Silverfox looked at him evenly, completely ignoring the

outstretched hand again. After a moment, Rich dropped it to his side.

"OK honey, bottoms up. Time to get this pup home!" Rich said, his voice a slightly higher pitch than normal. He gave a tug on the leash. G.M. looked at him with annoyance and then slowly backed away from Silverfox.

"Thanks again," Rich said, grabbing Dominic by the arm, pulling him stumbling backwards towards the bar. Silverfox nodded at them as other men eagerly filled in the space they'd vacated.

"What a prick!" Rich growled.

"I thought he was nice," Dominic deadpanned, and then laughed and leaned in to nibble on Rich's neck. "For an asshole." They each dug a hand into the other's back pocket and squeezed. "Let's go home."

J.B. STOOD QUIETLY AND regarded herself in the full-length mirror of Tintin's ladies' room. One last inspection before they opened the doors. The Uber-Cantelope nails were perfectly coordinated to her matching lipstick and complemented the smoke-gray fabric of her vintage Coco Chanel suit. She had debated over the makeup around her eyes, finally settling on just the lightest dusting of Lancôme Strut for a final counterbalance. She smoothed the fabric along her thighs, turned sideways just to make sure, and deemed herself ready. She strode out past the bar and paused at the stuffed dog Snowy, placing one hand atop his head. A perfect replica of the one from the Tintin cartoon, she hoped this Snowy would guard their venture. Pedro and his crew stood waiting, crisp in their white uniforms. The place looked fabulous.

"You know, except for that banner across the street," J.B. said, "I'd say we've done an excellent job. I think Allen would be pleased."

"Well, don't get too self-satisfied. The real work is just about to begin." Pedro was restless. He knew the importance of first impressions, especially in the restaurant biz. He'd seen more than one venture fail miserably because of the smallest of glitches: a martini with one olive instead of two or a napkin with too much starch. Without a soft opening to test their systems they would have to hit the ground running.

J.B. scowled until—remembering the increasingly deep ruts she'd noticed lately on her brow—she calmed her expression. "Not to worry, I'm on top of it," she reassured Pedro, her chest out and shoulders back. She picked up the guest list with the complex color-coding system and tapped the edges of the papers on into a neat pile. There was nothing else to say.

"OK, everyone. It's showtime!" Pedro moved forward to open the big oak doors.

The first guests started to arrive, some on foot, others by car. The valets sprinted to keep up with the flow, double-parking cars in front of nearby driveways until they could move them over to the lot around the corner. MUNI buses swung wide into oncoming traffic to get around, generating even more energy and buzz in front of Tintin.

"What's up with the sign?" a middle-aged gentleman named Walter and his sheepdoggish wife asked as they approached J.B. at the hostess podium just inside the door. J.B. recognized his name from the list. Blue—the hangers-on.

"The Mission has always been a lively center of political discourse. We love that they are continuing with that tradition," J.B. said.

"Seems like they are not terribly happy with their new neighbors."

J.B. had already rehearsed this "political discourse" angle. "No, but I'm pretty sure they're happy with the jobs and money we're bringing into the community." J.B. smiled, placing a hand on Walter's shoulder to move him along towards his table. A small line was beginning to form and she'd need to mete out her attention. Walter had already gotten more than his blue share. "Thank you for coming," she said with clear finality, passing him along to the waiter.

"Welcome to Tintin!" J.B. said brightly, reaching out her hand to the next guest, but a moment of silence hung between them. After one blink too many, the woman finally reached back and took her hand. "Beatrice Beale," she said dryly, "and this is my husband Bernard," indicating her basset hound of a companion. J.B. wondered why everyone was looking like dogs tonight, thinking that perhaps she'd been talking to Daisy too much. Beatrice was coded both green and red—a pissed-off influencer. J.B. had to make sure that Beatrice's experience was a good one.

"Beatrice, Bernard, we are so glad you could come!" she said, overcompensating for the rocky start. "Your table is right over here," she continued, leading them towards a prized window seat.

"We'd prefer something a bit farther away from the, um, hostility," Beatrice said nodding towards the banner across the street. The hauteur in her voice created a vacuum, pulling that same hostility inside Tintin, where it flowed and curled around J.B.'s ankles.

"Of course . . . Mrs. Beale." J.B. made eye contact with Isandro, who was leading a lower-tiered green couple towards a table closer to the bar. With a silent nod, as if they were performing a well-choreographed contra dance, they lead their respective parties towards their new tables. The switch was so smooth as to be unnoticeable.

"We're starting with complementary pastis." The words were barely out of J.B.'s mouth when she noticed Jeannine's scowl. "Of course, we also have a full bar, and I'd be happy to bring you whatever you desire," she said without missing a beat.

"I will have a kir royale and Bernard a scotch, neat."

"Very good," J.B. said, bowing slightly as she backed away. She wondered how this woman could already have made her feel lower than a barmaid. She grabbed Isandro. "Make sure that bitch is happy," she whispered, nodding toward Beatrice who was shaking out her napkin, her lip curled, as she struggled to flatten it onto her lap. A linen queen. Damn. We're screwed.

When J.B. hurried back to the front of the house to greet

the next guests, she noticed Daisy outside, who was waving from behind the velvet rope. "Hey there, J.B.!" Daisy's voice ricocheted off the tin ceiling. J.B. flashed an urgent look at the valet who immediately understood his new chore. J.B. watched as he bent low to speak with Daisy, who scowled, cleared her throat and spit into the gutter, but pressed the joystick and rolled away. This was an invitation-only event and J.B. only had time for those who mattered.

The evening continued on like this, J.B. filtering the front door, juggling blue and green and red, working the room like a pro while Isandro and the others moved efficiently and obsequiously in the background. The cassoulet was well received, they ran out of the mini escargot, and even the flummery was a big hit. The restaurant and the bar were filled to capacity and overflowed with good feeling as Serge Gainsbourg crooned in the background.

As the evening wore on, J.B.'s feet were achy and gravity had pulled the crotch of her pantyhose down to mid-thigh. She hated that feeling: while the bottom two-thirds of her legs glided smoothly and dryly over each other, the top third, the chub-rub section, stuck and grabbed. She was tempted to head back into the ladies' room and yank the damn things off. As she debated her course of action a distinguished silver-haired gentleman entered with a young man in tow.

"Good evening," he greeted her warmly, "I believe you have me on the list?"

J.B. stared silently.

"Silverfox?" he offered, nodding towards her guest list.

"Oh, sorry, one second." J.B. looked down. She was stunned by his unusual hair.

"And this is Jackson," he offered politely, sweeping his hand like an emcee towards the young man beside him who, eyes closed, was busy trying to find a dance beat in the French crooner's song. "We were both friends of Allen's."

"Yes, I have you both here," she said as her finger slid down the list. Red, she was surprised to see.

"We were very sorry to learn about his fate," Silverfox said sympathetically. "Does anyone have any idea what happened?"

J.B. was surprised and confused by his concern in light of the red code on his name on her list. That was for the pissed-off folks, the ones Allen had annoyed and wanted to win back into the good graces of Tintin. Maybe tragedy really did allow bygones to be bygones.

J.B. lowered her voice, not really wanting to discuss murder in this moment. "At this point, no. We're hoping they the police will soon, though."

"We?" Silverfox queried.

Jackson, the young man in tow, listened quietly as he moved in a subtle but complex rhythm to the music.

"We here at the restaurant, Pedro and me . . . and Daisy, the 'nosy neighbor,' I suppose." This last part about Daisy had come out almost in a whisper, said without thinking. Daisy must have been on J.B.'s mind after how she'd dismissed her so coldly earlier in the evening.

"Oh, I know Daisy!" Jackson brightened. "She comes into the coffee shop all the time. She does know everyone's business, doesn't she? Daisy told me she was going to solve this one!" he chuckled at the thought.

"Interesting. Well, I do hope they catch whoever did it," Silverfox added coolly.

J.B. picked up two menus and checked the seating chart.

"That's OK," Silverfox interrupted, "we're just going to sit at the bar for a drink."

"Please make yourselves right at home," she said, gesturing grandly towards the bar, relieved to move away from the subject of murder. "And thank you for coming. I'm sure Allen would have appreciated it."

She watched as they took the two seats at the end of the bar. Pedro had come out to make the rounds of the tables, the obligatory "chef-on-display" to make diners feel more like connoisseurs than cash cows. As he headed back towards the kitchen Pedro caught Silverfox's eye. J.B. could see the slight nod of acknowledgement between them but then Pedro passed right by without any further greeting. She wondered how Pedro could be acquainted with someone from Allen's pissed-off list, but before she could ponder this any further, her pantyhose took another dive south making a trip to the ladies' room no longer optional.

THE DAY HAD STARTED off bright and crisp, with a kind of still blueness that is a rare treat in San Francisco. Like a tollbooth agent unexpectedly waving you through because the car ahead has paid for you, this was the kind of day that made you think it just might be OK to be an optimist after all.

Daisy had done her usual morning rounds, greeting her four-legged friends and their human companions. Saturday mornings were usually pretty quiet, as San Francisco was a slow-to-rise town on the weekends. Fog usually blanketed the city in the morning, so no one rushed to start their day. Joe had been up early, though. He and Daisy had spent easy time chatting.

"Do you think they'll ever do anything with that empty lot?" Daisy gazed across the street towards the chain-link fence that had guarded nothing for as long as she could remember. Periodically, someone would come in to hack at the grass that had grown tall or pick up the trash that had been tossed in by wind or careless humans. It had always bothered her that the space went so neglected but now, since she'd found Allen's body there, its emptiness was unbearable.

"I know. It's weird that it's been like that for so long. With the price of real estate in this town, you'd think someone would have built on it by now." Joe had pulled his truck halfway out onto the wide sidewalk and was polishing the black hood as they'd talked. He paused and turned towards the lot, his arms held away from his sides, tin of polish in one hand, damp white rag in the other.

Daisy laughed, "You look like St. Turtlewax, patron saint of car polishers, offering blessings to those in need of a good shine!"

"Very funny," he said, smiling at Daisy as he broke the pose and changed topics. "Have you heard anything more about Allen, or who's going to take Skittles?" The dog was tucked into Daisy's lap, half asleep, looking more and more at home with each passing day.

"No. The cops are still missing in action as near as I can tell. Not a peep out of them. I did chat with J.B., you know the one who's doing that restaurant with Allen, but she didn't know much more either."

"Hmm." Joe went back to spreading thin circles of paste wax across the hood.

"You know," Daisy said, "I went by there last night, by Tintin. They were having their big opening." Daisy didn't hold a grudge for long. She had let go of the valet's rudeness last night by the time she'd rounded the corner. "I must say, their crowd seemed a bit snooty. The neighborhood is really shifting. But you know, it's not all bad . . . those new kids have lots of dogs!" Daisy exclaimed as she spotted yet another one of her new canine friends coming down the sidewalk, pulling an iPod-wearing, Google-working, twentysomething in its wake. The dog spotted Daisy too. It was like one long, slow-motion movie scene as they strained towards each other's affection.

SILVERFOX ALMOST ALWAYS SLEPT in. This morning he'd awoken early, bleary-eyed in a way no amount of coffee could remedy. He'd puttered about his loft until finally giving up and wandering up to Café Flore in the Castro for a late breakfast of mimosas. He had hoped that the eye candy of young homo hotties would revive him. He'd held court, gracing both friends and acquaintances with his attention, but even this task eventually became a bore. Restless and out of ideas, he headed back home.

For the last hour, he'd been lying on the long white sofa, trying to nap, but idleness did not suit his spring-steel temperament. Cocking his head to the left, he gazed out through the floor-to-ceiling windows of his "Swish Alps" loft. Thin clouds had started to sneak in over Twin Peaks, stalking the Castro below. Turning his head right, his eyes traced the curves of the Josiah McElheny glass sculpture hanging on the inside wall of his apartment. If he squinted, he could just see the clouds reflected in mirrored surface the sculpture. He turned back to the windows, then back to the sculpture. Back and forth his head moved like he was watching a tennis match. No matter how long most of his body lay still, his mind remained active.

He thought back to last Saturday and Allen. The play had been satisfying enough but the rest of the evening hardly worth it. He'd reveled in delivering pleasure and discomfort to Allen, put up with the necessary aftercare following the scene, then become annoyed as the evening wound down at his apartment. For Allen to go and get himself murdered was just one more annoyance.

"Fuck him," he muttered.

Silverfox was more annoyed by the intrusions Allen's death had brought into his world than death itself. Rich's questions were one thing, just his service to the community— so to speak—but that grotesque woman Daisy with her dyke companion, truly annoying. There was something about Daisy that irked him, got under his skin, some offense he couldn't quite name. Just thinking about her made it impossible for him to lie still a second longer. His frustration beyond bearing, he sat up with only one resolution: the Eagle. Mid-afternoon and the patio out back would be filling up by now. Bare skin and leather, sweat and body hair, the acrid scent of male heat competing with (and usually beating) the stench of raw meat combusting on the grill. Surely, these things would lighten his darkening mood.

He threw on a jacket and headed out, hoping that the long walk would smooth whatever ruffled him so. Pushing out from his front door he nearly tripped over a lump of homeless man propped against his front wall. He was having better luck at napping than Silverfox had.

"What the fuck!" Silverfox said angrily, kicking at the man's belongings. "Go find another place to pile your shit."

The man growled but reluctantly stood and moved on.

RETURNING FROM ERRANDS, DAISY opened the door to her apartment and found the shadows pulsating red from the bright number 2 blinking on the answering machine. She flicked on the lights, wheeled over, and pressed play:

"Hello Daisy, this is J.B. I just wanted to let you know that I heard from the police this morning. Seems they're finally making a little headway but it's not all good news. First off, the thing of most relevance to you: seems the family can't take Skittles right now, so I'm hoping you'll be able to keep him for a little bit longer . . ."

"Looks like you're stickin' with me, kid," Daisy said, looking down at Skittles who was snorting his way through a fresh bowl of kibble.

". . . I hope that's OK. Second, they finished the autopsy and it turns out he died from some weird thing called . . . hold on, let me look at my notes . . . hepatic subcapsular hematoma. The detective told me it's like a big bruise on the liver. Problem is, the coroner can't determine exactly when it happened. It's weird, autopsy showed he had several bruises—some fresh, some old—on that part of his body and any one of them might have been the cause. Oh, and they said that the X cut on his arm did happen after he died."

There was a long pause in the message. Daisy could hear papers rustling in the background on the recording.

"I'm not sure why I'm telling you all this other than you seemed interested and you're taking care of Skittles and all so I thought you might want to tell him . . ." another long pause then a muffled ". . . no that's weird . . ." and then a more assertive, "Right then. I'll be in touch if I learn anything else." J.B. hung up.

"She's a bit of an odd duck," Daisy reflected, looking around for Skittles. He had settled into the living room and was busy washing his nether regions. "Dessert?" she queried with a laugh.

The second message was from Detective Rendell himself. "Ms. Catsimatides, I just wanted to let you know that we've reached the family of Mr. Pontarlier, and they have asked that you continue to care for his dog for the immediate future, if you are willing. Should that be a problem, please contact me." He left his number and clicked off.

So there it was. She and Skittles were together, at least for now. That didn't bother her, but she worried that she might never know for sure how Allen died, and this bothered her to no end.

THEY SPENT the rest of the day in the apartment. Daisy worked the daily Sudoku from the Chronicle, put some beans and rice and a pork loin into the slow cooker for dinner, tidied up, but honestly, her place was so small there was very little tidying to do. After almost a week together, Skittles had settled in as if he were home. In his dreams, though, she could tell he was still working things out—he twitched and barked in closed-mouth laments.

By midway through the afternoon, the crisp clean air started to shift, to organize itself and move east dragging the first hints of fog trickling over Twin Peaks. Before long, the thick whiteness was spilling heavily down the hillside, splitting off into Noe Valley and Hayes Valley but skirting the Mission, leaving the skies there bright and clear. The fog was relentless as it poured down into the Castro. Condos on the Twin Peaks hillside looked like barnacles resisting a tidal flow.

Daisy watched Skittles as he dozed by the door. "You know, you probably shouldn't get too comfy. Allen's people may still come and take you away."

Perhaps she overestimated the esteem others held for four-legged relationships. She couldn't imagine how someone from his family, someone who loved Allen, wouldn't want to hold this furry reminder of him. Not everyone loved dogs as much as she did, though. It made her sad to think that she and Skittles might be separated. Her heart tore at the thought. And sorrow made her restless.

"Come on, buddy, let's go for a big long walk!" She picked up the leash—the tooling on the leather really was quite something—and clipped it to Skittles' collar. This dog was so even tempered. Moments before, he'd been sound asleep. Now, he shook himself stem to stern, preparing for whatever the afternoon might hold. He let out a loud mix of yawn and yowl, as if to say "Ready when you are!"

Daisy needed to shake things up a little and avoid the heartache of routine. Instead of doing the usual clockwise 15th Street–Church Street–Duboce–Dolores loop Daisy decided to head left on Church towards Dolores Park. This area had a strange deadness to it on a Saturday. One side of the block was filled by Everett Middle School while the other housed Mission Dolores Elementary. Without the energetic presence of children the residential street felt lifeless and dominated by the MUNI trains rumbling down the center of the wide street. Skittles trotted along though, content, startled only when the J-Church blasted its horn to warn that is was about to run another red light.

At the corner of 18th and Church, Daisy paused to consider. Up into Dolores Park or down along the flat sidewalk? The fog was looming to her right but hadn't yet drowned them in dampness. She looked down at Skittles

whose bright, moist eyes looked back with eagerness. "What the hell," she said, rolling into the crosswalk and straight across towards the park.

She stopped at the entrance to the park while Skittles peed on the first patch of grass they encountered.

"Yeah Little Man, that was a long stretch of cement, wasn't it?" she said sympathetically. She could tell that he found peeing on cement to be crass, something to be avoided at all costs. He preferred the delicate feel of grass under his paws and the muffled sound of pee on sod rather than the loud splatter on concrete.

As she waited for him to finish, she heard a voice.

"Daisy! Daisy, isn't it?" she turned to her right and saw the beautiful silver-haired man—the one she and Robbie had met at Mr. S. He shimmered like an apparition emerging from the backlit fog.

"Oh, hi there!" she stumbled. "You're the one from the leather store, right?" He was just about the most beautiful thing she'd ever seen.

"Is this your little dog?" he asked, ignoring her question.

"Well, it's Allen's dog actually."

"Of course," he said gently, bending down and calling the dog over to him. He knelt on her right beside her chair. "You must miss your master, little pup," he said, scratching behind Skittles' left ear.

He was so close to her, Daisy could get a better look at his beautiful hair. Silver didn't do it justice. Definitely platinum was a more apt description. As she pondered this subtle difference, she felt a bump on her chair.

"Oh, sorry," he said as he struggled back to his feet. "I'm a little stiff today." He smiled, offering no further explanation. "What's his name again?" he asked, gesturing towards the dog.

"Skittles. This is Skittles," she repeated.

"Well nice to meet you Skittles. Have a good day and stay warm. Looks like the fog is pouring in!" he said, nodding back to the west, as he continued east along 18th, disappearing as quickly as he had arrived.

"Well that was nice," Daisy said to Skittles, surprised at the chance meeting. "Ready to tackle this hill?" she asked, looking up into the park.

The electric motor on her Permobil Chairman HD whined loudly, struggling up the incline. She skirted around the Hidalgo statue and continued along the upper level of the park. The view was magnificent from here. The flat expanse opposite the MUNI stop was still full but people were starting to pack up their belongings as the temperature dropped. She spotted Jackson from the coffee shop and waved. He smiled and waved back from the center of a large pack of friends. It's like a YMCA-at-the-beach day, Daisy thought—nothing but men. Skittles looked longingly at a pair of King Charles Spaniels racing headlong down the steep hill in pursuit of a tennis ball. "Not today, babycakes," Daisy commiserated with the dog, tugging his leash to break his fixation. They continued along the upper path, curving left parallel to 20th, then back around towards Dolores.

At Dolores, they turned left again to complete their circumnavigation of the park. Daisy eased back on the joystick as the chair tilted down the steep grade. Skittles picked up the pace, trotting on the grass beside her. The engine continued to whir, the gearing automatically resisting the force of gravity pulling it downhill. The combined weight of the chair itself plus Daisy's considerable mass challenged the resistance systems. They bumped over a cracked block of the sidewalk where tree roots had pushed the pavement askew, caught the tiniest bit of air, and landed with a loud

clank on the other side.

Daisy *felt* the transmission slip into neutral as much as she heard it. To her horror, pulling back on the joystick did nothing. She rattled it back and forth but still no response. The whir of the engine relaxed into silence and Daisy began to gain speed. Beside her, Skittles broke into a gallop.

"Mother of god!" she cried out, "Hang on puppy!" Skittles was running flat out, ears pressed flat against his head. She had tied the leash to the chair's armrest and there was no way she could release it now—she clung tight with both hands, hoping against hope she wouldn't fall out of the chair or veer into the street.

"Watch out!" she yelled. A woman carrying a dozen hula hoops over one shoulder was walking uphill along the sidewalk with her head down, talking on the phone. "Coming through!"

The woman looked up just in time to jump aside, hoops and all.

Ahead, Daisy could see another uplifted block in the cement sidewalk, one that had created a huge lip, to her right, parked cars, and to her left, a row of palm trees and grass presented a slalom course that would have been far beyond her steering abilities, if she'd had any. Her choices had quickly narrowed to only one—she closed her eyes and let go, breathing slow and deep, knowing she was right with her God, come what may.

Just at that moment of surrender, she felt the chair begin to slow. She was still going downhill, she could feel that in the angle of her body and the press of her arms holding her in her seat, but she was definitely going slower and slower. She open one eye just a crack, seeking the source of this divine intervention.

"Damn, Daisy, you need to lose some weight!" Sam—the

same homeless, gray-blanketed, book-loving Sam that Daisy had talked just yesterday—was pulling on the back of her chair, guiding it to a slow roll.

Sam had been working his way through *To the Lighthouse* in the shade of a palm tree—his usual spot uphill taken by the weekend crowd—but was having trouble staying with the story. He'd been mired in one of Woolf's particularly indulgent stream-of-consciousness sections, having reread the same paragraph three times, when he had looked up and had seen Daisy rolling along at the top of the park. She stood out, even at a distance. In no hurry to return to Woolf, he'd continued to watch as she and the small dog moved past the gay beach then the family-friendly section, then came around at the top of the hill. He'd been mildly curious to see how her wheelchair would handle the slope. Had he been reading a better novel, he probably wouldn't have noticed that it wasn't simply her sense of adventure that made her drive down the hill at such breakneck speed. Sensing her distress, he'd leapt up and managed to intercept her halfway down the hill. Being homeless was not good for one's health overall, but it wasn't a sedentary lifestyle and it did tend to keep one limber.

Once at the bottom of the hill, Sam released the chair. He bent, hands on knees, trying to catch his breath. As he panted, Daisy could see his bony ribs and spine poking against his thin shirt. Skittles panted right along with Sam, both desperate for oxygen.

"Oh my God, Sam, you saved my life!"

"All in a good day's work, ma'am," Sam said dryly.

"What the hell happened there?" Daisy knew her chair inside and out. That kind of massive failure could only happen if both of the batteries on the back of the chair were completely drained, but she'd fully charged both of them this

morning. She reached down on her right, feeling for where the battery cables plug into the motor. To her surprise, she felt a loose cable.

"Sam, will you look over here and see what's going on," she said, rattling the loose cable that was out of her sight.

Sam squatted down on the cement beside Daisy's chair. In her hand was the cable that led from the second battery to . . . . It was unplugged.

"This is supposed to be connected to something, isn't it?" he asked.

"Hell, yes!" she replied. "Without it, I'm running on just one battery. Can you plug it in down here?" she said, pointing blindly to the electronic panel. Her hand was still shaking. "There are three prongs—you have to twist it a little to get them aligned."

Immediately the chair hummed to life.

"Well that's the darnedest thing. I know I plugged them both in this morning." She paused for a moment to think, "Unless that gentleman Silverfox knocked it loose by accident when he was talking to Skittles?" She and Sam looked at each other. His eyebrows rose.

"You know Daisy, there's a lot of strange things that go on around here. You'd be surprised by the things I see people do to each other. It's like there are two parallel universes. There's the one that we're told exists, where people are nice, stop at red lights, and put money in the meter. Then there's the other one, where people blow through stop signs, jam paper in the meters to break them, make fun of people passing by. When you're out here long enough you can't help but see both worlds."

Sam paused. "Let me show you something," he said, motioning her back towards his pile of stuff, halfway up the hill.

"Any chance you could bring whatever it is down here?" Daisy asked. She was still a bit shaken and in no hurry to regain elevation.

"Oh, yeah, sure. What was I thinking? My apologies." He climbed up to where he'd left his stuff, gathered it up into his battered stroller, and returned to the bottom of the hill.

"After we talked the other day, I got to thinking," he said.

Sam was being particularly polite today—and he *had* just rescued her and all—but Daisy hadn't forgotten the ire that had leaked out from him when they'd spoken last. She decided to see where this was going but toggled her joystick to check that her engine was still operating, just in case. She adjusted her tilt angle so she might listen more carefully.

Sam sensed her caution. "I'll admit it, I'm a little crazy. Who wouldn't be living out here? It's the old chicken-and-egg question—did being crazy make me homeless, or did being homeless make me crazy? I'm not sure."

"Sam?" Daisy interrupted gently. She was beginning to get a sense of his rhythm, a feel for how he could wax philosophical at the drop of a hat. She wanted to steer him back to the matter at hand.

"Right. So after we talked the other day, I decided to make a log entry to try and jog my memory—it's something I do, just to keep track of things. Then I went back a few days to look to see if I'd written something down the night your friend was killed."

"And?" Daisy sat up. She was curious now but still not sure how much stock to put in his random thoughts.

"Well, I had. Last Saturday, right?" he looked for her nod as he flipped through the pages of a dog-eared *How the Grinch Stole Christmas!*

"Uh ... Sam ... someone else wrote that book." She half expected him to tell her that, last Saturday, every "Who

down in Whoville" had been singing on the grassy median of Dolores.

"Oh, yeah," he laughed, closing the book so he could see the cover. "I love this book, but it's also got a lot of white space. I use that as my log." He opened the book again and turned it so Daisy could see. Indeed, amongst Dr. Seuss's red and black, was Sam's tight blue chicken-scratch.

"Last Saturday, I heard a bunch of punk kids. It says here they were laughing and messing about in the bushes. They spray-painted a giant R.J. on that abandoned house back on 15th." Sam pointed up Dolores towards Market as he searched for the next entry in the margin.

"Hey, I think I know which kids you're talking about," Daisy said, remembering her run in with the threesome. "I can sure understand why you want to steer clear of them." Remembering that night, she reached down and patted Skittles. He'd stopped breathing hard but still looked anxious after their downhill run.

"There's a note here about all the noise," Sam said.

Daisy frowned. She wasn't sure how noise was going to help her find Allen's killer.

"You'd be surprised," Sam said, sensing her skepticism, "just how much noise there is in the wee hours. Parts of this city come to life at around 4 a.m.: delivery trucks, assholes in the SUVs and Beemers rushing downtown—the ones whose work is timed to the East Coast markets, drunken folks coming home from the bars or that one night stand, even runners out before the sun has even come up. Most people are home snoozing, but it's a madhouse out here."

This was news to Daisy, but she couldn't think how this was relevant.

"Then, see, there's another little note here: 'Asshole operating without running lights. Collision course with

Chron. He's run aground now. Serves him right.' That's all I can make out. I can't even read my own handwriting."

Daisy was curious but didn't understand the nautical references. "What does that mean?"

"It means I remember that guy, your friend, the one in the suit coat who I said was an asshole. It really was 4 a.m., still dark out, and traffic was starting to roar. A Chronicle delivery truck had just honked as it drove by me—they do that sometimes, a little game to see if they can make the homeless guys jump—so I was awake. Your friend was talking on his cell phone and walking his dog—well, this dog here—when the same Chron truck just rolled right through the stop sign and turned right. Your guy had to jump to get out of the way. I'm not sure but I think the truck might have clipped him by the way he grabbed his back." Sam imitated what he remembered seeing, putting one hand on his side and arching back.

"Next thing I know, he's collapsing on the sidewalk. To tell you the truth I would have gone over to check on him but I heard those kids again. I figured I'd just lay low until they passed," Sam concluded.

"And so what happened next?" Daisy's doubt had faded. She was fully into the story now.

"After the coast was clear, I went to look but he was gone. I figured he'd gotten up and gone on his merry way."

"Is that it?" Daisy was excited and wanted to make sure that Sam hadn't left out any other pieces.

"Yup, that's it. The rest is just Who pudding and rare Who roast beast." He laughed at his own joke.

"Sam, this is great!" she said grasping his arm. "I think I know what happened now. And thanks for coming to my rescue, Sam. I'd be one flat Daisy right now if it wasn't for you. What say I buy you one of those rare Who roast beast

sandwiches over at Bi-Rite Market as your reward. It's the least I can do."

"Why Daisy, I'd be honored," and off they went—Sam, with his library in tow, and Daisy and Skittles in her chair.

DAISY AND SKITTLES WERE slow to get started. All the excitement of the yesterday had left them both so exhausted that they'd slept right through the early morning mass at Mission Dolores. It was well into midmorning by the time they finally came outside.

The overnight fog had left a cleansing dampness over every surface of the city. The sun had broken through and was nudging and prodding, transmuting all that moisture into a slow-moving steam rising in a chorus off of cars, sidewalks, branches, even off the gray wool blanket of a homeless guy asleep in the alcove near her front door. As she approached the corner at Dolores, a skittering pack of two-dozen Chihuahuas grabbed her attention up ahead. She followed the dogs and their owners south towards Dolores Park, where they were no doubt heading for one of those single-breed owner rallies. Their energy totally held her attention until she reached Joe's garage. He was standing outside the open door, sipping a steamy mug of coffee, equally fixated on something across the street.

Daisy slowed to a stop and turned to see what held his gaze.

"Holy cow! When did that happen?" said Daisy, suddenly seeing what Joe saw. She was a genuinely shocked.

"How did you miss that? They set it all up yesterday afternoon," Joe said, admiring their work ethic.

Yesterday's adventure through the park had taken Daisy on a completely different route than normal. She'd come back home along Guerrero rather than Dolores and had missed the flurry of activity in the empty lot at the corner of 15th and Dolores. A whole swarm of day laborers had arrived and cleared the space of trash and debris, mowed down the long grass, and raked up the clippings. The lot had looked clipped and clean, like a freshly shorn flattop. By the time the flatbed truck had arrived, they'd already hung strings of lights and attached the sign (P.A.W.S. Benefit—Christmas Trees) on the wall adjacent to the Obama poster that had been plastered there some weeks before. By proximity, the signage made it look like newly elected Obama was blessing this fundraiser, and a little of that Obama-magic certainly couldn't hurt. The workers had unloaded the whole flatbed of trees and wreaths, filling the entire space with pungent evergreen.

"Well, heck, let's go check it out!" she said. Joe pulled his garage door closed and followed Daisy back across Dolores.

The piney scent of fresh-cut trees met them halfway across the street. "Wow, this sure does smell better than the urine smell that's usually on this corner!" Daisy said, never one to mince words.

Twelve-foot tall trees, still corseted in their bundling wire, leaned against the chain-link fence, created a square forest. Inside of this, smaller trees were fluffed out and nailed to crude wooden stands in a haphazard labyrinth. Daisy and Joe bravely ventured into the space. Almost immediately, the wheels of Daisy's chair caught in a rut on the rough ground and spun. She rocked the joystick from forward to reverse and back again, the maneuver finally pulling her free.

"This place ain't exactly ADA-compliant," she said to Joe as he wiped the mud splatter from his pants, "but I sure do like the smell. It reminds me of the piney woods back in Kentucky."

"Hey, Daisy!" a nearby tree called.

"Who's that?" she queried back.

In answer, the bottom branches began to shake and then a black, wet nose poked through.

"G.M.!" The black shepherd yearned towards Daisy's outstretched hand and, moments later, Rich too popped through the tree, a gift from the sylvan gods.

"How's my girl?" she said, scratching at the dog's stiff black ears.

"She's useless, that's how!" Rich said, exasperated. "We're volunteering, and she can't seem to get the hang of this customer-service thing. Every time I try and help someone pick out a tree, she seems to have her own opinion. Either she herds them away from a tree or she wraps them to one using her leash. It's driving me crazy." Rich pulled gently on G.M.'s tail, feigning anger.

"Volunteering?" Joe asked. From his garage he couldn't see the sign on the wall indicated that this was a fundraiser.

"Yeah, this whole thing is a fundraiser for P.A.W.S. It's something we've never done before. We got this surprise donation—ten thousand dollars worth of wreaths and trees—from an anonymous donor. All very last-minute. It could have been a disaster if the city hadn't been super cooperative about the permits," Rich leaned forward and lowered his voice, "I think they're trying to wipe away any association of this lot with Allen's murder."

Skittles had hopped down from Daisy's lap and, after sniffing noses, had moved directly through G.M.'s legs towards her back end. His low stature made it possible for him to slip under G.M.'s belly and sniff from this unusual angle. In turn, G.M. simply bent her head between her front legs to reach Skittles' butt—a modified 69-sniff. Skittles recognized anxiety in G.M.'s scent. He could tell it was related to Allen.

It was almost as if Daisy picked up on the scent too. "I know, I can't stop thinking about him either. I heard from J.B. yesterday, Allen's business partner. She told me that they'd finally gotten the autopsy results. Turns out he died of some sort of liver injury. Hepatic sub-something."

Rich blanched. His mind immediately went to the missed flogger strike. He swallowed hard. "Do they know what caused the injury?" he asked slowly, his eyes narrowing to ward off the answer he most feared.

"From what J.B. said, they couldn't tell. He had a bunch of bruises on that part of his body—some fresh and some older—and any one of them, or even the combination of them all, could have caused the injury."

Silence from Joe and Rich. G.M. looked up at Daisy with a gentle sense of curiosity. Skittles peeked out from under G.M. and waited. Daisy continued, "The funny thing is, I talked to Sam yesterday . . . you know Sam? The homeless guy who's always reading a book? He often sleeps over there," she said pointing towards the green PG&E box barely visible through the forest of trees.

Rich hadn't noticed, but he nodded anyway.

"Well he said he saw Allen the night he was killed."

"Really?" Joe and Rich said in unison. This seemed like important news.

Daisy ignored their eagerness and plowed on slowly with all the lurid details. "He told me he saw Allen that night, that he was crossing the street while talking on his phone, and that this Chronicle delivery truck almost ran him over. Sam thought it might have it actually clipped him, with the mirror or something. I'm wondering if maybe that's what caused the bruise that caused the liver injury. Sam did say Allen was holding his back right afterwards."

Rich let out an audible sigh. He'd been holding his breath the entire time Daisy had been speaking. "Yeah, I guess that could explain it too," he said.

Daisy cocked her head, catching the "too" but deciding not to inquire.

It dawned on Rich that he might never find out for sure which bruise had killed Allen. It might have been his mishit or the glancing blow of the truck or something entirely different. Or it might even have been the combination of them all. He realized that he'd just have to find a way to live with that mystery, never knowing for sure if their brief encounter at the Castle had contributed to Allen's demise.

"The weird thing is, though they're sure that hepa-sub-whatever-it's-called is what killed him—even if they can't say what caused it—they do know that the X mark in his arm came later, after he was dead. Isn't that strange?" Daisy let this gruesome fact hover between them.

After a moment, Rich asked, "Did Sam tell you anything else?" He felt shy about being so nosy but ever since he and Dominic had talked with Silverfox at the Eagle on Friday, he'd been even more confused about Allen's death. He wasn't sure if Silverfox had been telling the truth about that night, about Allen leaving when he did, about Sketch . . . but if what Sam said was true, then probably Silverfox's story was too. Still . . . .

"The only other thing Sam said was, he heard those punks at about the same time as he saw Allen," Daisy added.

"Punks?" Rich asked.

Joe continued to listen quietly, as he so often did in Daisy's presence. He dug at the dirt with the heel of his boot, creating a small trench.

"Didn't I tell you about my run-in with them? Those three kids almost killed poor Skittles! But he gave them what-for, right buddy?" Daisy said proudly.

Rich remembered the story, remembered that he'd only been half listening on Friday morning when their paths had crossed and Daisy had first recounted it, but now something tickled at him. "Tell me again what they looked like?"

"There were three of them—black hoodies, black baggie pants, white shirts, white kids . . . nothing different from what you usually see around here with the Mission High kids—but these kids were mean. The one that seemed like the leader, his friends called him R.J., had a tattoo on his neck that looked like an X."

The connections started to snap into place. "I know this is going to sound weird," Rich hesitated, "but I think those might be the same kids that jumped my CCOP patrol Wednesday night. And one of them had an extremely sharp knife. Do you think . . . ?" Rich waited for Daisy to catch up.

A half-beat later, she did. "So you're thinking they might have scratched the X onto Allen's arm? But why would they do that?"

"The night they attacked us, they didn't strike me as the brightest bulbs—their insults were so, well, unsophisticated. Maybe they're in a gang and they thought the leather flag tattooed on Allen's arm was a rival gang's tag. I've heard that one gang will cross out the symbols of a rival gang with an X over it."

Rich shook his head at the stupidity of the punks if that had been their thinking.

"Of course, they could have just been homophobic assholes!" he continued.

Sadly, this seemed the more likely explanation. Between Prop 8 and the street patrol attack, Rich was feeling depressed by the state of the world these days.

"Excuse me!" Another disembodied voice, female this time, filtered through the needled branches, "Is there anyone here who could help me with some wreaths?"

"Yes, right over here! Just follow the sound of my voice!" Rich launched into a full-throated rendition of *Somewhere Over the Rainbow*, the singing as much to buoy his own spirits as guide this new arrival.

"They really should arrange these trees so it isn't such a maze in here," Daisy whispered to Joe as they waited for the thrashing of branches to reveal the woman who had called for assistance.

She finally broke through.

"J.B.! What are you doing here?" Daisy exclaimed.

J.B. brushed the pine needles from her sweater. "Daisy? Fancy meeting you here. Actually, I'm not quite sure."

"Well then, first let me introduce you. J.B., this is Joe and Rich, and you know Skittles, and that," she said, pointing to G.M.—who had pressed her nose directly and insistently up between J.B.'s legs—"is G.M. which is short for Gay Marriage." The dog pulled back, swiping her tongue across her own nose and jowls, and sneezed in satisfaction. They all laughed at G.M. as J.B. discretely tried to wipe dog slobber from her inseam.

"Well, umm," Rich giggled, "maybe I can be of more assistance than my ill-mannered dog. I actually work here so how can I help?"

"Like I said, I'm not quite sure. I got a call this morning from the Executive Director of the Women's Building. That would be weird enough, it being a Sunday and all, but it gets weirder." J.B. gave up dealing with the needles and slobber and dropped fully into the confusion of her morning. "She said she wanted to thank me for 'our generous donation.' But, to the best of my knowledge, neither Allen nor I made one."

"Might not be such a bad idea," Daisy suggested, remembering the impoliteness of the valets at Tintin and Farina. "A little generosity in the community can go a long way towards keeping the peace."

Rich and Joe stared at her, then at each other, surprised

by her political savvy.

"I know, I know. You're the second person to tell me that. To be honest, it never even occurred to me." J.B. didn't want to get distracted by her lack of social responsibility. Instead, she plowed on. "The thing is, it gets even weirder. The E.D. told me this morning that she got a call from a guy at Ali Baba Falafel on Friday saying he was delivering lunch to the staff. Free, prepaid, courtesy of Tintin." J.B. shook her head at the twists and turns of her saga. Her audience was rapt.

"Along with the lunch, there was a big envelope with 'our' donation—forty thousand dollars! The envelope included instructions that she wasn't to contact me until this morning and that, when she did, she was to tell me to come here to buy 'Christmas decorations.' Even she was confused by that."

"That's fantastic!" Daisy exclaimed. "Sounds like generosity is in the air. Did you know that P.A.W.S. got a surprise donation of ten thousand dollars to set this up?"

"Fabulous indeed!" Rich said, emphasizing it with a three-snap gesture that zigzagged in front of his body.

J.B. relaxed as she realized no one else was the slightest bit perplexed by this turn of events or the coincidence of the fifty-thousand-dollar total. Her business brain couldn't help wondering if blackmail often resulted in some sort of positive externality.

"So how can we help?" Rich queried.

"The instructions said 'Tintin needs Christmas decorations' and that I should head over to 15th and Dolores to get some. I didn't even know there was a tree lot here. I always go to the Guardsmen at Fort Mason." J.B. looked around, taking in the abundance of evergreens.

"Well actually, this is the first time we've done this. Kind of fortuitous, eh? It's a benefit for our four-legged friends," he said, scratching G.M.'s head.

"OK, then I guess I'll need ..." she scanned Tintin's space in her mind's eye "... twenty wreaths and about two hundred feet of fir garland ... oh, and one small table-top tree." She could picture the Hergé drawing of a Christmas tree on a small sled. They could recreate that perfectly by the front door.

"Alright, then, let's do it! Daisy, if you wouldn't mind holding G.M. then I'll be able to actually help J.B." Rich handed Daisy the leash and took the still-bewildered J.B. by the arm. "Now honey, we're going to find you and Tintin the loveliest decorations."

As they disappeared through the branches, Joe and Daisy stayed silent, sharing easy camaraderie.

Finally, Joe spoke. "I'm gonna head back now. Janet and I are going to try something new and take a drive down to Pacifica. Figured it's kind of silly to keep waxing my truck if I never take her out for a spin."

Daisy understood that this was about more than the truck.

"I'll see you tomorrow," he said, turning away and not waiting for her answer, trusting in the steadiness of their friendship.

Daisy smiled at Joe's back as he threaded his way out of the lot towards Dolores Street. Well you old dog, who knew you could learn new tricks! She watched him pause before stepping out onto the sidewalk, gesturing to a homeless man—who was pushing a shopping cart overflowing with colorful detritus—to pass by first. The man nodded at Joe for his politeness, handed him a bent Mylar pinwheel from his collection as a reward, and proceeded on his way.

Through the branches to the 15th Street side of the lot Daisy could just see Robbie heading home, bagel and coffee in hand. Probably her second round already, essential sustenance for her a long days of writing.

The acoustics in this temporary forest were surreal. She thought she could hear Lisa calling gently to her shepherd Rocco and the scrape of his arthritic paws and long claws as he meandered down the sidewalk. Daisy knew she could hear Rich's lilt calling out "Yoohoo!" to Jackson as he flew past on his bike, late for work at Maxfield's. While she sat and listened, G.M. and Skittles circled her chair in opposite directions, wrapping her completely in their leashes. They settled in at her feet where Skittles began licking G.M.'s forehead, styling up a striking shepherd Mohawk.

Ensnared by the leashes, forested by the trees, alone for just a moment in the midst of one of the liveliest cities in America, Daisy reached for the lever and adjusted her tilt angle. She put one hand down to just reach the soft fur on Skittles' ears. Daisy took a deep breath of pine and smiled, fully aware of the fragile, tangled threads that linked them all together. She'd seen so many changes in this neighborhood, yet she still felt rooted here. She knew this moment was just another in a long list of ones that anchored her to this spot. All of these memories, all of these people, all of these dogs were a part of her . . . as she was of them.

From her chair, she surveyed all she could ever want.

"Who could have imagined that this wheelchair would be the best seat in the house?" she asked, to no one in particular. Skittles' warm tongue across the back of her hand the only and sweetest reply.

Acknowledgements

Writing a first novel is an audacious and humbling undertaking. Characters emerge from some strange interplay between the real world and the imagined, take on their own identity, dig in their heels, start acting out, and then deign to collaborate on a story. It was my job to capture that tale, to manage the fuzzy boundary between reality and fiction, and to put it all down on the page as best as possible. The extent that the effort falls short of aspiration is wholly my responsibility; the extent to which is succeeds is in no small part due to the support of these fine folks.

To all the neighbors (Joe, Frieda, Andy & Chaise, Marisa & Sherika, and many whose names I do not know) who create the rich context of everyday.

To Steven and the wonderful people at Maxfield's House of Caffeine, the best coffee house for writing in SF! It's like being at home but with a better dance mix.

To Chris Baty and everybody at NaNoWriMo (National Novel Writing Month) for making the insane, heroic undertaking of the first draft so much fun.

To Alexis Lucas (always the first reader), Sandy Guevara, Heather Stewart, and Rachel Lavengood, who waded through early drafts, providing honest feedback and encouragement. I couldn't have taken the next step without you.

To Teresa Mejía, who helped me speak two languages.

To the various writing teachers over the years who have helped improve the quality of my words on the page: from Prof. Sussman (who I think of every time I use a semi-colon), through Michelle Tea, and finally to Jen Cross, whose fierce words and generous ear always give me courage.

To Carol Queen and Jen Cross and the Erotic Reading

Circle at the Center for Sex and Culture, where the transgressive power of erotic writing comes to life, and where parts of this work got its first audience.

To my editor Brent Calderwood (and I love being able to say "my editor"), who took the manuscript to task and made it so much better for the effort (once I learned to decipher his handwriting).

To the whole BS Group (Pat, Susan, Barbara, Suzanne, Janice, Denise, and Lynette) who came up with best title for this book.

To everyone in Hamm Gramm & the Wham Bamm Thankyou Ma'ams, who picked the final cover design.

To Zed Meade—boyfriend, booking agent, and so much more—who bestowed the most critical imprimatur: published author.

To Tina Stromsted and Wickie Stamps, who helped me wrestle with the inner daemons, the very ones who made this project possible but who, at the same time, can be the most unruly of psychic houseguests.

To Laura Tabet—my most favorite imaginal playmate— who insisted on calling me an artist, and did so long and hard enough that I finally had to listen. My gratitude is enormous.

And finally, to all the dogs—Tucker, especially—who are a daily reminder of what really matters: long walks, fresh air, and interesting butts to sniff.

About the Author

Amy Butcher is a writer, artist, bodyworker, business consultant, and liminal guide who lives and works in San Francisco. Her debut novel *Paws for Consideration* showcases her varied skills in graphic design, illustration, and writing in order to capture a unique slice of San Francisco life. She is proud to say that this novel got its (very rough) start during National Novel Writing Month.

Butcher's short story "Touched" was just published in *Best Lesbian Erotica 2012*. Follow her many adventures at www.amybutcher.com.

Author photo © 2012 Marisa Aragona

❏ Some people find Daisy a hard character to like. What is your first impression of Daisy? Did your relationship to her change over the course of the story? What do you think motivated her to try and solve the crime? What personal qualities helped Daisy in her citizen-detective quest? What qualities got in her way?

❏ Which dog in the story was your favorite and why? Which human character did you sympathize with the most? Were the characters real and believable? Do they remind you of anyone you know? What do you think will happen next to the main characters, both the people and the dogs?

❏ Were you surprised by the ending? Were you satisfied by it? Why or why not? Ultimately, where would you place the blame for Allen's death?

❏ Discuss the mystery aspects of the story. Were you able to figure out things before they happened or did the author keep you guessing? Were there points where the author failed to hold your interest in the story?

❏ This story takes place in San Francisco in November 2008, immediately following the election of President Obama and the passage of California's Proposition 8, banning gay marriage. Did the author provide enough information to understand these events as they related to the story? What do you remember from your own experience of that time period? Did this setting enhance or detract from the story?

❏ Robert Frost wrote in his poem "Mending Wall" that, "good fences make good neighbors." In this story, the author explores the complex relationship of neighbors, both the positive and negative aspects. What is your relationship to your neighbors? How does that relationship support your daily life? How does it frustrate it? What would life be like without neighbors?

❏ Did certain parts of the book make you uncomfortable? If so, which ones and why? Did this discomfort lead to any new personal understanding or awareness you might not have thought about before?

❏ Daisy's adventures take us through a variety of class experiences, all of which appear to exist simultaneously in the same place and time? Which class experience did you relate to more: the working-class restaurant staff or its high-end customers? How did that affect your reading of the story? What did you think of the message protesters stenciled on the sidewalk ("Mission Exploitation: Trendy Google Profs Raise Housing Prices!")? Does gentrification and decreased class diversity help or hurt a neighborhood?

❏ Have you ever witnessed a crime? How did that affect you? What would you do if there were an unsolved murder in your neighborhood?

Q: *You've never written a book before. What gave you the audacity to think that you could?*

A: Well, I honed my craft by writing a lot of erotic short fiction, a discipline I highly recommend. I hoped that writing a book would be very much like that, only requiring more paper. Honestly, I had no idea if I could write a book. Who does, really, unless filled with hubris? Without the support of NaNoWriMo (see below), I'm not sure I would even have tried. From the beginning, I knew I wanted to write a murder mystery. It's my favorite thing to read. It felt cozy and familiar like a bunch of friends hoisting a pint together. In my imagination, it also set the bar low—especially in other people's eyes—so that I was free to just try. Whether I tripped over that bar or soared over with room to spare, you'll be the judge, but either way, I'm damn proud of the effort.

Q: *What surprised you most about the NaNoWriMo process?*

A: Pretty much everything about National Novel Writing Month (NaNoWriMo) was a surprise—how crazy and fun it was, that a person really can write 50,000 words in 30 days, that so many other foolish people are trying to do the same thing at the same time. One of the NaNoWriMo mottos is 'quantity over quality.' This freaked me out until I discovered that firing the inner critic could liberate some very creative ideas. I am so grateful to the mad scientists at NaNoWriMo for making an arduous task feel not just fun, but down right heroic.

Q: *How did the role of neighbor become so important to you?*

A: When I was 11, I moved from a neighborhood where I was the leader of a gang of kids to one with no kids at all. It was a lonely shock. I've paid attention to the relationships we take for granted, the ones that are just the background, ever since. I moved to San Francisco in 2004 and didn't know a single person when I arrived. Neighbors were very important in helping me to feel at home.

Q: What was the strangest thing about writing a novel?

A: You know how they say that characters take on a life of their own? Well they really do. And they can be recalcitrant too if they don't get their way.

Q: What was the hardest thing about writing a novel?

A: Keeping track of it all! I had to come up with a system for organizing the details of names, ages, apartment locations, decorations, etc. It just wouldn't do for Skittles to be a Boston Terrier in one scene then a Great Dane in the next. People notice these kind of things. In the end, I built a spreadsheet for it all.

Q: Are your characters based on real people?

A: Legally, my answer is no. In reality, the folks around me definitely inspired the characters. There is probably also some of myself in all of them. The only character who is almost completely fictional is Allen. Maybe that's why he dies.

Q: How do you describe the theme of this book?

A: First and foremost, it's a murder mystery and so must follow the conventions of that genre; however, I was definitely trying to explore something more. I'm interested in the various connections that I see all around me—my neighbors, my neighborhood, and the different social strata existing simultaneously in space and time and yet often functioning as if they were in completely separate worlds. I was curious about what would happen when thing got a little leaky at the boundaries between worlds, how one might impact the other— for good or for evil. Without being heavy handed, I wanted to point out that we're all in this together.

Q: Who are some of your favorite mystery writers?

A: Dick Francis, Ruth Rendell, Sandra Scoppettone, Cara Black, and Laurie King for starters.

Q: What do you want readers to get out of this book?

A: I hope it's a story they enjoy, that they meet some characters who stick with them, that there are some laughs and surprises along the way. I hope that they are curious about the world I see, at least for a moment. To me, I know I'm in the thralls of a good book when I can't wait to climb into bed and read. So I really hope this book and its readers get some good pillow time together.

Q: Describe the process for illustrations and design of your book.

A: I'm a graphic artist and have done book production, so I had some ideas of where to begin. I looked at other mystery novels and stole liberally from the work of Cara Black's designer. It's really about visual clarity and creating a hierarchy so the reader knows where they are. For example, you might notice that each day is a whole new chapter, each scene starts at the top of the page with a header (in Cracked and right justified) and the first four words of the paragraph in small caps, while each change of vantage point within a scene is marked by an extra space between paragraphs and then the first two words of the next paragraph in small caps. Like theatrical lighting changes, these help the reader stay located in space and time. The illustrations were done either from memory or based on photos. I tried to make sure there was a dog in almost every picture, even if I had to add one. Usually, I sketch in pencil first, then ink in using a Rapidograph (if the ink hasn't dried up) or Pigma Micron to get a nice fine line, then do the shading with Faber-Castell's awesome PITT artist pens. They're like a using a paintbrush without all the cleanup. Then comes the right brain part of the process—I start wrangling scanners, Adobe Photoshop, Illustrator, and InDesign to pull it all together. The flipbook illustrations were done with the aid of the super helpful Anime Studio Pro.

Q: Where did you come up with Tintin the name of the restaurant?

A: I used to work as a bicycle tour guide in France, leading gay and lesbian tourists through Provence. Tough job, but someone had to do it. My fellow guide Andrew was a big fan of Tintin and he introduced me to the books. Somehow they just stuck in my imagination. Guess they stuck in Steven Spielberg's too—since he made the animated feature *Tintin* in 2011—but I'm pretty sure he was never on one of our homo tours.

Q: Where is the best place for you to write? Do you have any writing rituals?

A: I love writing in coffee shops, especially the real Maxfield's. When I'm having a particularly tough bout of writer's block, I wear my underwear inside out. I find that helps.

Q: Your book is love child of Agatha Christie and Rita Mae Brown wouldn't you say?

A: Perhaps. Or maybe just an immaculate conception, mothered by Dick Francis . . . that is if he'd been an American growing up watching Lassie reruns rather than a Brit learning to be a jockey.

Q: Which media personality do you want to interview you?

A: Ellen, of course.

Q: Will you be getting Meryl Streep or Glenn Close to read for the audiobook?

A: I think Glen will be all over this one. And Kathy Bates will snatch up the movie rights. Daisy is a luscious part!